"I'm sorry I asked _____ I'm not ready for you— I mean, I'm not dating anyone. I mean—I made a mistake, asking you out."

"And you make a lot of them, don't you?"

Emily seemed to ignore the comment. "The reason I left so quickly on Friday had to do with my sister. Otherwise I might have stayed to see if you were okay. But I thought I should get Molly out of there. She tends to cause trouble wherever she goes."

"*She* does?" Stone felt a grin coming on. "From where I stand, you caused the trouble. I wouldn't have walked outside if it wasn't for you."

"And I thank you for doing that, but I didn't ask you to." Emily raised her chin.

That put her lips in decidedly much closer territory to his. "No, you didn't, but you didn't exactly stop me." Now he moved till he was only inches away from her, and their gazes locked.

Dear Reader,

For many authors, a finished book is the result of a dream come true. I'm no exception, but I do wonder how many can say that a book is the result of a literal dream. Sometime in 2013, I dreamed about a woman who discovered during a genealogical search that she was the descendant of the first licensed female pilot in California. What if this young woman was at a crossroads in her life, and the idea of following in the footsteps of a pioneering woman appealed to her spirit of adventure?

That's how this book was born. Eventually the result became *Breaking Emily's Rules*. Our heroine sets off on a journey, never expecting her destination to be true love. But then again, isn't love the greatest adventure of all?

I like writing strong alpha heroes, and so the idea of three Air Force pilots who must adjust to civilian life was born. Welcome to the Heroes of Fortune Valley. In this first book we meet a tough hero who is battling his personal demons and never planned on falling for his first student. I hope you will enjoy it!

I love hearing from readers. You can find me on Facebook, Twitter (@HeatherlyBelle), Instagram (Heatherly.Bell) and Pinterest, or email me at Heatherly@HeatherlyBell.com.

Sign up for my newsletter on my website to get all my latest news and updates, plus receive a free novella.

Heatherly

HEATHERLY BELL

—

Breaking Emily's Rules

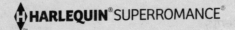

HARLEQUIN® SUPERROMANCE®

Recycling programs
for this product may
not exist in your area.

ISBN-13: 978-0-373-64016-4

Breaking Emily's Rules

Copyright © 2017 by Maria F. Buscher

Printed in U.S.A.

www.Harlequin.com

Heatherly Bell tackled her first book in 2004 and now the characters that occupy her mind refuse to leave until she writes them a book. She loves all music but confines singing to the shower these days. Heatherly lives in northern California with her family, including two beagles, one who can say hello and the other a princess who can feel a pea through several pillows.

Books by Heatherly Bell

HARLEQUIN SUPERROMANCE

Breaking Emily's Rules

Other titles by Heatherly Bell are available
in ebook format.

To Alice Ramona Font, aka Mom,
for inspiring a lifelong love of books.

CHAPTER ONE

ALL THINGS CONSIDERED, Emily Parker would rather be at the cemetery.

Instead, she pointed her truck in the direction of the Silver Saddle because when her sister, Molly, got an idea in her head, she was like a pit bull with a bone. Today that bone was dancing, and she'd cornered Emily into going along.

"You can go to the cemetery any ol' time. All those dead people aren't going anywhere." Molly pulled down the passenger-side visor and smoothed on bright red lipstick.

As if Molly needed any help channeling her inner hussy. "A little respect, please. Some of them might be our relatives. I have a lot of gravestones to inspect if I ever want to complete the Parker family tree."

Emily pulled into the gravel parking lot filled with cars and eased her truck into a space in the back. Maybe this wasn't such a good idea. There might be men in there. There would certainly be plenty of smart women glancing in her direction and whispering. *Did you hear? Poor Emily. She didn't see it coming, but maybe she should have. After all, didn't everyone?*

"Awesome. Friday night and this place is crazy." Molly unclicked her seat belt. "What are you waiting for?"

Emily didn't move as she glanced out the windshield from the safe place inside the cab of her truck. Couples were milling around the entrance, fools on a quest for the impossible. "I'm not so sure about this."

"Why not? You're not still on the giving-up-men thing, are you? I thought you were kidding."

"You know, there are more important things in life than men." Emily fiddled with her keys, still safely in the ignition. She hadn't made any firm commitments to getting out of this truck.

"Name one."

Think, Emily, think. "Family, of course." There was more, but she didn't work well under pressure.

Molly scowled. "Fine, but you can't do the really fun stuff without a man."

Spoken from a woman who loved men a bit too much. "What did being man-crazy ever get you?"

"Don't start with me. I swear the condom broke. Why won't you believe me?" Molly slapped the dashboard, reminding Emily of the little girl she'd once been, raising hell wherever she went. The red hair fair warning to anyone crazy enough to tangle.

The fact that Molly was seven years younger than Emily and already had a child shouldn't have bothered Emily. Except, sometimes it did. As usual, Molly didn't appreciate what she had.

"Let's not talk about this now." Emily resisted the urge to pound her head on the steering wheel.

"You brought it up. You might want to be a mom, but that doesn't mean every girl wants that."

"Who says I want to be a mom?" When Molly got mad she tried to hurt anyone within spitting distance. Pulling the keys out of the ignition, Emily grabbed her purse, opened the door and leapt out of the truck. She needed to blow a little steam off now, thanks to her bratty sister.

"Well, your biological clock is ticking." Molly followed.

"It. Is. Not. Ticking!" Emily could give as good as she got with her sister, even if her blond hair wasn't the slightest shade of red. Even if she'd always had to look out for the little squirt.

"You're twenty-eight. I think it's started to tick."

"Twenty-eight is the new eighteen."

"What does that mean?"

"It means if fifty is the new forty, and forty is the new thirty, then what the hell do you think the new twenty-eight is?" Emily spoke loud enough some of the patrons hanging outside the entrance turned to stare at them.

Emily grabbed her sister's hand and pulled her toward the entrance. "I'm doing this on one condition. All we're doing is dancing, and then we're going home. Alone. I don't go home with anybody, and neither do you."

As the big sister, it was Emily's duty to remember Molly only served up her parade of big hits when she hurt inside. Sooner or later Emily would have to figure out what bug had curled up inside Molly this time and probably help her with it, too. But for now, Denial was a river they would drown in together.

Opening the door to the Silver Saddle felt a little like opening death's door. A bit like entering a battlefield without armor. No self-respecting woman would do that, and yet, Emily was here.

Bertha, the broken mechanical bull, sat in the corner, warning the games were about to begin. From somewhere within, Emily drew a deep breath and placed an imaginary shield on her chest. There. Let someone get through that.

"Hey, it's the Parker girls." Thomas Aguirre sidled up to Molly. Everyone knew he'd had a crush on her since third grade.

Emily shoved her body between them. "We're here to dance. And nothing else. Right, Molly?"

"Right." Molly may have said what Emily wanted to hear, but her eyes said Open for Business.

"How about this dance?" Thomas didn't even

wait for a reply as he grabbed Molly's hand and pulled her onto the dance floor. Molly shoved her purse in Emily's hands before going far too willingly onto the crowded dance floor.

Emily had just wandered over to the bar and checked their purses in with the bartender when Jimmy Hopkins, the bar's owner, appeared at her elbow. "Hey, girl. How about a dance?"

As luck would have it, Jimmy was a harmless sweetheart. Best of all, he was engaged to one of her oldest friends, Trish. He'd recently taken six months' worth of dance lessons in preparation for their wedding, and Trish let him dance with any willing girl for the extra practice.

Maybe she could manage to dance with Jimmy all night. "You got it."

Jimmy spun her around the dance floor. Without a doubt, he was the best dancer in the place. Every other guy was shuffling his feet around and grabbing his partner's ass. This was going to work out better than she could have hoped. No ass-grabbing for Emily.

"Hey, are you okay, hon?" Jimmy asked between turns.

"I'm all right." As long as she didn't pay attention to the whispers, and with Jimmy it was easy. "I wish everyone would stop talking about me."

"They have nothing better to talk about. This year's been rather lean with scandal."

"Henry stopped peeing on the gazebo?" Henry

Turner, the town drunk, did his business where and when he wanted. Lately he seemed to favor the gazebo in the town square, and their mayor was up in arms about it. Apparently she wanted a new town resolution against public urination, as if the old one wasn't good enough.

"Think he's moved on to greener pastures, pardon the pun." Jimmy winked.

"It would help if you and Trish would finally set a date," Emily said. "Maybe wedding talk would keep them busy for a while."

"Are you kidding? Trish still hasn't decided on the venue, much less picked a date."

"You are going to consider the ranch. Right?" She hadn't made the decision to add weddings to her family's event company so her friends could get married somewhere else.

"It's up to Trish. But the reception is here."

"Perks of owning a bar. Have her give me a call."

After three dances, even Jimmy needed a break, but Emily was just getting started. She'd forgotten how much fun Western dancing could be. Fortunately, she had willing partners stepping up. They didn't want to talk, just dance. One hard look and she'd managed to keep the ass-grabbing off limits, too.

Dancing turned out to be the right recipe after all, especially since she'd known these guys since grade school. None of the men inspired the slightest amount of desire in her.

But then she caught a glimpse of *him*.

He sat on a stool against the perimeter like he'd been hired to enhance the wall. Dark wavy hair curled slightly at his neckline and, even from a distance, his eyes shone steely blue. The way he gazed at her both piqued her interest and made her want to smack him. His thoughts were so clearly written on his face and in those piercing eyes. He was practically undressing her in front of all these people. And she didn't even know the man.

Between stealing long PG-13–rated looks at her and taking sips of his beer, he spoke to Jedd, an old friend of Dylan's and a regular at the Saddle, except tonight Jedd's wife, Casey, was nowhere in sight. Emily continued to dance with anyone who asked and occasionally peeked at Hot Guy. He never seemed to take his eyes off her, and it was making her neck sweat.

"We need to get home soon," Emily took a moment to say into Molly's ear as she passed by in Thomas Aguirre's arms. Not a good sign she'd danced the entire time with one man. She'd keep an eye on that scenario.

"Sure, whatever you say," Molly sang out.

Emily stole another look at Mr. Studley, who now lifted his beer bottle and grimaced in the direction of the band playing Garth Brooks's "Friends in Low Places."

The heat pulsating all the way to the back of her knees had nothing to do with the dancing, and everything to do with that man. It wasn't like she'd never seen his kind before, the type of man who might as well have yellow police tape draped around him to serve as warning.

But for twenty-eight years, she'd stayed away from his kind, and she wouldn't likely end that streak tonight.

SHIT. I KNEW this was a bad idea.

Stone Mcallister sat nursing his beer at a bar someone had the moxie to name the Silver Saddle. Everything in this town had whimsical names like The Hair-Em, and The Drip. It felt like he'd been dropped in the middle of Whoville. And even after he'd avoided this joint for six months, tonight his luck had run out. Jedd, his mechanic, wouldn't take no for an answer. So now he was stuck staring at the blonde with the wavy hair that seemed to dance as much as she did. Dressed in a short white dress, showing off the best pair of legs he'd seen in years and wearing a pair of blue cowboy boots, she had the attention of every male in the place.

She tempted the hell out of him. Something he didn't need.

What he did need right now was some financial hocus pocus, and sitting here staring at the girl wasn't going to help.

She was tearing up the place, dancing with anyone who asked. None of his business. He didn't plan on staying in town for long. That reason, more than any other, made him wonder if maybe he should introduce himself to the young lady. Women were more trouble than he could handle right now, but if the girl wanted a warm bed for the night, he certainly had one. Jedd brought him another beer though he still wasn't done with the first one. Stone set the old one aside and grabbed the cold one.

"Thanks for coming out with me, boss," Jedd shouted over the live band playing some kind of nonsense song about friends in low places. Another thing he could barely stomach about this place. Country music.

"Told you not to call me that."

"Aw, but if it wasn't for you taking over the flight school, I'd be out of a job right now."

"Not true. You're a great mechanic and you'd find work, no matter what." The last thing Stone needed was the pressure of the distinct possibility that if he didn't fix this mess and fix it soon, Jedd would be out of a job. But he was young. He'd find other work.

"I don't know about that. But anyway, I'm not here to talk business. I wanted to give you the good news. I'm going to be a daddy." Jedd reached across to Stone's bottle and they clinked together.

Stone swallowed, in part because the blonde had just passed him on the dance floor, leaving a trail of her sweet scent behind, but mostly because he wondered what Jedd would do with a pregnant wife and no job.

"Congrats." He slapped Jedd's back. Monday Stone would start the ball rolling for Jedd and make a few inquiries. Couldn't hurt.

"Are you going to dance? I can't because Casey would kill me. But don't let me stop you. I see you eyeing Emily." Jedd elbowed him.

"Who?" *Emily. Vanilla. Yeah, she smelled like vanilla.*

"Uh, yeah, the blonde you can't take your eyes off. That's Emily Parker," Jedd said with a wink.

Another thing. People in this town winked too much. He wasn't interested in Fortune, California, this Peyton Place of towns, but Emily did have his attention. In the next moment, she caught him staring, but rather than look away, he locked gazes with her. She smiled back a little and continued to dance.

Stone gulped down the ice-cold beer, hoping it would reach his bloodstream and cool him the hell down. "About the flight school. You know we've been having problems. I had a buyer for the school lined up, but my sister is causing trouble."

"I heard. She wants to sell to that big corporation." All the blood seemed to drain out of Jedd's face. "But there's no chance I could lose my job, right?"

"No, of course not." He couldn't tell Jedd. Not tonight. But if his sister kept it up, Stone was worried his buyer would walk away, afraid to get caught up in a lawsuit.

"Don't worry. I have faith you'll figure it out. If anyone can, you can." Jedd's cell phone rang and he whipped it out, checked the caller ID and smiled. "My wife."

As Jedd walked outside, Stone wondered why anyone would put their faith in him. And as if he needed to prove the point, Stone took one last swallow of his beer, got up and headed straight for the girl.

HOT GUY MARCHED straight toward her, like a man on a mission. Unfortunately Emily was between dancing partners, as vulnerable as a lamb. One quick glance toward the bar and Jimmy chatted quietly with the head bartender and some of their coworkers.

A little tingle went down her spine, and Emily drew in a shallow breath. What was Jimmy doing when she needed him? She could just pull up her big-girl panties and deal with it, but she wouldn't do it alone. Mentally, she picked up a sword to go with the imaginary shield. Yep, she was as ready as she'd ever be. *Go ahead and let me have your best shot, Mr. Hunk.*

On second thought…

Before he reached her side, Emily veered to the right, toward the bar. She'd get Jimmy's attention one way or another. Pretend Jimmy was her boyfriend and scare this guy off. Even if he didn't look like he scared easily. It was worth a try, because her imaginary sword's blade felt a bit dull and the shield a little tarnished.

But the bar was crowded and loud with couples and singles flirting, drinking and shouting over the band. She waved in Jimmy's direction. No luck. One would think she could at least get the attention of the bartender working, but she was striking out tonight. Just her luck. She was invisible to everyone but the dangerous guy.

Emily waved again, two-handed this time. "Doesn't anyone see me?" she asked no one in particular.

"I see you," said Mr. Danger from behind her. Quickly catching the attention of the one female bartender with nothing more than a finger, he pulled out his wallet from his back pocket and set a couple of bills on the bar. "I'll have a beer and whatever the lady's having."

"I'm not drinking," Emily sputtered.

"Then why were you waving your arms around like ground control?"

"I'm trying to get the attention of my boyfriend

over there." She jutted her chin in Jimmy's direction.

He winced. "Don't look now, but your boyfriend is kissing another woman."

"What?" Emily turned.

Jimmy was in a lip lock with Trish, who must have sneaked in at some point.

"Oh. Well, that's disappointing."

"I guess he's just not that into you." He took a swallow and set his bottle down. Studied her.

She wilted in two seconds flat. A record. "Fine, he's not my boyfriend."

He quirked an eyebrow. "Really."

"I'm here with my sister. I'm Emily."

His navy blue eyes held an intensity which threatened to knock her figurative sword right out of her stone-cold hands. "I know." He smiled, the naked desire never leaving his steely eyes.

"If that's your way of introducing yourself, your momma didn't teach you right."

He blinked but stuck out his hand. "Stone Mcallister."

A big hand, warm and rough. "Stone Mcallister, I don't know what I've been doing in your mind, but you should know I'm not that kind of girl." Defensive Training 101. Make light out of it, joke around. *I've got this.*

"No, you're a liar with a fake boyfriend. I get it." Here came that wicked smile again. It should be made illegal in all fifty states. She fervently wished he'd put it away before somebody got hurt.

Emily swallowed, suddenly feeling both parched and guilty. "I don't usually lie, either. But you make me nervous. I'm only here to dance."

"And what do you think I'm here to do?" He took another pull of his beer and then set it down.

Create mayhem with a woman's body, heart and mind. "I don't know, but I don't like the way you're looking at me. And you don't look very innocent."

"I'm not."

"Right. But listen, I prefer to keep my clothes on in front of all these people so if you don't mind, at least imagine me in a swimsuit." Mentally she wore full body armor, but let him imagine her in a swimsuit. It had to be better than naked.

"All right, a swimsuit it is. One of those string bikinis."

Not exactly what she'd had in mind. "No. Have you ever watched *Dr. Quinn, Medicine Woman?*"

"Yeah. She's hot." He smiled again.

"Imagine me in a skirt like the one she wears, with one of those high-neck tops that go all the way to the chin." Emily put her hand under her chin.

"Still pretty hot."

"Anyway, nice meeting you, Mr. Subtle." Emily turned, but he grabbed her hand.

"I think you should dance with me."

"That's what you get for thinking."

"One dance." He put his bottle down and pulled her onto the dance floor.

For the next few minutes, he proved he could dance, strong large hands wrapped around her waist as he stayed in step. Emily danced three dances in a row with him; though, she suspected no one else dared interrupt. A couple of times Ronnie Walter approached as if he would cut in, but Stone's glare chased him away.

When the music slowed to "Let Me Down Easy," Stone pulled her against him. Fast tunes had played all night, which meant his hands only briefly lingered on her waist, but she couldn't risk a slow song. She should stop the torture of a slow dance now, but she found his rock-hard chest and the way her head fit under his chin too seductive. He smelled like a man. Leather and some kind of light aftershave that didn't make her dizzy. Not what she had planned for tonight or any night since she'd decided to be done with men.

"I haven't seen you here before," Emily said against his chest as she tried to pretend for one moment she might go home with this guy. Never times infinity to the tenth power. This kind of guy couldn't be controlled.

"I haven't been here before." His hand lowered to the small of her back, and she might have trembled a little bit.

"Why not?"

Here was the problem, because there was a problem with every handsome man from here to Poughkeepsie. Of course he was married, probably with a wife and kid at home. She'd call that strike, one, two and three. If this guy was single, then Emily was the tooth fairy.

A veil went over his eyes and he stopped smiling. "New in town. And I don't like bars."

"You're married."

He stopped moving, like she'd slapped him. "I would be at home with my wife if I was married. And we wouldn't waste time dancing. Or if we did, it would be the horizontal kind."

Emily cleared her throat and tried to dispel the image of Stone dancing. Horizontally. "So you think we're wasting time here?"

"Not if I do this right." He grinned and twirled his finger in a strand of her hair like he had every right to do it.

She stared at his finger like she would cut it off, but this seemed to have no effect on him. "What don't you like about bars?"

He was probably an alcoholic and it was too hard to be around booze. Stone was up to bat, unaware he was about to strike out.

"People. Noise." He threw a glance in the direction of the band.

"That's music." She glared at him.

"If you say so."

"Where did you learn how to dance?" For a man who hated country music, he knew his steps.

His eyes closed for a brief second. "Long story. Let's just say it involved a dare, a G-string and a six-pack of beer. I'd rather not say any more. What about you? Looking for something? Or someone?"

"What makes you think I'm looking for someone?" Heavens, her shield had slipped.

"You're kidding. Every guy in this place has his eye on you."

Not possible. She whipped her head around, wondering which one of them had fooled her. Stone, at least, was obvious. "No, they don't. I went to school with half of these guys. They only want to dance with me."

"Uh-huh."

"And you. What about you? Who gave you subtlety lessons, because you should really get your money back."

"Hey, I'm only trying to protect you. From the others."

Emily managed to crack a smile. "My sister and I come here whenever we want to dance. That's all." She wanted to spell it out for him because he didn't look like the kind of guy who was used to hearing the word *no* from a woman. "And do you have to look at me like that?"

"Like how?"

"Like I'm a steak and you're not a vegetarian." Maybe if he'd stop looking at her like she was a T-bone, she could stop sweating. Already, a trickle had slid down the inside of her thigh straight into her boot.

"True, I'm not a vegetarian. But I don't bite unless I've known you for at least a month."

Someone get her the smelling salts. "A whole month?"

"Yep," he said with a grin as the song ended.

The longest dance in history had ended. Time to get Molly home. Besides, if Emily didn't get out of his arms, the rest of her resolve might weaken. Maybe all she needed was one night with a man like this to help her forget the way Greg had humiliated her, and this guy would do it, no question about it.

Too bad she wasn't that kind of girl. Rules were in place for a reason. "I need to get my sister and get her home."

"Are you sure?" He lifted her chin so it was inches away from his lips, and his warm breath reached her.

She wasn't sure of anything as she stared into those eyes. They were kind eyes, and not the eyes of a man on the prowl, which made him all the more confusing. She could kiss him, if she was a different woman. If she wasn't Emily Parker, currently researching her family tree, and if she was willing to forget who she was for a second, she could. Maybe. Might even let him kiss her. In another life.

It wasn't going to happen tonight. Emily pivoted out of his arms and turned in time to see the back of Molly's head.

Leaving the bar with Thomas.

CHAPTER TWO

"MOLLY!" EMILY HEADED after her sister. No way would this happen under her watch. Molly had obviously had too much to drink and ignored her promise. Either that or she'd lost her ever-lovin' mind.

A man was the last thing Molly needed right now. She used men to distract her from the real work she had to do on herself. Sooner or later Molly would have to face the mess she'd left behind.

Emily stomped through the couples on the dance floor, and they parted like the Red Sea. She thought she heard some of their whispers:

There she goes, and she's mad. Boy, I tell you, she almost looks like Molly right now.

I mean, there's no way you can keep it inside for so long. Before you know it, blast, you've got a disaster on your hands.

Yes, sir, Emily's about to let someone have it. Should we go watch?

She threw open the bar's side door and spied Molly about to get into Thomas's car. A few quick purpose-filled strides and Emily stood next to Thomas' old beat-up Ford.

"Where are you going, young lady?" Emily grabbed Molly's arm.

"She's going home with me." Thomas bowed. The smell of tequila nearly knocked Emily off her feet. He sure wasn't driving her sister, or anyone else.

"No, she's not. She promised me. Right?" Emily pulled at Molly on one side, and Thomas pulled on the other.

"Sorry, mister, but I have a sister." Molly swayed a bit to the right, demonstrating her own level of intoxication.

"Why you gotta be such a killjoy?" Thomas tapped Emily's shoulder hard enough to make her wince. "If you don't want to have any fun, that's your business. But don't ruin it for Molly."

"You should take your hand off her right now," a voice said from behind Emily.

Emily turned. All the planes of Stone's face were set in hard lines, his jaw rock hard. He looked different. Still dangerous, but in a whole other kind of way.

"What did you say, buddy?" Thomas sidled up to Stone, clenching a fist in the air.

"The lady is not going home with you. And you're not going anywhere until you sleep it off."

"That's right. Thank you." Finally, someone had come to her aid instead of the other way around.

He shot her a hot look she felt down to the heels of her boots. Not to mention how it began to melt her shield.

While she tried to take her focus away from his lips and back to the matter at hand, a flying fist seemed to come out of nowhere and connect with Stone's jaw.

Stone reacted Ninja-style and had Thomas on his back within moments.

"Cool," someone said from the back of the crowd. "Did you see that move? I can do that."

"Emily!" Molly, as if she'd suddenly realized the mess she'd made, reached for her.

Emily pulled Molly to her side as others spilled out from the bar to witness the fight in the parking lot. Except, from the looks of it, there wasn't much fight left in old Thomas there on the ground, twisting and writhing under Stone's pin. A fresh pint of guilt seeped through Emily's veins, knowing Stone had probably taken a hit because she'd distracted him for a moment.

What she should do is stay behind and thank him. Properly. But there were two problems. First, she'd never kissed a man she didn't know, even if this might be a good time to start. Second, she'd given up men, and this one would be trouble. Trouble rolled into fun with a heaping side of heartache.

Jedd soon joined the fray to help Stone, not that he seemed to need any help and, between the two of them, they had the situation under control. Right now Emily had her own damage control to do and needed to get her sister back home. Her drunk and sad sister, who had fooled Emily into coming here tonight.

"Let's get out of here." Emily pulled her sister away from the commotion, throwing one last glance in the direction of her hot hero. His back was turned to her as he restrained Thomas, who was now calling out every expletive Emily had ever heard, and some she hadn't.

This wasn't the way she'd envisioned parting tonight, and her chest tightened with the mess she'd left Stone to handle. She should have explained that she couldn't take it any further with him, not now. Not ever. Casually drop in the fact she didn't do risky and didn't do strangers. She didn't do much of anything, period. Not anymore.

Emily pulled her sister away from the chaos and shoved a sobbing Molly in the front passenger side seat of the Chevy truck.

Good thing Molly was already crying or Emily would have said something to make her. Emily gripped the steering wheel and high-tailed it out of the parking lot, kicking up gravel. She turned left on Monterey Road and headed toward Fortune Ranch.

"I'm so sorry. I didn't mean for it to happen," Molly bawled.

"Look at it this way. Thomas won't be driving

anyone home tonight, which is the way it should be. But I thought we agreed. Why did you do this?"

"I wanted to feel good, even for a little while. Do you know how long it's been since a man wanted me? I mean, really wanted me. And only me."

"We're not going there. You are *not* going to talk to me about being lonely."

"I'm sorry. But you know how to be alone, and I don't. I feel like crap. And I probably look like it, too." Molly pulled out a tissue from the glove compartment.

"You ought to feel bad. The man took a hit to the jaw, and you don't even know him." Neither did she, but after tonight, she almost wished she did.

"I have to apologize to him." Molly rubbed at her mascara-smeared raccoon eyes.

"Don't worry yourself too much about it. Something tells me the man can handle himself." Or had Molly missed those special forces–like skills he'd displayed? Emily didn't even know what the man did for a living, but she'd bet her family's ranch it didn't involve sitting behind a desk.

"Before you say anything, I know I have to start making better choices." Molly rocked back and forth in her seat.

She sounded so pathetic and broken. Emily

wished she understood, but she still wasn't sure she could put her finger on what exactly had gone wrong. Of course, Molly wasn't talking about it, either. For the first six months of her daughter Sierra's life, Molly isolated herself from the rest of her family. The next thing anyone knew, Molly had taken off to Hollywood, leaving Dylan and Sierra behind. To a place so foreign to the Parker family, she might as well have gone to Mars.

"You have to get your mind off men. They're not going to make anything better for you. Work on yourself first, like I am. Everything else will fall into place then."

Emily turned her truck at the large sign that welcomed one and all to "Fortune Family Ranch: Events/Weddings/Picnics." Once a large cattle ranch, present times meant the Parker family had to diversify. Enterprise.

The new family business.

The truck rolled down the long dusty driveway, past the empty lots designated for parking, past the red barn that served as a gift shop and up to the main Victorian house sitting on the hill.

Emily parked and turned in her seat to give Molly her full attention. "Does Dylan know you're back in town?"

"I hope not. You know how he hates me."

"He doesn't hate you. He's just not happy with you right now. Can you blame him?"

"It's his fault, anyway. Maybe if he'd come after me."

"When you didn't tell anyone where you'd gone? Don't do this, Molly. It's not his fault you left."

Emily should have paid more attention to the situation at the time, and she still blamed herself for that. She should have seen that Molly was in over her head and going under. But a few of the times Emily had wanted to come over and help, Molly claimed the baby was sleeping, or the apartment was a mess or any one of many other excuses why they didn't want company. The times Emily had managed to make it inside, the small efficiency had looked like a bomb had gone off. Stacks of baby diapers all over the house, clothes strewn in every corner, piles of dirty laundry practically tall enough to be a teepee, other clean clothes folded in the basket, dishes overflowing in the sink.

Molly and Dylan had managed to keep mostly to themselves, and whether it had been intentional or not Emily had never been sure. Dylan's mother could barely stand Molly, and the unexpected pregnancy hadn't helped. But Emily didn't fully understand why Molly would have shut her own family out. Unless it had been because of Dylan, who thought Molly had been spoiled by their father for too long.

And true enough, had he had one look inside,

he would have likely hired Molly a cleaning service. Not how Dylan rolled.

"You needed help, and maybe you didn't know how to ask for it," Emily said now.

"I know you tried, but Dylan always thought we should do it on our own. And of course, he was never around much to help me."

"There was no shame in either one of you needing help. You're both so young." Emily now wished she'd bulldozed her way in more often. What if Molly had suffered from postpartum depression? Dylan, as a trained EMT, should have seen the signs. But maybe he'd been too close to the situation.

After Molly had gone, Emily tried for a few months to help Dylan with a colicky and often inconsolable Sierra. Eventually, due to logistics and family ties, most of the babysitting shifted to Violet, Dylan's mother. Dylan stopped calling, and Emily, ashamed of her sister and tired of making excuses for her, stayed away.

"Maybe if he'd loved me more. It felt like the only thing we had in common anymore was Sierra. He barely touched me for six months. Do you know what that's like?"

Molly didn't want to go there with Emily right now. Did she know what it was like to have her heart ripped out seam by precious seam? "Does a broken engagement count?"

Molly didn't look at Emily. "I'm sorry, Em."

"It's all right."

But it wasn't. Emily had never been engaged before Greg. Greg was reliable, safe, structured. A software engineer. If a girl couldn't trust a man like Greg, who color-coded his ties, then whom could she trust? No one.

MAYBE NEXT TIME you'll stay home.

The night wasn't over until a cab service took Thomas Aguirre home, black eye covered with a bag of ice from the bar. But the real cherry on top of this sundae had been when Stone looked for the stacked blonde that had caused him his sore jaw and found her nowhere in sight. Not like she owed him a thing, but a simple kiss would have been nice. Maybe even a short "thanks."

It usually took a woman at least a month to be this kind of trouble to him.

Now he had a bruised lip and sore jaw, thanks to being temporarily distracted by the way she stared into his eyes with a kind of trust that sent lava-level heat running through him. More to the point, the whole thing was his fault for being stupid enough to follow her outside and become mixed up in drama that was clearly none of his damn business. That should teach him.

Jedd brought out a bag of ice. "It's a good thing we caught Thomas trying to leave with Molly, 'cause he had no business driving."

"Yeah. Glad I could be of assistance." Stone

took the ice and placed it in on his jaw since he couldn't put it on his sore ego. He should have seen that flying fist coming. Six months out of the service, and he'd let his guard down.

"I wish I'd been out here sooner."

"Don't worry about it."

"I hope you don't blame this on Emily. If you blame anyone, blame Thomas. As for Molly, that girl is hell on wheels. Almost forgot she was back in town." Jedd fell into step beside Stone, as he headed toward his truck.

"My fault. Shouldn't have followed Emily outside."

"But you thought she was in trouble."

Stone didn't want to be anyone's hero, or pretend he'd had anything on his mind other than finishing what he'd started with Emily.

"To tell the truth, I didn't do enough thinking tonight." He massaged his jaw and managed to crack a smile.

Jedd laughed. "Yeah, Emily has a way of doing that to a guy."

Stone looked sideways at Jedd.

"Naw, Emily's older than me and never gave me a second look. She was going to get married to some guy from Palo Alto. But it didn't happen." Jedd lifted a shoulder.

"I don't need her damn biography. I won't ever see her again." He clicked his key fob to unlock the truck.

"If you say so," Jedd said.

Stone should have followed his first instincts and kept to himself. Probably should have searched harder for an excuse as to why he couldn't come out with Jedd. "I do. I'm out of here."

"Thanks for coming out with me. See you Monday, boss—I mean, Stone," Jedd called out.

Stone threw open the door and climbed in his truck, throwing the ice pack to the side. He'd be sleeping alone tonight and that would be okay. It would have to be. With damage like this in thirty minutes, who knew what she could do with a little more time? He didn't need the distraction. All he wanted tonight was a warm body under him, and Emily wouldn't stop there. She wouldn't stop until she was another in his long list of commitments.

Speaking of commitments...

A few minutes later, he'd pulled into the driveway of James Mcallister's sorry-looking single family home, shut off the truck and stared at his inheritance. The place needed a new coat of paint. Hell, it needed to be bulldozed down to the ground and started over. He didn't have the time or inclination to do either. But he, along with his sister, Sarah, was heir to this mess.

Six months ago when he'd separated from the air force, Dad had said, "You didn't have to come."

"The hell I didn't." The air force might have been his life for the past twelve years, but when it came down to the AF and Dad, there had been no real choice.

The fact that it had taken him too long to make the choice? No use revisiting that scenario now. It had been tough to think anything could be strong enough to knock his old man down, but he'd been wrong about that. Should have separated earlier, when he'd first heard of the diagnosis. It seemed to be the first in a long line of mistakes he'd made lately.

Back then, Stone thought he'd have time with Dad. Time to say a long goodbye, fly their Cessnas in tandem a few times and maybe take a couple of fishing trips. But colon cancer had a way of sneaking up on a man. Four months. It was all the time they'd had, and Dad spent most of it telling Stone about his last wishes.

"I know this isn't what you planned to do with your life. But stay long enough to sell the school so Cassie and Jedd can keep their jobs. Don't listen to Cassie. She loves the place."

She could have fooled Stone. "Don't worry. It's all taken care of."

"When I die, Sarah will get my letter and half of everything. Be nice to her. I didn't want her to know about the cancer. What would be the point? I sure don't want her to see me like this."

In the end, it had been a quiet death, not at all

like all the other deaths he'd witnessed. There were no screams, no blood and no raging hot anger. No one fought death harder than a young airman. But Dad had been ready. The hospice nurse had nudged Stone out of a light sleep, and he'd been by Dad's bedside to hear him take his last breath.

A few days later, Sarah had been notified, and the proverbial shit hit the fan.

Both the house and school would be sold and the proceeds split down the middle. He had a buyer lined up for the school, someone who loved planes and planned to keep everything the same. The way it should be. The way Dad wanted it.

Unless Sarah had her way.

He stuck his key in the front door, turned it and slipped inside. He wasn't fooled by the silence for a second as he slipped into warfare mode. Granted, he hadn't done any hand-to-hand combat in the air force. A good thing he'd been trained, though.

Stone flipped on the light switch in the family room. Winston, Dad's ninety-pound golden retriever mix, flew around the corner and jumped on Stone. If licking could kill, he'd be a dead man walking.

Standing on his hind legs the beast nearly reached Stone's height of six feet. But Stone had a knee, and he put it to good use by nudging Winston's middle. "Off!"

Winston jumped down, his brown eyes wounded. It would take a lot more than a knee in the chest to hurt the monster, and he wasn't fooling Stone.

"Don't give me that look. I swear I'll find you a new owner if you don't stop jumping on me. The licking is bad enough. This is not going well."

Within seconds, Winston had followed Stone into the kitchen, his food bowl in his jowls. Whoever said dogs weren't smart had never owned a Winston.

"Yeah, yeah." Stone fed him and watched Winston go to town. "With manners like that, you'll never get a girl."

Unfortunately, that made him picture the way Emily had moved in his arms and the curves she had in all the right places. It was possible that if he stepped back into that country music–infested den, he might see her again. Why that mattered he didn't know, but if he didn't get his mind off her, he might wind up making another trip to the Silver Whip, or the Silver Saddle, or whatever the hell they called it.

Stone stripped in his bedroom, took a shower, toweled off and didn't bother with the boxers. Instead, he plopped on the California king, rolled into the covers and let sleep take him away.

DAMN, THIS GIRL can kiss. Emily straddled him and kissed him long and deep. She moaned, which ripped out a groan from him as his hands lifted the skirt of her dress, searching for heaven and finding nothing but silk. Soft. Smooth. Curves. Skin. Yeah.

Suddenly, she licked his face. *This is strange, but if she's into it, I'll learn to like it.*

The bark was what finally woke him. Winston on his bed. Again. The beast's paws on Stone's chest as he lapped at his face.

"Off!" Stone growled and opened one eye against the ray of light breaking through the window blinds. He pushed Winston off, rubbed his aching jaw and glanced at the clock. Crap, eight already. Time to get up.

He'd have to cut his workout short this morning. Usually he ran five miles before work and hit the punching bag in the garage for an hour. Couldn't afford to get too soft. He might be out of the air force, but the air force would never be out of him.

Last night he'd dreamed of the girl who made him forget he was a short-timer in this town. No need to start rescuing people. Served him right, even though it had been a cheap shot. His own fault for paying too much attention to the girl and not enough to the other man's fists. *All right. Get over it, Chump.*

Winston stayed next to the bed and stared at Stone, panting, brown eyes questioning. He cocked his head and barked.

"I told you, this is my bed and over there is

yours." Stone pointed to the cushion that sat in the corner of the bedroom.

Winston barked again. Stone loved dogs as much as the next person, but Winston was less of a dog than an inconsiderate roommate. A hairy one who demanded his meals on time and whose only contribution to household chores was creating more of them. Another treasure he'd inherited from Dad. Everything he'd handed down seemed to come with complications. And commitments.

Dad had loved this dog and swore it could read his thoughts. Right now, Stone wondered if Winston could read his, too, because they were less than charitable.

"You interrupted a great dream, monster." The first decent dream in months.

Stone pulled on a pair of jeans and headed to the kitchen, Winston following close behind. True to form, he performed his shameless circling dance as Stone scooped out the dry dog food and placed it in his bowl.

"Wish I could be that happy to have breakfast," Stone mumbled, placing the bowl on the cold terracotta kitchen floor. "Do you realize all you do is eat and sleep?"

He'd not only inherited Winston, the flight school and his father's ramshackle ranch house, but pretty much James Mcallister's life. And if he often felt like there wasn't enough oxygen in the room, it was probably because too many people, dogs and inanimate objects depended on him.

He'd arrived in town with one large duffel bag and everything he owned in it. He was always ready to leave at a moment's notice.

The doorbell rang, and Winston ran out of the room like a scared schoolgirl. *Doorbells.* Winston was afraid of them. Then again, Dad's doorbell played a haunting rendition of "Grandma Got Run Over By a Reindeer." Stone kept meaning to disconnect the thing.

Stone peered through the peephole. Staff Sergeant Matt Conner, wearing his civilian clothes, held a couple of cups. "Let me in, asshole. These are hot. Coffee."

Stone swung open the door and accepted a cup from The Drip (Rise and Shine and Have a Drip, the annoying cup said) as Matt walked inside.

"Is he—?" Matt asked, eyebrows raised.

Stone nodded. "Put the cup down now if you know what's good for you."

Matt set the cup on the short key table by the door and squatted like a wrestler. Yeah, he knew the drill. Like he'd heard his name called, Winston flew around the corner and tackled Matt.

Fortunately, Matt was a dog person, not to mention the size of a linebacker. "Hey, I love you, too, you big lug."

"Don't encourage him." Stone walked into the kitchen, taking a gulp of the coffee he had become addicted to. He'd never been there himself, but coffee from The Drip was first-rate; although, he'd never get used to saying that name. "Want something to eat?"

"You have food?" Matt followed.

Stone didn't answer. All right, so he was stalling.

"Yeah, I didn't think so. Let's get to it. Where do we begin?" Matt threw him a look.

"Yeah." Stone knew that look. It was a *get your shit together, airman* look. If he'd given it once, he'd given it a hundred times to the newbs. And it had been more than a few years since he'd been on this side of it. It didn't sit well with him.

Sure, he'd helped pack up the barracks bags of airmen who were never going home again, but this was different.

My father's house. Where to begin? No matter how he sliced it, it didn't feel right to get rid of Dad's things. Like maybe he'd be back later, pissed Stone couldn't see the sense in hanging on to ten old fishing rods. Crazy.

"*Yeah*'s not an answer, dude." Matt threw him a pity look, the kind bestowed upon the widows and orphans of the men who weren't coming back.

"Where do you suggest, moron?"

"The clothes." Matt met Stone's gaze.

They were still in the closet. Pretty pathetic. Clothes were always the first thing to go. It wasn't like he was going to suddenly start wearing plaid shirts and polyester pants.

"Right this way."

Winston followed them in the bedroom and lay like a rug near Dad's bed. Stone made himself shove shirts and pants, even an old suit he'd never seen before, into a plastic garbage bag.

Matt worked faster, bagging up two to every one of Stone's. "I'll take all these to Goodwill Industries."

"Sure." Stone didn't look at Matt. They were just clothes. It shouldn't make any damn difference. He didn't understand why his chest felt tight.

"By the way, she came by to see me again yesterday." Matt said it like it was nothing, like he might as well be talking about the weather.

"Why?" Stone didn't even have to ask who "she" was. She'd somehow decided Matt was her new best friend.

"You know why. She wants to talk to you."

"I have nothing to say to her."

"She's your sister," Matt said with an emphasis on the word *sister*, as if it was supposed to mean something to Stone. It didn't.

Not his fault. His parents had made that decision, and he'd had no say in the matter. Only now, he was left to pick up the pieces. All in the past, and best left there. He wasn't going to start singing "Kumbaya" this late in the game. "Here's the thing. I don't know her anymore."

"You could get to know her. Again." Matt threw another bag in the pile.

But it had been Sarah's choice to stop visiting summers after that last one when she'd been thirteen. He'd been fifteen at the time, and sue him if he'd been a little busy. Their parents had each agreed that by fourteen each kid could decide where they wanted to spend their summer. That summer Stone chose to stay in California where he had a job and a learner's permit. It meant that he'd spent the summer with his sister for the first time since the divorce. Looking back, he probably hadn't paid her enough attention but what he'd remembered of that summer was a teenage girl with attitude. Not much different from now.

Dad didn't know what the hell to do with her, either, when she didn't want to fish or camp anymore. Every morning she'd glare daggers at the both of them as if they were doing something to offend her by simply breathing. Then she'd gone in the bathroom for three hours where she did something to her hair.

It was about all he remembered of that last summer from hell.

The next summer Sarah chose not to visit again, nor any summer after that. There had been cards over the holidays and a few strained phone calls. Stone had unfortunately had a front-row seat to his father's confusion and pain at feeling shut out of his daughter's life. It had served to remind Stone to call his mother and not just wait for her calls to him. He might not have thought he needed her much as a stupid teenager, but he'd always loved his mother. Which was why he couldn't quite understand Sarah's anger now. She'd made the choice. If their father hadn't begged, it was because the Mcallister men didn't beg.

Stone surveyed the closet. They'd made a dent in it, but not much more. He'd leave the boxes on the shelves for another time. Had his father thrown anything away? Ever?

Stone reached for a tie that looked straight out of the seventies. Probably not. "Maybe we should have a family reunion. Picnic, maybe?"

"Don't be a smartass."

"She wants to sell to a developer. There's nothing to talk about."

"You could talk and explain this is what your Dad wanted."

"She knows that. All she wants is more money. She doesn't care that people are about to lose their livelihoods." It wasn't just Cassie and Jedd. The airport had a small air museum, the only one of its kind for miles. There was also the Shortstop Snack Shack, owned and operated by a retired firefighter. Dad had owned the hangar building and leased the space to everyone else. The aviation school was the anchor, and if it was sold to a developer all the other businesses would go, too.

"I get the feeling your sister might be reasonable. Why not meet with her?"

"I did." All she'd wanted to do was hurl insults and accusations at their late father. He carried enough guilt about those last months without Sarah adding to it.

"Again, I mean." Matt slid him a look. "One meeting that didn't go well isn't enough. It's worth a try."

But Stone wasn't sure of that anymore. He should talk with Sarah again, to see if he could get her to see reason. Matt seemed to think she was open, but that hadn't been Stone's experience. Some people were a lost cause, and he felt fairly certain the sister he didn't know anymore was one of them.

CHAPTER THREE

"Wake up, Emily."

Emily opened one eye.

Grammy stood over her, dressed in her sparkly blue jeans and leopard-print top. It was one of the most irritating things about her grandmother. She refused to give in to convention and wear track-suits like all her friends did.

Emily hadn't even heard her come in. "What good is it to give me the loft for privacy if you keep barging in on me like this? What if I had company?"

"Emily, dear, please. I don't have time for jokes. We have the Chamber of Commerce party today. I'll need you to help George. He's an old man now."

"Don't let him hear you say that."

George Carver had worked for the family for as long as Emily could remember. Old or not, he was still their handyman, their gardener and a long-time family friend.

Emily's dog, Pookie, a Poodle and Chihuahua mix, peeked out from the under the covers.

"You're letting Pookie in your bed? What's wrong with you?"

"She'd old, Grammy, and it was cold out last night. I caught her shivering." That was Emily's story and she was sticking to it. Growing up on their pseudo ranch usually meant dogs lived outside, but Emily liked it better this way. If Grammy was going to let Emily have the loft over the garage, then Emily could let Pookie have a spot on her bed at night.

"Girl, your heart is just too big. Pookie has you fooled. She's fine outside and has a warm dry place in the pen. Cuddles up next to Beast every chance she gets. Anyway, the meat is coming in at noon, and I'll need you to check it. You know what happened last time." Grammy started to make the bed with Emily in it.

"Hey. Why don't you let me get out of bed first? What time is it?" Fighting to push off the last dregs of sleep, Emily pulled the covers up to her nose. She wasn't sure, but she might have been in the middle of a dream that made her blush, even thinking of it. It might have involved Stone and some of that horizontal dancing.

"It's time for you to get up. And there's something I want to show you first." Grammy walked toward the front door and put her hand on the doorknob.

"What is it?" Emily rubbed her eyes and looked at the clock. *Eight thirty.* Too bad Grammy didn't believe in sleeping in even on the weekends, because right now all Emily wanted was another few minutes. And she wasn't going to get them.

"Wait till you see. I ordered it and it came yesterday. I'll meet you at the house for breakfast." Grammy let herself out, but not before picking up Pookie and carrying her out. "Dogs stay outside."

Emily rustled her feet from under the warm covers and let them touch the cool hardwood. She shrank back and resisted the urge to bury under the blanket and go back to her dreams. Dreams in which she'd gone home with Stone.

Forget about him. I'm not ready for someone like that, and maybe I never will be. No, she was never going to be "that girl." The girl who didn't worry about consequences. The one who took a chance. She was too sensible for all that.

Emily showered, tried not to think of Stone, dried off and dressed in the working jeans and Fortune Ranch company shirt she wore while working on the family's ranch. Not that it was a ranch anymore, unless one counted a petting zoo and three ponies. But Grammy insisted on keeping the name, a testament to the former glory of the Parker family's four-hundred-acre cattle ranch of days gone by.

After eminent domain and the freeway extension had made its way through, they'd been left with forty acres and the house. Thank God for ever-resourceful Grammy, who claimed she hadn't lived through the depression for nothing. And even if the family business now came down to outdoor company parties, picnics and high school Sadie Hawkins dances, they still had their home.

Thank heavens for that, because right now Emily needed home. The place where she'd grown up and the last place she'd lived with Mama. She'd been gone seventeen years, but her absence still ached if Emily thought about it too much.

Emily made her way down the creaky steps of her second-story apartment loft above the detached garage and jogged over to the main Victorian house on the hill. She threw open the side door to the kitchen and walked in to the sounds of Molly's high-pitched voice. "That's it—you've finally taken the last train into Crazy Town, and this time I'm not sure you'll be back."

"What's up?" Emily grabbed a mug from the cupboard.

Molly and Grammy stood before some type of large vase on the kitchen counter.

"Grammy has done it now." Molly looked like she'd woken only minutes ago and stood in the middle of the kitchen wearing her oversize Hairdressers Do It with Style T-shirt, hair mussed and eyes bloodshot with the after effects of too much tequila.

"Once again, your sister is demonstrating how

short-sighted she can be. This is where I'll be buried—my ashes will be, anyway. And I want you girls to pick the perfect place where I'll be seated for all eternity. I was thinking somewhere in the dining room."

That thing sitting on the kitchen counter was an urn? No wonder Molly was freaked out. Emily wasn't sure she could ever eat food in here again. "Can we take it off the kitchen counter?"

"For the love of Pete, you girls act like I bought a used urn. This was ordered from the most highly regarded crematorium in the state. Don't you think it's nice?" Grammy ran her hand along the little pink roses that decorated the border.

Emily couldn't look at the place where her Grammy's bones would someday lie. "Can't we do this another time?"

Grammy waved a hand. "Fine. I'll find a place in the dining room. This way I'll be in attendance at every Thanksgiving and Christmas even after I'm gone. Now, I'll be watching over you all, so don't forget to say grace."

"Oh, Daddy is going to love this," Molly said with an eye roll.

"Your father isn't any of my concern. He spends half his time in Texas pretending he's a cowboy when he ought to be home with his family," Grammy shouted over her shoulder as she left the room with her urn.

The subject of their father and his reluctance

to let go of the cattle ranch days was one Emily couldn't handle before noon. Or plenty of coffee.

She eyed the bacon and eggs Grammy had left on a warming platter, considering whether or not she still had an appetite.

"I was thinking—" Molly said with a grin.

"Don't you dare." Emily pointed a finger.

"I'll be good this time. Okay, I should have stayed away from the tequila shots. And Thomas."

"That would have been nice."

"But we should go see if we can find that nice man who helped us with Thomas. And then I can apologize."

Emily sat at the kitchen table and thought about how much she'd like to thank Stone. But she wouldn't need Molly for that. "I'm not going back there for a while."

"Why? I saw you dancing with him. And you looked happy. What have you got against happy?"

"I don't have anything against it. I have something against starting a relationship right now. I have to work on myself."

"Who said anything about a relationship?" Molly drew the last word out, emphasizing every syllable. "Why does everything have to be a big deal to you? Can't you just have fun?"

Of course she couldn't have fun. She had plans to make, and they didn't involve a man. Emily opened her mouth to answer, but Grammy walked back in the kitchen and spoke first.

"What you need to do is learn from your big sister, young lady. Sometimes a lady needs to take a good long look at her life to find out where she's going. It wouldn't hurt you to do the same." Grammy reached for a mug and poured some coffee in it.

Molly rolled her eyes. "Sorry. I forgot Little Miss Perfect does everything right."

Emily winced at the moniker, but what was so wrong with setting goals and controlling one's future? For so long, she'd been the only one with any good sense in this family. Dad out in Texas playing cowboy, Molly pretending she hadn't screwed up the best thing in her life and Grammy planning her own funeral.

Either way, it was time for Plan B, since none of her best-laid plans had worked out.

Like real estate. She'd bought the course on the late-night infomercial, but nothing was like the book said it would be. Her attempt at writing a historical romance hadn't done any better. And if it wasn't for the stage fright that kept her from returning to the stage, maybe she could get that country music career off the ground.

Either way, she had to figure something out, because she was running out of time.

Molly had struck a nerve when she talked about ticking clocks. It wasn't that Emily wanted a baby—she'd given up that dream—but reminders of how little she'd accomplished in her twenty-eight years weren't welcome. She'd recently read in one of her college alumni newsletters that a former classmate had founded her own clothing company and another was running for a congressional seat in her district.

Emily needed something like that. Something big.

Grammy patted Emily's back. "Nothing wrong with being a good girl, right, dear?"

Good Girl. Yeah, that was her. Another name might be *Doormat*. "Never said I was perfect."

"Don't forget tomorrow is our monthly meeting with the Pink Ladies. I know you won't want to miss it, Emily." Grammy sat across from Emily.

"Why are you encouraging her?" Molly slammed her coffee mug on the table. "That's exactly what Emily needs. Hanging out with a bunch of geriatric women. That should do it."

"Your sister has a hobby, and maybe you can find one, too," Grammy said with a scowl.

"I have a hobby. It's called dancing. Meanwhile you waste your time talking about dead people that can't do a thing for you anymore." Molly took a gulp from her mug and gave Emily a pointed look.

Emily shook her head. "I love when you both talk about me like I'm not here. What if I'm interested in our family history? What's wrong with trying to find out all about my namesake?"

"That Emily Parker isn't going to help you. Because there's a little problem. She's dead."

"Listen, young lady. Never speak ill of the dead. Someday I'll be one of them." Grammy reached over and swatted Molly's hand.

Molly walked over to the sink with her mug. "Someday we'll all be one of them. But before that, let's have a little bit of damn fun before we all die, why don't we?"

Grammy laughed at Molly's back as she walked out of the kitchen. "Oh, Molly, dear, you are so dramatic. Learn to be a little bit more like your sister. Level-headed. Grounded."

Emily almost choked on her coffee. Was that what she was? Level-headed? Grounded? Why did that sound boring?

Emily had spent the past year in a kind of self-imposed hibernation with little interest in anything other than eating, sleeping and watching reruns of the first three seasons of *Homeland*.

But then a few months ago Grammy had come to her with some genealogy research. She wanted to find out whether her family had come from Ireland or Scotland. One of Grammy's Historical Society friends had traced her ancestors back to the Revolutionary War. Naturally, Grammy was convinced they could do better than that. They only needed to trace the family lineage back far enough and the truth of the spunky and steady Parker spirit would be revealed. It had all started out simply, with a bit of online searches, and before Emily knew it, she'd been spending most of her spare time with Grammy's friends.

Then Molly had come back home. Suddenly genealogy research was a hobby for the geriatric crowd.

"I'll quit when I find out what happened to the first Emily Parker." Time to reevaluate, perhaps, the amount of time she spent on this hobby. A little diversity couldn't hurt. Getting out from under this "good girl" image couldn't hurt, either.

MOLLY TRUDGED UP the steps to her bedroom, and threw herself on the trundle bed. Everyone in her family was officially bonkers, fascinated with the past and dead people when there was so much living to be done right now. Emily was too young to hang out with all those old women, but Molly couldn't seem to get through to her. Yet.

She'd get Emily back out on the dance floor, or her nickname wasn't Trouble.

She reached under the mattress and pulled out the photo of Sierra at six months old. She'd just learned to sit up and wore a bib that read Daddy's Girl as she smiled her toothless grin. Molly traced the angle of her baby face. Oh, how she remembered that smile. It was the last picture Molly took of Sierra before she left town. Dylan had been working long hours and left her alone with Sierra night and day. They could have all lived at the

Parker family home and Molly would have had help from both Grammy and Emily, but Dylan had insisted they live on their own. Raise Sierra on their own. Insisted he'd support his own family, and that meant they were stuck in a studio apartment.

That same studio apartment had felt more like a Love Shack when they'd first been married, right after they'd learned of her pregnancy, and made love every night. But once Sierra arrived, everything changed. Dylan had been too tired to do anything but collapse in a heap at the end of the day.

Emily had offered to help but Molly was so ashamed of her mess. Ashamed that she couldn't stop crying some days. She couldn't figure out how to take a shower and at the same time take care of her baby. And after every time Emily had come over, Dylan had nothing but praises for her big sister. *Emily sure knows how to clean a house.* Or, *Did you fold and put away all this laundry, or did Em?* On and on he'd go about her wonderful big sister and how Molly could learn a lot from her.

Emily wasn't a spoiled Daddy's girl like Molly, Dylan would say. And now that she was a mother, she had to give up on being Daddy's girl. But Daddy seemed to be the only one who realized when Molly was way in over her head. Which, according to him, was pretty much always.

Molly swallowed the sob in her throat and picked up her cell phone. She dialed her father, who was out at their Texas cattle ranch instead of at home where he belonged.

"Daddy?" Molly whispered into the phone.

"What's wrong, baby?" Daddy answered with the Texas twang that grated on her nerves.

But leave it to her daddy to always realize when something was wrong. "I'm bored here. When are you coming home?

"I'll come home next week, for sure."

"I've been back home two months and seen you once."

"The ranch out here keeps me busy. Doesn't Emily keep you company?"

"She's no fun anymore."

"Your sister has been through a rough time. You go easy on her. Have you seen your daughter yet?"

"I don't know if Dylan is going to let me." Dylan had been furious when she'd left. She was still a little bit afraid to face him.

"It's not for him to let you or not let you. You're that baby's momma and nothing can keep you from seeing her."

That's what Daddy thought, but Molly knew Dylan wouldn't make it easy. He'd warned her when she'd left that if she didn't come home immediately, she could forget about coming back. "I'll try, but I can't promise anything."

"You do that, little Trouble. You made a mistake and some people just have to be big enough to forgive you."

More than anything, she wished Daddy was right about that. Molly hung up and stared at the ceiling, trying to swallow the golf ball in her throat. *I'm not going to cry. Not today. I should be all cried out by now.*

She stuffed Sierra's photo back under her mattress.

What she wanted to do and what she could do were two different things. Right now, a little fun wasn't going to kill her.

Anything to forget about the photo that lay pressed under her mattress of the little baby girl with red hair, just like her mommy's.

THE PINK LADIES Genealogical Society gals were in good spirits on Sunday, mostly because Grammy had whipped up her famous wine-based margaritas. It didn't matter everyone knew the recipe originally belonged to George, who called them Po'man Margaritas.

Emily sat at the dining room table with the ladies, her laptop in front of her. She was their online researcher, and the ladies had come to count on her. She searched census records and online gravesite markers for those with ancestors in other states. So, even though she'd had second thoughts about tonight, wondering if maybe she should go back to the Silver Saddle, she was here tending to her obligations. Good girl and all.

Grammy set the pitcher at the end of the table, away from all the papers. "Dig in, girls."

Luanne Hinckle leaned in to Emily. "I can drink now, because Dr. Taylor took me off the pills. You know, from the hysterectomy?"

Emily winced. "Are you doing all right?"

"Oh, honey, I won't miss those parts. Don't need them anymore." Luanne gave a wave of her hand.

"Speaking of pills," Marjory Lewis said, "I've got a new supplement which could help with your arthritis, Jean."

"You don't mean that pool scum thing?" Grammy scowled.

"It's made from blue green algae."

"It's pool scum." Grammy poured a margarita and set it down in front of Emily.

"Emily, are you back on the dating scene again or is it too—ah, too soon? Because if you are, my nephew is on the hunt for the third Mrs. Dr. Logan. And, honey, you would enjoy being a doctor's wife." Luanne winked.

Emily reached for the margarita and took a large gulp. "No thanks, Luanne."

"She's still in recovery, Lu. What's the matter with you?" Marjory patted Emily's hand.

"I'm not in recovery," Emily protested. That would give Greg too much power over her. No way would she let the slimeball control her, even now. "But I'm working on myself."

"Of course you are," Marjory and Luanne said at once.

"If we could get back to the matter at hand," Julia Bush spoke now.

Leave it to Julia to get the meeting back on track. Now a member of the Daughters of the American Revolution, thanks to her family tree, she seemed to believe she was the Grand Pooh-Bah of their little club. Emily didn't dare disagree, and probably no one else would, either.

"Yes, please, Julia. Get us back on track. Where were we when we left off?" Grammy opened the notebook she used to take notes.

Grammy's official parchment family tree was probably still under lock and key. It wouldn't be coming out anytime soon, not when the ladies were drinking. Grammy guarded the document like it was the US Constitution.

"I'm still trying to find out about my Uncle Bob, the one who owned the barbershop back in Maine. I can't find a certificate of death anywhere," Luanne said.

"We'll get to that," Julia said with authority. "But you won't believe this. Remember how Emily hasn't been able to find out much about her namesake, the first Emily Parker?"

"I can't find her on any census records except for the one in nineteen hundred, and by then, she had married." Emily had tried to find out the name of her great-grandmother's parents, but time after time reached nothing but a dead end.

"We know she had a son, Lonnie, and then she died shortly thereafter. Her husband remarried and they had six more children," Grammy added.

"It's like any record of her before her marriage doesn't exist. Where did she come from? Who were her parents?" It bothered Emily to think that a two-year-old had been left motherless, but what bothered her most was it seemed no one would ever remember the first Emily Parker.

Julia smiled and peered over her bifocals. "I've got good news."

Emily's heart did a little squeeze, and her fingers froze on the keyboard. News for her? "What did you find?"

"You won't believe it." Julia looked through the binder she carried with her everywhere—the Bible, she called it.

"Don't keep us in suspense!" Grammy said.

Julia pulled out a piece of paper she'd covered with a plastic sheath.

She did that with all official documents. Emily stopped breathing.

"Now it wasn't easy to find this, but you all know how I have connections now." Julia probably wouldn't spill the beans this century.

"Yes, yes we know!" Luanne leaned forward,

like she might reach across the table and rip it out of Julia's hands.

"This little piece of paper is a private pilot's license," Julia said, her chin rising slightly as she placed it on the table for all to see. "For an Emily Parker."

"Let me see that," Grammy reached for it, only to earn a glare from Julia.

"Careful." Julia slid it over to Grammy.

Emily watched, not moving, as Grammy read it over. "My goodness. How about that." She handed the document to Emily.

It really was the official pilot's license of an Emily Parker. Frayed around the ages, yellowed and worn. "This is my relative?"

"It is," Julia said with authority. "Same date of birth, as you can see. She was only twenty-one at that time."

"And she would have died only three years later," Grammy added.

"Imagine that. A pilot. Isn't that the funniest thing you ever heard?" Marjory elbowed Emily.

"Funny?" Emily put down the paper. It was a connection all right, to a woman who sounded as different from her as any two women could be. Emily had never done anything even remotely that adventurous. The first Emily Parker sounded like a maverick. A rebel.

"You have to admit it. This Emily Parker sounds like she was a risk taker, maybe a bit of an eccentric." Grammy leaned over Emily's shoulder now.

"It's true," Julia said. "At that time, there weren't many women pilots. Amelia Earhart comes to mind, but that was much later. And that's about it."

"A woman at that time, flying a plane. That's dangerous. Irresponsible. What if she had crashed and left her children behind?" A second after the statement, Marjory clapped her hand over her mouth.

They were all aware this Emily had died of consumption and left a young son behind. But at least she'd lived her life fully before dying. Something the new Emily wasn't sure she could say about herself. Then again, hadn't she decided she would change some things?

"It's true. I've always played it safe," Emily said to the license. Maybe that was what Greg had been all about. Greg and his 401K, sensible shoes and plans for a rock-solid future. A future that would have included their 2.5 children. She could have never guessed that he, of all people, would humiliate her the way he had.

"I wouldn't call it playing it safe, dear. I'd call it being practical. You're by far the most dependable girl I know." Grammy patted Emily's shoulder. "Why, I'd trust you with anything."

"Which is why she'd make a good doctor's wife," Luanne said with a nod.

"Why does everyone want to marry me off?"

Emily's voice rose. "Maybe I don't want to get married anymore. Ever."

"Don't say such a thing," Marjory grimaced and then waved her arms in the air. "Cancel that, cancel that."

Marjory believed every word spoken had power, and that if one waved their arms around like they were shooing away a bug, the Universe might forgive it. Wipe it away, so to speak.

"Don't cancel it." Emily waved her arms around in the other direction. "What if I mean it?"

"Hear that, Universe? She said *if*." Marjory cast her eyes heavenward. "She's not thinking this through."

Emily stood. "I'll tell you what I want. I want you all to stop thinking about me as good ol' dependable and steady Emily. I'm not a vacuum cleaner. I'm ready to be a wild woman now. Take a risk." There. She'd said it out loud. It didn't sound as crazy as she thought it might.

"Oh, Julia, look what you've done," Luanne shook her finger.

The Daughter of the American Revolution stood up now, hands on her waist. "I'm merely a conduit to the past. We all have our path to take. I'm happy if this leads to personal insight."

"But there's nothing wrong with being sensible," Grammy said, practically wringing her hands.

"Nothing wrong at all," Luanne agreed.

"Did I say there was anything wrong with it? It's just that maybe, for the first time in my life, I want to do something crazy. Something none of you would expect of me." Emily crossed her arms.

From now on, she was going to do what she wanted, when she wanted, like Molly. No more Little Miss Perfect.

She'd show her family. She'd show everyone she could, at a moment's notice, if the mood so struck her, be a wild woman.

CHAPTER FOUR

"LET ME GET this straight. Your great-grandmother, your namesake, was a pilot." Emily's oldest friend, Rachel Harwood, leaned across the booth and touched the official pilot's license, still wrapped in the plastic Julia had put it in.

Emily was still a bit surprised she'd been able to wrestle it out of Julia's hands. "What do you think? Are you going to laugh, too?"

"Laugh? Why would I do that?" Rachel stirred her coffee. "Please. Let me just have a nice whiff of your leaded coffee. This decaf is killing me."

Emily pushed her mug over and let Rachel take a nice long sniff. She obviously wanted Emily to feel sorry about the awful caffeine withdrawal, but she couldn't dredge up even an ounce of pity. Rachel had switched to decaf because she was eight weeks pregnant.

It was Monday morning, and they were sitting in a booth at The Drip, one of Emily's favorite places in town. Nothing could cheer her up like the strongest coffee in the Bay Area. "You don't want to tell me that she doesn't sound anything like me?"

"I didn't expect you to have anything in common with a woman who lived in the first part of the last century," Rachel said with a mini eye roll.

"Don't you think she sounds wild and carefree?"

"Sweetie, women in that time were never wild and carefree. Get a clue."

"But she was a maverick, for her time."

"She sounds like she was bored," Rachel said. "When you can't vote, can't work, can't get birth control, I guess you get a little stir-crazy. Lesson learned."

"I can't believe you're not impressed. I know I am. And from now on, I'm going to be a wild woman, too."

Rachel froze and closed her eyes for a second. "You're going to be a—what?"

"You heard me. I'm going to take chances and throw caution to the wind, and most of all, I'll be the most impractical person you've ever met. Rachel, meet your new best friend. She's going to be fun and carefree. Like a *Rebel Without a Cause*, but not so James Dean-y. I think you're going to love me."

"Where is my Emily and what have you done with her, you impostor?"

"I'm the new and improved Emily."

Rachel put her hand on Emily's arm. "Don't let Greg do this to you."

"This isn't about him. This is all me."

"Oh, the hell it is. You didn't do anything wrong, so why change who you are?"

Emily sighed. "Because maybe I want to?"

"Only if you want to change for the right reasons. I've always said you can't control everything. Sometimes the fun is in letting go and going for a ride." Rachel rubbed her temple. "Okay. I get where you're going with this. And I think I'm on board."

"Thank you!"

"Why don't we try this 'new you' on for size." Rachel, who faced the entrance to the café from their booth, turned to point to a man who now stood in line behind her. "What about him?"

Emily glanced at the back of the man. Her back to the entrance, she hadn't even noticed anyone come in. Still, she couldn't see how a stranger had anything to do with this. "Him?"

"I'd like to see this new wild woman go up to that man and ask him out. Then I'll believe you mean it. That will show me you're willing to do this thing by relaxing Emily's Dating Rules."

"Can we start with something that doesn't have anything to do with a guy? This new me doesn't have anything to do with men."

"Meh. I hear a lot of excuses. I don't think you have it in you. It's all right. Not everyone does."

"I'm not afraid. There's no point to it." Besides, what if the man said yes? What then?

"Okay, okay, never mind."

"What if he's married?" That would be where she'd draw the line with this rebel thing. No married men. No thank you.

"Then he'll say no."

Emily raised an eyebrow. "Now who's being naive?"

"I'll have him checked out at the paper if he says yes. It's one date, and it won't kill you. And after that, you can go back to your dry spell."

"Fine. I'll do it. But if he says yes, you'll have to find a way to get me out of it." Emily planted her hands on the table, wrenched herself up and marched over to the man's back.

It was a pretty good-looking back, as those went. Broad shoulders tapered down to long lean legs. Definitely fit, not that it mattered. Ask the man out. She could do that.

Rachel was worried about her, which was kind of sweet, actually. But even if Emily had stayed in bed for the better part of six months, she was back now and better than ever. Except, she wasn't sure how she would ask this man out.

She'd watched Molly do this a bazillion times. Emily had to channel her inner Hoochie Mama. She was in there somewhere, under lock and key, and would now be released on an unsuspecting world. And this unsuspecting man. She'd prob-

ably come staggering out, waving cobwebs out
of her way, but come out she would. Just for a
minute.

Emily drew in a deep breath. In a voice as drip-
ping with sex as she could conjure up, she said to
the man's back, "Hey, I think you and I should
go out sometime. What do you say?"

The man had just paid for his drink and turned,
coffee in hand, eyebrows up.

It was Stone.

Emily threw up her hand in surprise, and it ac-
cidently collided with his hot coffee. Like watching an accident unfold in slow motion, he tried
to right the cup while her hand did the same.
But when her hand slapped against his, disaster reigned supreme as coffee won the day and
spilled all over Stone's brown cargo pants.

"Here, let me help you." Emily grabbed napkins, and the barista threw over a dishrag.

Emily blotted for a minute before she realized how close she was getting to his crotch. She
turned in desperation to Rachel, only to see her
doubled up in laughter, wiping her eyes.

Stone shook his head, scowling. "You're dangerous, girl."

Oh, epic fail. As if she was Cinderella at the
crack of midnight, Emily turned, grabbed her
purse from the booth and ran out of the café. She
could barely hear the sound of Rachel behind her,
calling out Emily's name.

Maybe if she was lucky, really blessed, Emily would turn into a pumpkin.

She reached her truck and climbed in, ready to peal rubber out of the parking lot. *Ask a man out? When will I listen to that inner little voice? A klutz should never ask a guy out in the vicinity of any kind of liquid.*

Rachel banged on the passenger-side window, so Emily unlocked the door.

"Are you happy now?"

Rachel opened the door and let herself inside. "I'm sorry I laughed. That wasn't fair. But, hey, you did it."

"I made a fool out of myself."

"Who cares? I've never known you to even approach a stranger, and there you were, doing it. So what if coffee and gravity won? I do think he would have said yes, had you not run out on him."

Emily hit the steering wheel with her head. She'd run out on Stone. Again. No point in telling Rachel this was round two. "I *did* run out on him."

"I don't blame you," Rachel continued. "With a man like that, you want to put your best foot forward. Maybe you should go back in there and try again."

"No way, Rachel. I'm done listening to your bright ideas."

Rachel elbowed Emily. "You know what? You've proved it. You're a wild woman. Why don't you do something really wild, like get your pilot's license?"

"Are you nuts?"

"Why not? Your namesake did, so there's some connection to the past there. It has nothing to do with men, right? And if you want to do something different, step outside your comfort zone. Does it get any more different for you than that?"

As a matter of fact, it didn't. She'd always had her feet planted firmly on the ground, both literally and figuratively. But flying lessons? Emily thought about it while she peeled out of the parking lot. "It would make a nice human interest story for the alumni newsletter."

"You bet it would."

Pilot's license. Crazy, yes, but wasn't she courting crazy? "I'll think about it."

"Are you okay?" The barista handed him another coffee, a sheepish look on her face. "This one's on the house."

His first visit to the establishment and he'd been bathed in the stuff. Damn Matt for getting him hooked on the coffee here. "Yeah. Thanks." Now he'd have to turn around and go back home to change, and he could look forward to another encounter with Winston when he did.

"Emily's always been a klutz. But I will say, I've never seen her ask a guy out before. This is one for the books," the girl said as she came around to mop the floor.

And what the hell had that been about? Emily's eyes had widened in shock when he'd turned to see who had asked him out in a voice that sounded like that of a phone sex operator. Hadn't she told him she was not in the habit of going out with strangers? And why the hell was she constantly running out on him? He still hadn't heard "sorry" come out of her mouth, but at least this time, the apology had been written all over her face.

"I'm guessing she comes in here a lot," Stone said, dumping the napkins in the trash can.

"Emily? You could say that. Her family owns Fortune Ranch, if you're interested in following up on that date request."

A tempting thought, admittedly, but maybe best to stay away from the girl. First his jaw, then hot coffee spilled inches from his crotch. He couldn't afford to lose a limb at this point. "Fortune Ranch?"

"It's not a cattle ranch anymore. Mostly where we have the high school's Sadie Hawkins dance, picnics and big company parties. She's going to add weddings now."

He looked out the storefront and saw Emily hit her head on the steering wheel of her truck. He recognized the woman who had run after her, since she'd come in a couple of weeks ago to talk to them about newspaper advertising.

Stone headed back to his truck, brand-new cup of fresh coffee in his hand. With no traffic, he was back home within minutes.

After wrestling Winston down again, changing and driving to the airport, by ten Monday morning Stone was back at the flight school. No one here to bother him but the planes. *That* he could handle.

Finally, a few moments of relative silence. Not common at airports, but there was a lull between landings and takeoffs at San Martin Airport in the afternoons. The airport and its strip were small and located out in the middle of the empty field, formerly zoned for agricultural use alone.

Stone stared out the window at the two Cessna planes, Magnum Flying School printed on the side of one of the planes. Dad's dream had lasted a good ten years, but it threatened to fizzle out with Stone at the helm. He'd never claimed to be a damned businessman. He knew how to fly a plane. Happened to love flying a plane. Teaching and running a small business was another story.

He shut the window because he smelled shit again, or as his office manager, Cassie, explained, the fertilizer for the mushrooms. It was a fact of life here in Fortune, home of the mushroom, but only mattered depending on which way the wind blew. There were days when the wind shifted and Stone wanted to pack his bags. But then he'd see his father's photo and be reminded he'd made a promise, and he intended to keep it.

Cassie stuck her head in the door. "Got a minute, boss?"

"Told you not to call me that."

Cassie Helms was sixtysomething, and nearing retirement. By way of introduction a year ago, she'd told him exactly how old she was and announced she and her husband had a pleasant-sized nest egg and planned to retire to Mexico. In case he got any bright ideas about making any significant changes, he assumed. They'd already bought the hacienda, which made Stone wonder whether perhaps he paid Cassie too much. More than likely, the previous owner had, for many years. Come to think of it, that sounded just like Dad.

Then again, Dad hadn't been any more of a businessman than Stone. Not when his biggest concern had been that both Cassie and Jedd keep their jobs.

Cassie walked in with a glazed donut, which she placed on his desk. This meant she had semi-bad news, since she often liked to present her news with food offerings. Candy meant good news, donuts semi-bad news. Stone expected in a few weeks he'd find a cake on his desk.

"What is it now?" Stone raked a hand through his hair.

"Mr. Burton wants a meeting," Cassie said as she eased into the chair across from his desk.

"I should have seen that coming." In Burton's place, Stone would have done the same.

Burton, a wealthy retired CEO from Silicon Valley, had been the only one to express interest in buying the school as one of his investments. They'd been in the middle of working out salaries for keeping Cassie and Jedd on staff. Stone could almost smell his freedom, and then his sister had slammed into town. She'd been approached by a developer for almost twice the amount. But that would mean the loss of many local jobs, and likely another strip mall. "I doubt it's good news."

"You've done everything you could, and I know your father would say the same."

"He was so proud of you. Had pictures of you and your unit all over the office. I used to like coming in here and seeing all those handsome soldiers. An old lady needs to get her thrills somewhere. But then you took them all down."

He sure didn't need any reminders of that time. "Yeah. Sorry."

"I miss your dad more than I want to admit. The ol' fart."

Stone grinned. "I should have put that on his headstone."

Dad's presence was here in this office and everywhere Stone looked.

He had a meeting with Sarah and her attorney next week. Matt had talked Stone into it, do-gooder that he was. There should be a job waiting for Matt at the United Nations if he wanted it. Stone supposed it was his own fault for putting her off so long after that first contentious meeting. But on the other hand, she'd been the one to hire an attorney first, forcing him to hire one, too. Still, there was no point in avoiding the inevitable. Maybe with some luck Sarah's attorney would help, though Stone doubted it. A meeting was all he'd agreed to.

Sarah might be his sister, but in name only. They didn't know each other anymore, and the fact she only cared about money made him think he didn't want to know her. She didn't feel like family since only biology connected them, and he had no obligation to her. The one thing he knew without a doubt was that his obligation was to the only real family with which he'd had a real and lasting connection. The United States Air Force, and James Mcallister.

CHAPTER FIVE

A MORNING OF ERRANDS followed Emily's spilled coffee fiasco. She'd been way too close to Stone's crotch, and not at all in the way she would have preferred. He'd stared at her with those edgy blue eyes that said he now believed she was toxic. And maybe she was to men. They were certainly toxic to her.

She'd just hopped in her truck when her cell phone buzzed. Trish. Emily couldn't miss this call, or this wedding. Jimmy and Trish were two of her best friends and she wanted to see them married at the ranch. Besides, knowing Trish, they'd spare no expense. Emily pulled over in the parking lot of the Snow White Drive-In to take the call.

"Hey, Trish."

"Hi, hon. Jimmy tells me you'd like to host our wedding."

"Yep. I'm expanding. We have a weddings package now."

"Okay, but Emily, are you *serious* about this?

Because this is the biggest day of my entire life.
Bar none."

"Right."

"And I want everything to be perfect."

"Oh, of course and it will be."

"I mean, I went to that company party you
guys gave last year where you ran out of meat. I
can't have that."

Oh, sigh. Don't remind her. While half of the
staff had claimed to be vegan, many had changed
their minds at the party. Hence the lack of preparation.

"That was not our fault. It—"

"Uh-uh. No excuses."

Emily bit her lower lip. "I promise to give your
wedding my undivided attention. I'll handle every
aspect of it myself."

There was a long, silent pause on the other end
of the phone.

"I've decided to trust you with my wedding
day," Trish finally spoke.

"I'm honored."

"I'll call you in a couple of days with my list
of demands."

"Um, what?"

"I mean, all the little tender touches and per-
sonalized effects that I've decided will make this
day special. Beyond compare. Oh, Emily, I can
hardly wait."

Emily swallowed. She had a bad feeling about

this. But no. This was Trish, for crying out loud. No, it would be fine.

When Emily finally got back to the ranch, she recognized the out-of-place vehicle parked next to the barn immediately. The same silver luxury sedan he'd insisted he had to buy for appearance sake, because an engineer who worked for one of the software giants in Silicon Valley had an image to maintain. The last thing she needed right now. *Greg*.

He was still sitting in the car, no doubt because Grammy wouldn't let him inside. She'd once said her hospitality could be pushed only so far, and that would include ex-fiancés who cheated on her granddaughter. She'd spent the better part of a year crying over the idiot, and now the sight of him churned emotions she didn't want to have. Regret and shame, to mention two, but anger and hostility might win the day this time around.

Emily marched over to the sedan as Greg rolled down the window. "What are you doing here?"

"I need to talk to you."

"There's nothing to say."

Greg got out of the car and shut the door. "Can't we talk about this?"

"Now?"

"You walked out the door and stopped taking my calls."

"And that was a year ago. What's there to talk

about? Nika's been your maid for over a year, so the transition to live-in girlfriend shouldn't be hard."

"Okay, I guess I deserve that."

"And so much more." She'd never realized before how close together his brown eyes were—made him look a bit like a weasel.

"But some couples survive these kinds of… bumps in the road."

"*Bump in the road?* Is that what you call her?"

"It was pretty clear how much you cared about me. You never for one moment stopped to think that we could work this out. You walked out the door and never looked back."

She didn't answer, just glared at him. He didn't know how many times she'd looked back and wondered how Greg could have fooled her. She thought she knew the signs of a cheating partner. Had read all about them in *Cosmopolitan*, color coded them and put them on index cards. And yet, with Greg, she'd never seen sign one.

"We both miss you." Greg shuffled his feet in place. He wore penny loafers and slacks, and he was a vegetarian. And come to think of it, he'd always made her feel like a plate of overcooked vegetables.

Out of the corner of Emily's eye, she saw Molly, a red streak, headed straight for Greg. She'd hopped on his back before Emily realized it or was able to stop it.

"You son of a bitch!" Molly's legs were wrapped around his waist, her hands wrestling with his neck.

"What the hell?" Greg turned in circles as he tried to throw her off his back.

"Molly!" Emily put her hand to her mouth and strangled a laugh. This wasn't the way Emily would have thought to handle it, but nothing less than what Greg deserved. And she wasn't enough of an angel not to thoroughly enjoy the spectacle for a minute.

"I'll hold him while you punch him. Go on, I think I've got him." Molly appeared to have a death grip on him with her legs as Emily marveled at how much strength a woman could muster when she was angry enough.

"Get this lunatic off my back," Greg yelled, while he tried to move Molly's hands from his eyes.

"Molly, get off him. This isn't helping." Emily put a hand over her mouth and tried to keep the laugh out of her voice, with great difficulty.

Molly finally jumped off him. "Fine, you're too easy. A real man would be able to wrestle me off. Get on out of here, jerk." Molly waved her arm as she marched up the steps.

"I didn't want to hurt you." Greg squared his shoulders and smoothed his wrinkled khakis. "If I'd thrown you off like I should have, you'd have landed on your back."

"Yeah, right. You're lucky my daddy isn't here. He's the one with a shotgun. If you see his truck pull up, I'd run if I were you." Molly slammed the front door shut.

Greg ran a hand down his rumpled cotton shirt, and Emily wondered how she'd ever felt this was a man who could love and take care of her. A one-hundred-pound ball of fire had knocked him for a loop.

"I'm sorry about that. You're not very popular around here."

"You told everybody what happened?" Greg's face drained of color.

"She's my sister." Emily decided not to add that everyone in her family knew exactly what he'd done, even if she'd left some of the more sordid details out for Grammy's sake.

"I don't feel safe here anymore," Greg said as he opened the door to his sedan. "Can we go somewhere else?"

He wanted her to go talk somewhere else, a place where he felt safe. What a man. "I would, Greg, honestly. But I still have a few working brain cells left."

Greg smoothed his hair back into place. "This is important, and I don't want you to hear it from anyone else."

GREG LOOKED A LOT more comfortable at The Drip, and Emily began to wonder if maybe her attraction to him at the time had more to do with location. Being a well-respected engineer, Greg commanded a certain presence she found attractive. He was good with computers and Power-Point presentations, and that had seemed sexy at the time. Besides, Greg had been patient with her dating rules. He'd gone along with each one of them, remarking how refreshing it was to be with a woman who realized what she wanted, who took control of her life.

He'd ordered his usual espresso and remembered her double-shot mocha as if it had been yesterday when he last ordered her one.

"Here you go, jerk. Your triple shot espresso. I didn't spit in it or anything." Annie, the head barista and one of Molly's best friends, nearly slammed the cup down. The fluff of steamed milk rocked. Annie gently put down Emily's mocha, sniffed and turned away.

Greg's eyes widened. "Does everybody in town know?"

"I used to work here," Emily lied. All right, so Molly had a hard time keeping her mouth shut. What else was new?

Greg turned his mug and inspected it, taking a whiff as though he might be able to smell spit. After a few moments, he dared to take a sip. "I've missed you."

"Cut to the chase, Greg. What do you want to tell me? That can't be it."

"We're both sorry it happened. Especially Nika. She's fully aware of everything you did for her. You got her the job."

Yes, way to add salt to the wound. Emily had met Nika at a Bay Area nightclub, where she'd been hired as a bartender. But when it was clear she'd lied to get the job and didn't know a screwdriver from a mimosa (adding vodka to everything, Emily later heard), she'd been fired on the spot.

Emily had heard the commotion, saw a statuesque blonde sobbing and yelling in a foreign language and stupidly followed her into the ladies' room. Emily blamed it on her years of fixing Molly's messes, but before she'd known what she was doing, she was comforting Nika. Trying to fix it for her.

"What can you do?" Working as the head event manager at her family's company gave her a lot of connections.

Unfortunately, it had turned out Nika wasn't good at much of anything, but Greg needed a maid. Emily had taught her how to clean the house the way Greg liked it, and Nika was reliable and energetic, showing up three times a week. The house was always spotless.

"Watch out for that one," Rachel had said to Emily the first time she'd introduced Nika.

"Why? You think she'd be interested in Greg? I mean, look at her. She used to date an NFL player." Emily never dated über-handsome men. Too much temptation to other women.

"All that money he makes is attractive, even if Greg isn't." Rachel had said in a thinly veiled warning.

It was true Greg's software start-up was about to go public and his shares would put him into an entirely different income tax bracket. Not über-rich, though. Not athlete-rich.

But hindsight was twenty-twenty. Nika, like most women, wanted security. Being swimsuit-model gorgeous didn't take that need away, it turned out. Greg was the marrying kind. Nika saw that, and loyalty was not part of her repertoire. Survival was.

Now Greg reached for Emily's hand. "I didn't want you to hear about this from anyone else. Nika and I, we're getting married."

Greg already getting married? To the woman he'd cheated on her with? "Married?"

Greg studied his cup. "She's pregnant."

Emily swallowed the golf ball in her throat. It had been a year. Emily didn't want to think about how Nika and Greg had spent that year and whether they'd eventually made their way to the bed for some of Greg's paint by numbers sex. Or maybe he and Nika enjoyed something altogether different than Emily and Greg had had.

"I see." If there's one thing Greg did know, it was how much Emily wanted to start a family. Right after the wedding, had been the plan. He'd reversed the order with Nika.

"I'm so sorry." Greg shot her a look filled with pity.

Oh, no you don't. "Don't be sorry. You're having a baby." Nika would hopefully be a better mother than she had been a friend.

It was better this way, and Emily needed to keep telling herself that. After a few more torturous minutes, Greg left and Emily watched from inside the coffee shop as he drove off.

"What did that douchebag want?" Annie stopped by the table to ask.

"To tell me he's getting married to Nika."

"The maid? No way!"

"Yep. It's for the best." She stood, picked up her purse and walked outside into the warm spring day.

Greg was getting married to Nika. Emily slid into the driver's seat of her car and rested her head on the steering wheel. So much new information. Her head felt heavy and thick from the overload.

More to the point, Greg had moved on. But

Emily was still stuck where she had been a year ago. She hadn't dated anyone or moved forward. Still stuck at home, spending most of her weekends with the Pink Ladies. A bunch of wonderful women, sure, even if the youngest was seventy-two.

Maybe she had to stop working so hard at hiding and throw herself back into the world full tilt.

Rachel was right. Getting her pilot's license was at least something she could do in her free time. And if it didn't work out, if for some reason the whole thing made her sick, she'd find something else to chase. Maybe she could make another list, kind of like a bucket list.

One way or another, Emily had to start living again.

AT LEAST STONE'S passenger was on the quiet side.

But then again, once you'd been released from death row in Texas and were about to get a second lease on life, you might not want to jinx it by being loud and inappropriate. Or possibly his passenger wasn't saying a word because he was clearly terrified, shaking in the seat next to Stone.

"We're almost there. Take it easy." He spoke softly, hoping to sound soothing.

It was noisy in his Cessna and having been sprung from death row, loud and sudden noises were probably not comforting to his passenger. Supposedly, this was a match made in heaven.

He'd been united with a family in California, but since they were separated by a few thousand miles, they needed a plane.

And that was where he came in.

"Yark!" said his passenger.

"Ah, so you're talking to me now."

"Yark! Yark! Yip!"

"Yippee is right, buddy. You're about to meet your forever family. Nothing like being small, cute and furry to find you a good home."

Unlike Winston, who was large, ugly and farted at will. Which was how Dad had wound up with him when the person who'd thought Winston might be their forever dog changed their mind. Just one of Winston's farts could do that to a person.

Pilots and Paws was an organization Dad had contributed his time and talent toward, and now so did Stone. A few minutes later, he landed his Cessna, took off his headphones and unstrapped his hairy passenger. The furball licked his hand in gratitude, and Stone carried him out. The family was waiting at the airport and as he walked toward the hangar, all three of them spilled out.

"Fluffy!" one of the kids ran toward him.

"That's original," Stone said to the poor dog. He handed him over to the kid.

"Can we take a picture of you with the dog?" the mother asked. "It's so wonderful of you to do this."

"I'm one of four thousand pilots. No big deal."

"Can I go in your plane?" the kid asked, handing the dog over to his mother.

Short attention span, that one. "Ah, no."

"Of course not, Justin. We're not here to see the plane. This is our forever dog," the mother said.

"I like the plane better," said Justin, who it turned out was a pretty smart kid. Still, he wasn't going anywhere near the plane.

"Let me have Fluffy," the younger boy said.

Fluffy was handed from the mother to the boy and promptly began shaking like he had when he'd first been placed on the plane. Stone thought it looked like an epileptic seizure, but he'd been assured by the shelter it was normal small-dog nervous energy.

"Let's have our pilot hold the dog while I take one picture. Please?" The mother turned to Stone.

"Sure." Stone smiled as the dog was handed back to him. Just as the mother took her picture, the dog tongued Stone.

"Thank you so much," the mother said.

Stone tipped his head and walked toward his office. The things he did for Dad. Pilots and Paws being one of them. He'd been flying dogs back and forth for a couple of months, all in the line of sainthood. Just carrying on the Mcallister legacy. Right.

It didn't help that he wasn't sleeping well, and this time he couldn't blame it all on Winston's incessant snoring. Six months ago he'd done the right thing, the only thing he could do in the face of his choices. Dad needed him. Stone hadn't hesitated. But that still meant that he wasn't where he should be right now, with the rest of his crew. He wasn't flying jets or having daily adrenaline rushes. For now, it felt like he was coasting. Existing. And barely, at that.

Every now and again his thoughts went back to Emily and that deer-in-the-headlights look in her eyes when he'd turned around. She'd asked *him* out and not waited around to see if he might take her up on that offer after drying himself off.

Because he would have. Maybe.

After he'd downed three Red Bulls, Stone helped Jedd with some engine work on Dad's old Cessna until nearly noon. The early spring sunshine warmed his back, and a bead of sweat rolled down.

Cassie opened the outside door leading to their hangar and shouted, "Get over here."

"What is it?" Stone squinted in the bright sun. He wiped his grimy hands on a rag and threw it back on the cart, walking toward Cassie.

Cassie grinned ear to ear. "We have a customer. She says she wants a lesson and has been waiting for an hour. Didn't want to come back later. I'd say all that waiting makes her patient. She'll be a good student. Your students need patience."

He let that insult slide off his back since there

was more than a kernel of truth to it. "I'll talk to her."

"She's waiting in your office." Cassie followed him inside the hangar. "And don't give her the fifth degree. Be nice."

Stone turned and stared at Cassie, hand on his chest. "Have I ever been anything but nice?"

Cassie rolled her eyes. "Let's not go there."

Stone opened the door to his office, and when the woman turned in her seat to face the door, his groin seemed to recognize her before his eyes did. Emily from the bar. From the coffee shop. The same Emily who took off on him twice.

"You."

And she seemed just as surprised to see him. She stood and stepped away from the chair. "Are you—*you're* the pilot?"

"I'm the pilot." Stone marched toward her. Oh, man, he was going to enjoy this. She wouldn't be running out on him again anytime soon. He considered locking the door to his office to make sure.

"But I thought—"

"You probably thought an old man still ran the place?" Stone stopped when he was a foot's distance from her.

"No. I know Mr. Mcallister died. I heard his son was running the place. But you're—you mean *you're* Mr. Mcallister's son?"

This did surprise most people. "Yeah, that

would be me. But let's talk about you. You want to get your pilot's license? Are you tired of starting bar fights and spilling coffee on poor unsuspecting men?"

Emily chewed on her lower lip, and damned if that didn't drive him crazy. "I didn't get a chance to tell you how sorry I was about the coffee spill. And the fight. How's your jaw?"

"Nothing a little ice couldn't cure, but thanks for asking. So what about this date?"

Emily took a step back while she clasped and unclasped her hands. His spirits soared higher than they had in months as he witnessed her obvious discomfort, and he wasn't done playing with her yet.

"I'm sorry. I've never asked a man out before."

"No kidding. I would have never guessed. You were so smooth."

"That's not funny. I got kind of flustered when you turned around."

"So I wasn't supposed to turn around?"

"No, I didn't say that. I didn't expect—I mean I didn't know you—"

"You didn't know it was me when you asked my back out on a date."

She didn't speak, but her mouth opened and closed a few times. Nothing.

"Try again. I have all day."

"Okay, look. I was trying something new on for size. And it didn't work out too well, as you know."

"The coffee I could have done without. But what about the date?"

"Maybe we need to forget about that? You have to admit it's been less than a stellar beginning." She stared at the ground, and a blush the size of Texas crossed her cheeks.

"Running out on me didn't help."

"Maybe, but you didn't look too happy with me. And by the way, I'm sorry I asked you out because I'm not ready for you—I mean, I'm not dating anyone. I mean—I made a mistake, asking you out."

"And you make a lot of them, don't you?"

She seemed to ignore the comment. "The reason I left so quickly that night had to do with my sister. Otherwise, I might have stayed to see if you were okay. But I thought I should get Molly out of there. She tends to cause trouble wherever she goes."

"*She* does?" He felt a grin coming on. "From where I stand, you caused the trouble. I wouldn't have walked outside if it wasn't for you."

"And I thank you for doing that, but I didn't ask you to." Emily raised her chin.

That put her lips in decidedly much closer territory to his. "No, you didn't, but you didn't exactly stop me." Now he moved till he was only inches away from her, and their gazes locked.

"So—um, can we talk about me getting my pilot's license?"

"You want your *pilot's license*?" This stunned him. He thought for sure she wanted to take a onetime lesson for kicks. So many people did just that—either they were gifted a onetime lesson or they chose to cross it off some list of things they'd always wanted to do at least once.

"Is that a problem?"

"To get your pilot's license, you'll have to log more than twenty hours of flight time. That means with me. Next to you. In the plane."

"You're the only regional airport for miles." Emily backed up another step and hit the wall. He had a small office.

He pushed one solitary flyaway hair off her forehead, even though what he wanted was a fistful of that hair in his hands. "I'm not sure I should let you anywhere near my plane."

"Don't you have insurance?"

Not a comforting thought. He had boatloads of insurance, thanks to his dad, but the plan was never to use it. The thought of his father pulled him front and center.

What the hell am I doing? She wants her license, and I happen to run a flight school. Be professional, idiot. No matter how great she smells.

Stone forced himself away from her and walked behind his desk. "What made you decide you want to get your pilot's license?"

She gave an audible sigh and sat back down on

the chair across from his desk. "You're not going to believe this."

"Go ahead and give it a shot." He crossed his arms and leaned back.

"This begins with my great-grandmother and namesake, Emily Parker. I traced her back to the early nineteen hundreds."

"This sounds like a long story. Can we fast-forward to the new millennium? I do have a business to run."

"Short version coming right up. See, it turns out my namesake was a pilot. At a time when there weren't many of them."

"How nice for you, but what has that got to do with anything?"

Emily blinked. "I wasn't aware I needed a great reason to get my license. My friend Rachel seemed to think it was a neat idea. The first Emily Parker was a maverick, and I want to follow in her great footsteps."

"And that's it?"

"What do you mean, that's it?"

"What do you know about flying?"

"Not much. That's why you're here."

"It could take a while to get your license. Depending on whether you take long breaks between lessons. And in order to qualify for your pilot's license, you'll have to take three solo flights between airports."

"By myself?"

"That's the idea. There's also lots of course-work and passing the FAA written test."

"I'm good with books and tests." Her first hint of confidence.

"There's a lot more work to do if you ever want to carry a passenger. The more hours you log flying, the faster you can get your license. Like anything else, you need lots of practice."

"I can handle all of that. I'll do my lessons three times a week so it'll stay fresh in my mind. Anything else?"

The facts were he needed more students. Not only was he getting tired of hiring himself out for chartered flights to keep the school afloat, but a good roster of students would make the school a better investment for the buyer he'd lined up. Maybe she'd inspire other people in town to give it a try. She probably wasn't serious, but at least seeing her would be a nice break in his week. Emily could make things stimulating for however long he had left here. Interesting, and also challenging.

It had been a hell of a long time since he'd been useful to anyone. But God help him. Why had he always had a thing for the wacky ones?

He almost couldn't believe he was about to say his next words. "One more thing. I'd like to take you up on that date."

"But—"

"It was your idea. One date." He held up his finger.

"One? That's it?"

"One." He only needed one date to get her out of his system. There were no white picket fences in his foreseeable future.

"Okay." She took a deep breath. "I can handle that."

CHAPTER SIX

JUST HER BRAND of luck Stone was the pilot of the only flight school in the area. Hunky Stone Mcallister who, thanks to Molly, Emily had left without even saying thank you, or goodbye. Thanks to Rachel and gravity, she'd asked him out and then spilled coffee all over him. He'd obviously not taken either one of those well. At all.

But the new and improved Emily living life full tilt couldn't let this distract her plans. The only thing that might distract her would be those eyes that made her feel naked. She'd need him to sit far away from her and stop looking like he was about to have a three-course meal. But surely that could be arranged. It would have to be.

Even if from the moment she'd seen the small planes on the tarmac and stuttered out the words, "I want my pilot's license," she hadn't had a good solid breath of air. Those small planes were an accident waiting to happen, like a strong gust of wind would blow them off course. She'd eventually have to fly one of them by herself. Sure, that made sense, so why hadn't she stopped to consider what it might feel like all the way up there, all alone?

She'd taken a week to think about Rachel's idea. It appealed to Emily's new call to adventure, without a doubt. Maybe she could even blog about the experience. An experience that wasn't supposed to involve men. Not younger men. Not hot men.

The door to his office opened, and Jedd popped his head in the door. "Hey, boss, the—" Jedd stopped midsentence and stared at her with a slacked jaw. "Hey, Emily. What are you doing here?"

Emily stood. "I'm here to take lessons."

"You've come to the right place. This right here is the best teacher you could ever find. He's former air force. He's the man." Jedd pointed in Stone's direction.

The silence in the room was deafening until the roar of a plane lifting off filled the room.

"I'm taking the plane out. Is she ready?" Stone stepped past her on his way to the door.

"She's ready and willing," Jedd said with a wink toward Emily.

She followed, because Stone wasn't getting away from her that easily, and almost bumped into him when he turned around, stopping her in her tracks. "Are you coming?"

"Now?" They hadn't even set the parameters for their supposed date. Was this a coffeehouse date or a dinner date? Was it denim or silk? Should she shave? Wax? Did she need to? *No! I'll decide and I won't need to shave. Decision made.*

"Isn't that what you're here for? Lessons?" Now the confounded man looked annoyed. With her. "Ready?"

"Uh, yes. Why would you think I'm not ready? What a stupid question." She didn't think they'd start today, but even if the thought made her heart race, she couldn't rethink the situation now. She was about to walk straight into history and maybe make some of her own. Hopefully it wouldn't involve a crash.

Stone stopped her at the door, laying a hand on her shoulder. "I'm going to do something I rarely do. I want to give you a free lesson, because I think once we get up there you'll change your mind. And there's nothing to be ashamed of. So, let's give it a try."

"I'm not going to change my mind." Boy, this guy was a piece of work. For someone so damn good-looking, too bad he suffered from a personality disorder.

"Leave your purse with Cassie." Stone waved a hand in the direction of her desk.

"Have fun," Jedd called out as they made their way through the hangar.

Once she stepped outside, Emily blinked in the bright sunlight and wished she'd brought the shades from her purse. Stone had pulled a pair of

Top Gun–looking shades out of his shirt pocket. She followed his long, purposeful strides in the direction of a small plane a few hundred yards in the distance. When her legs didn't want to cooperate, she silently willed them to move forward before they made a fool out of her.

This is it. I'm going to do it. Now that she was about to take her first flying lesson, Emily had a million questions she hadn't had a chance to ask. But now she was afraid to ask, worried he might start arguing with her again.

He opened the door to the plane and stepped aside. "Sit."

If he was going to churn out commands like she was some kind of dog, this wasn't going to work. She gave him a stare that she hoped looked as mean as it felt. The charming man from last Friday night was gone, the one who knew how to dance and make a girl feel like she was the only one in the room. Probably he'd left for parts unknown when he realized he wasn't getting in her panties. And he wasn't. She never put out on a first date.

How would he fit his long legs into the tiny cramped space beside her? The cockpit was an intimidating assemblage of buttons and knobs, but eventually they would all make sense to her. That was why she was taking lessons. She took a shallow breath of what was left of oxygen in this tiny hole.

Stone sat next to her and their shoulders literally touched, way too close for comfort.

"Seat belt." He pointed to hers and then put on his own.

So. Man of few words. No matter, she was here to learn how to fly, not make a new best friend.

"There's not much room in here, is there?" The seating arrangements gave new meaning to the word intimate.

"What did you expect? The Taj Mahal?" He didn't smile.

Emily tried to concentrate as Stone explained all the instruments and what all those confusing knobs and dials were all about. She had a difficult time concentrating when he was so near. When he asked if she had any questions, the only one floating through her mind was how someone could make mechanical things sound so sexy. It was probably his deep, gravelly voice. This would all be so much easier if her instructor was old and decrepit, but beggars couldn't be choosers.

"Is there a book I can read that has all this information?" There was no way she'd remember all of this, especially not when he sat next to her looking like an extra from *Top Gun*.

"You won't need to know all this right away. Anyway, after this flight you might change your mind."

"I won't." *You jackass. But I'm rethinking the whole date thing.*

"We'll see." He placed a headset with a mic on her head and set one on his own. "I'm going to talk to you through this headset so you can hear me."

"Okay." Emily adjusted the headset. "But aren't you going to contact traffic control before we take off?"

He turned to her. "Where do you think we are? This is a county airport in the middle of nowhere and I'll watch for 'traffic' myself. I guarantee there won't be any jams."

Maybe she should have checked this guy's references. She didn't want to die up there. Unmarried. Childless. But Jedd seemed to trust him, and if he was an air force pilot he could surely handle a small plane.

She put out her hand to touch an interesting-looking knob.

"Don't touch that," he snapped and grabbed her hand. "Don't touch anything."

The quick but warm touch of his hand sent a charge through her that did nothing to calm her down.

Once he started the plane, the need for the headsets became apparent. His voice sounded strangely intimate. She began to imagine situations she had to push out of her mind if she wanted to concentrate on flying. It helped when they started taxiing down the runway and he continued to explain preflight checks, dials, proper speed and way too much for her to remember.

"You're going too fast. Are you trying to confuse me on purpose?" That wouldn't surprise her.

He sighed, like a man overcome with the woes of the world. "I'll go over all this again. If you're serious."

"I am serious. Why won't you believe me?"

"Shut up if you can and concentrate." He picked up speed and, in a matter of seconds, they were off the ground and lifted into the skies.

Emily let out a strangled breath as she viewed the green hills and farmland below, her Fortune Ranch in plain view. Once she got her pilot's license, she'd fly over the ranch on her own. Sure, that was what she'd do. Maybe she'd even carry a banner advertising their private company parties and petting zoo.

Stone was the picture of concentration, his brow furrowed. He looked too serious. Which meant there might be something wrong with the plane. Oh, Lord, she was about to die up here with Mr. Hot Guy, and he'd never even kissed her.

Breathe, Emily, breathe.

"It doesn't feel like there's that much between us and the ground down there." She swallowed.

"That's because there's not. Don't let anyone fool you. This is a bunch of tin strapped together. Any minute now we could both plunge to our deaths." He turned and smiled, and that was when she noticed the dimple.

The jerk was trying to scare her when her hands were already shaking. "W-when do I get a chance?"

"Grab a hold of the control column." Stone touched a large column between them. "You can steer the plane for a while."

"Steer the plane?" Maybe this wasn't such a good idea after all. "Are you sure?"

"Second thoughts?" He quirked an eyebrow.

"No, but that would make your day, wouldn't it?"

"Steer. And don't do anything crazy."

The amount of faith he had in her was positively touching. "I can do this."

"I'll keep control of the rudder pedals, and you steer."

Emily placed trembling hands around what he'd called the control column. She reminded herself he probably didn't want to die, either, so he wouldn't have her do this if it wasn't perfectly safe.

This is it. I'm flying, and I'm not even afraid. Even though they were several thousand feet in the air, and a drop would mean certain death.

He tried to talk her through making a turn, but she didn't do it smoothly and the plane jerked, which made her breakfast threaten to make its reappearance. She couldn't handle that right now.

The last thing she needed was to get sick and prove his point.

"We'll head back now," he said.

How could she possibly keep this up? She already felt like she'd run ten miles, and they'd only been up for twenty minutes or so.

"You okay?' He glanced at her, brow furrowed.

"Of course I am. Why would you ask that?"

"You're white-knuckling it."

They finally landed, and Emily had never been so happy to see the ground again. Legs shaking, she took off her headset and flung the door open. She needed a drink of water, an aspirin and maybe her head examined.

She managed to make it a few steps from the plane before she heard Stone's voice behind her. It sounded tinny and distant.

"Still want to fly?"

She turned to see his dimpled smile. It was the last thing she saw before everything went black.

HOLY SHIT. THIS was not going according to plan. His new student had passed out, just missing the tarmac. With what felt like seconds to spare, he'd made a dive for her and caught her by the shoulders before she hit the ground.

Wonder how many of Dad's students had passed out after a plane ride?

He gathered Emily in his arms, ready to carry

her back into the airport, when her eyelids fluttered open.

"What are you doing? Why are you holding me?"

The color had returned to her formerly ashen-white face, and he managed to relax a little. Maybe he hadn't killed his first student. "You fainted."

Her eyes were at half-mast. "I guess this means I can't fly."

That made him want to laugh. Maybe she was still searching for an excuse to get out of this and save face. "You'll feel better in a few minutes."

He proceeded to carry her inside, but she wriggled, trying to get away.

"I can walk, you know?"

He didn't let her. "I'm aware of that. Humor me."

Cassie threw open the door to the hangar and stared from Stone to Emily. Then she glared at Stone, because, of course, this was somehow his fault. "Great. What did you do to her?"

"She'll be all right. Maybe a little altitude sickness." Stone carried Emily into his office, where he set her down on the chair. He walked over to the water cooler and poured her a cup, which he handed to her.

She accepted it, a look of resignation on her face. "Maybe I'm no good at this flying thing after all."

Cassie followed with a towel, which she placed on Emily's now-rosy cheeks. "Don't worry, hon. This happens sometimes." Then she left.

"Does it?" Emily turned to him, wide-eyed, as though she wanted confirmation.

"Sure." Somehow, he couldn't say no to her.

"I'll be better next time. Probably." She took the towel and patted her forehead.

Time to put all his cards on the table. Or at least a few more of them. "Here's the thing. I'm not sure how much longer this flight school is going to be around. Not sure how long the airport is going to be around, actually."

"Why isn't it going to be around much longer?"

"A developer wants to buy the airport."

"What? This airport has been here for decades."

"I'm aware of that. But it's valuable land and some people only care about money." Like his sister. "I had an investor lined up to buy the flight school, but I'm afraid he might be backing out due to the lawsuit."

"Lawsuit?"

Yeah, he thought that would get her attention. "My sister is suing me. Seems she'd rather have more money. I know what our dad wanted, and I can't let her get away with it."

Emily only stared at him. Probably rethinking the whole thing. Not that he blamed her. He didn't know why in hell he was telling her any of this instead of just taking her money.

He was obviously as great a businessman as his father. "Why don't you go home and think it over?"

Emily worried a nail between her teeth. "I don't need to think it over. I kind of liked being up there."

"Even with me?" He crossed his arms and leaned against the desk. "The guy you ran out on—twice?"

She squirmed in her seat. "You don't see me walking out now, do you?"

No, he didn't, even though it appeared that, at this point, she'd need to wobble out of here.

"Look, if after you go home and sleep on it you still want lessons from me, come back. I'm not going anywhere for a while."

"I don't have to sleep on it. I know what I want." She patted her lips with the towel.

The problem was, so did he. He wanted to bury himself inside her, not teach her how to fly. But if there was one thing he understood, it was discipline. Yeah, he could do this. One tempting blonde who'd been nothing but bad luck so far wouldn't stop him.

"Fine." He held his arms out to the sides, resigned. Somehow, he had a feeling he would regret this. "As long as I have a flight school, you'll get your lessons."

He decided not to add that the way things were going, it wouldn't be for long.

CHAPTER SEVEN

MOLLY SAT ON the park bench and waited. It was Sunday, and the Pink Ladies' meeting had literally driven her out of the house this time, but she'd had plans to come here anyway.

The scent of pine wafted through a light breeze, and Molly put on her baseball cap. Dylan brought Sierra here every Sunday. It had taken a month to find the right time, but Twilight Park happened to be closest to the house Dylan now rented, so that part had been easier. She found out where he'd moved by asking around at the Silver Saddle. Emily thought all Molly wanted to do was dance and hook up with men, but she'd also found time to talk to some of her old classmates about her ex. And found most of the women were more than willing to talk about Dylan.

The moment she saw them walking hand in hand down Monterey Street on their way to the park, Molly pulled the cap's bill down farther. Normally she wouldn't be caught dead wearing a hat, but she couldn't risk Dylan spotting her red hair, a dead giveaway. Anyway, if her so-called friends had managed to keep their mouths shut like she'd asked them to, he might not even know she was back home. Still, she sat on the bench farthest away from the play structure that she'd already noticed Sierra loved to climb.

Her baby had grown so much Molly hardly recognized her. Sierra didn't just walk now, she ran with unsteady steps. Two weeks ago at the park, Molly had witnessed Sierra fall on her behind and resisted the urge to run and help her up. Dylan seemed accustomed to watching their baby fall down on her butt several times an hour. Watching her, Molly was reminded of how much she'd missed.

And Dylan—he looked better than ever. Now he looked like a man. His honey-colored hair was closely cropped, but he sported a beard that made him look like he had a permanent five o'clock shadow. She'd once made fun of that stubble and teased that he didn't have enough testosterone to grow a full beard. About that time Dylan hauled her off her feet and carried her into the bedroom to demonstrate just how much testosterone ran through him. A lot.

Molly shook her head. The last thing she wanted was to think about having sex with Dylan. Her inability to resist him had gotten her into trouble more than once, even though it had produced their beautiful baby girl.

Sierra squealed from the bucket swing as Dylan

pushed her. Pretty soon she swung so high Molly had to bite her lower lip. That looked dangerous. Leave it to Dylan to push it to the limit. It was probably why they'd been like thunder and lightning together and bound to explode eventually.

Still, her baby needed to be kept safe and if Dylan couldn't do it, she would step in.

Oh, who am I kidding? I could never do as good of a job as Dylan has done. Look at her. She's healthy and happy.

Sierra obviously didn't need her. Neither did Dylan, for that matter, even though she'd asked around and he wasn't seeing anyone. Her classmates said Dylan had sailed through EMT training and now worked toward becoming a paramedic. But then again, school had always been easy for him.

The mother with a little boy in the swing next to Sierra's began to engage in conversation with Dylan, flipping her hair and laughing at everything he said as though it was the funniest thing she'd ever heard. *Flirting at the park? Really?*

Molly's face felt hot as Dylan appeared to flirt back with the pretty mother. He should be paying attention to their daughter and not trying to pick someone up.

Suddenly, a car backfired behind her, and both Dylan and the mother looked in Molly's direction. Too late, Molly turned her head away but realized that Dylan had already seen her.

She rose and half ran, half marched toward her truck. If she was fast enough, she'd make a clean get away and maybe Dylan would think he'd only seen her look-alike.

"Molly!" he shouted with his no-nonsense voice. That tone meant business.

She stopped in her tracks and turned around, taking the ridiculous hat off and letting her long hair spill out. Then she couldn't breathe because Dylan had closed the distance and he held their baby in his arms, inches away from Molly. Closer than she'd been in one long year.

"Hi, Dylan." She didn't take her eyes off her baby. Sierra leaned her tiny head on Dylan's shoulder and smiled shyly at Molly. She had teeth now. Little precious baby teeth.

"Jedd told me you were back, but I didn't believe him. Told him it had to be some other redhead that caused a fight at the Silver Saddle. What was I thinking?" Dylan's intense brown eyes glared at her. "It had to be you."

Damn Jedd. People in this town needed to learn how to shut up. "I wanted to call you."

"What are you doing here? Are you spying on me? On us?"

"It's a free country. And I like parks." She folded her arms across her chest.

Dylan narrowed his eyes. "Since when?"

"Since I was a little girl, if you must know. And I've decided those swing sets over there are too dangerous for babies. What if she falls out? Did you ever think of that?"

"She's safe in there. I wouldn't do it otherwise. I hope you don't think you can come back and—" Dylan stopped and glanced at Sierra, his eyes filled with tenderness. His voice softened. "Take up where you left off."

"No, I don't." She didn't need Dylan to fly into protection mode.

"Good, because it could be confusing. For someone."

Molly knew exactly who that someone was. She looked at her baby longingly one more time. "Can I hold her? For just a minute?"

"That's not a good idea."

Sierra had lost interest in Molly and now fingered Dylan's shirt collar. Molly considered grabbing her out of Dylan's arms. He didn't have the right to keep her away from Sierra, even if she had abandoned them. But she didn't want to make her daughter cry. After all, it was obvious she didn't remember Molly. She might as well be a stranger.

"Right. You know best." Tears flooding her eyes, Molly turned and walked away. This time Dylan didn't call after her.

AFTER THE WEEKLY Pink Ladies' meeting, Emily stood in front of the gift shop red barn with bride-to-be Ashley Hawker. She had to make this work.

Running Fortune Family Ranch wasn't easy with Dad's penchant for buying cattle and all the upkeep required on the cattle ranch he'd bought in Texas. Not to mention all the flying back and forth he did. Last month she'd taken a good look at their ledgers, and if they didn't do something to increase Parker Inc.'s net worth, her father might have to lose some land in Texas. Maybe even some cows.

Besides, if Emily could handle weddings after her own almost-disaster, then so could everyone else. "Is this it, then?" Ashley checked out the barn. "It's a gift shop."

"We turned it into a gift shop a few years ago. We have two ponies left, and we moved them to the pen on the back side of the house. So now we can sell the work of local artists. Anything that's in some shape or form related to the town, or a Western theme." As it so happened, that was a lot.

While Ashley inspected the outside of the barn, Emily studied Ashley's arms. She'd never read someone's arm before, but she couldn't take her eyes off the future bride's full-sleeve tattoos. It wasn't polite to stare, which gave her limited time to read. Most of them were drawings of roses, butterflies and a woman's face, but there were words, too, and Emily was dying to read them.

She'd always wanted a tattoo, a small butterfly on her shoulder. Or maybe a flower. But her father was against body art, and when she'd suggested it to Greg, he implied only loose women had tattoos. Now that she was a wild woman, sooner or later she'd get that dang tattoo. In fact, maybe she could ask Ashley where she got hers done.

"So what will you do with all this stuff?" Ashley asked.

"We'll move it in time for the wedding and put it back later. Unless you'd like to at least see the gazebo out back. It hasn't been used since my father built it for my sister's wedding."

"No. No gazebos. This is perfect. We're going for spooky. I love being scared."

Emily stared at Ashley's purple painted lips. She was a striking girl, with jet-black hair and alabaster ivory skin. Her dramatic black eyeliner would have commanded attention at a nightclub, let alone in the bright light of the day. "You want spooky?"

"I wanted to get married on Halloween, actually, but my mom insisted that wasn't going to happen. Delilah doesn't think it's a good idea, either. We had to scramble to get another date. As long as Billy and I get married, I don't really care about the date that much." Ashley might not look like any other bride Emily had ever seen, but funny how her eyes lit up when she said Billy's name.

Emily hadn't heard the car drive up until she heard a door slam. Turning, she saw whom she assumed would be the wedding planner/minister walking toward them.

Emily had only spoken with Delilah over the phone when she'd committed to the dates. The deposit had cleared, and as far as Emily was concerned, that meant a wedding would take place. The wedding planner didn't look like anything Emily would have imagined. She wore a colorful caftan and some kind of square hat on her head.

Ashley and Delilah exchanged a hug, and Delilah introduced herself. She walked into the barn and studied the rafters. "This will do fine. Thank you for working with us, Emily. I realize this isn't the norm for you, and it's short notice."

"We're expanding." Emily hadn't pictured the barn as the best venue, but now that she appraised it with new eyes, it could work. Amazing she hadn't thought of it earlier.

"You were so right, Delilah. This is a sick, classic red barn. And if we do this at night, with only candles, it will be scary. Like, *Wrong Turn* scary." Ashley rubbed her arms like she'd just scared herself.

Why someone would want to be scared on her wedding day was another story, but Emily didn't want to ask.

Delilah pointed to a notebook she carried. "I've done the numerology charts, and now that we've got the right date, this is important—the wedding rehearsal must take place the day before the wedding at precisely six."

Ashley nodded like that made all the sense in the world. "You got it. I don't want to start this marriage off on the wrong number."

"The wrong number?" Emily dared to ask.

Delilah nodded. "It's how we picked the wedding day. Will that be a problem?"

Emily took out her tablet and made a note. "No problem at all."

The sound of Molly's truck blazing up the trail kicking up dust like a whirlwind drew Emily's attention. "Would you excuse me?"

She met Molly at the bottom of the hill, because Emily didn't have time for this now. Sure enough, Molly looked ready to throttle someone. "What's up?"

"It's Dylan, that bastard." Molly kicked the gated fence.

"When did you see Dylan?"

"At the park."

"What happened?"

"Oh, forget it. I can see you're busy." Molly stalked toward the house. "I don't want to waste your precious time."

"Go talk to Grammy, and I'll be there in a few minutes. I told these people I'd do whatever they need to make this wedding day memorable for them, and I have to do that."

"Talk to the hand." Molly turned once to hold up a one-handed gesture. "Or the finger."

Great. A pissed-off Molly was the last thing this day needed.

When Emily walked back to the barn, Ashley and Delilah were inspecting the rafters and speaking to George, who looked confused.

"Is everything all right?" Emily smiled.

"There are no cobwebs because I do my job," George said, eyebrows meeting what was left of his hairline.

"No cobwebs?" Emily turned to Ashley.

"I was hoping," Ashley said with a frown.

"George takes care of that. It *is* a gift shop." Emily wasn't sure why she felt like she should apologize.

"That's okay, we can add some fake cobwebs if we must," Delilah said with a wave of her arm.

"Ma'am?" George looked from Emily to Delilah and back to Emily again.

"I want to make sure your experience here is satisfactory in every way." Next on the list: buy cobwebs.

She whispered to George that he shouldn't worry and she'd explain later. He walked away, muttering under his breath. Finally Emily concluded the meeting, and both Ashley and Delilah were on their way, with an appointment to come back for the wedding rehearsal.

Now to deal with Molly.

Emily found Molly in her bedroom, half underneath the bed.

"So what's going on?"

"I want my boots. The pink ones. You seen them?" Molly came out from under her bed, holding what looked like a library book in one hand and a sandal in the other. "I can't find them."

Emily bent down to pick up the matching sandal from where it lay behind Molly's trash can. "You could clean up in here once in a while."

"I could. But right now, I need my boots. Are you going to help me, or what?" Molly opened her closet door and started tossing shoes out.

Emily caught a flying stiletto pump before it impaled her forehead. "Hey, watch it. What's wrong? Do you want to talk about it?"

"No, I don't want to talk. I want to dance. And I'll need my boots."

"Let's retrace your steps. Think about where you last saw them."

"I'm looking for my boots, not solving a mystery. Help me look or stop talking."

Emily should let Molly learn the hard way, but right now she seemed so upset. A quick trip down to the laundry room and sure enough, Molly's boots were under a pile of her dirty clothes. Emily ran back upstairs with them.

Molly's room now looked like a monsoon had been through it. She stood in the middle of a pile.

"You had my boots all along? Why did you let me make this mess?"

"I didn't— Oh, never mind. What happened at the park today?" She handed the boots over to Molly, who slipped them on.

"Nothing. Forget about it. I saw Sierra, and Dylan wouldn't even let me hold her for a minute." Molly picked up her hairbrush and pulled it through her hair. "No big deal. Maybe I would have dropped her. Lord knows I can't take care of her."

Molly had mastered her poker face to the point where Emily almost believed her. But she'd been upset about it enough earlier. Now she wanted to forget it. If there's one thing Emily understood, it was how difficult it could be to talk about the pain of a humbling experience. In Emily's case, it had been a derailed wedding day but Molly was dealing with so much more.

"You don't really believe that. You took care of her for six months, maybe even the most important months."

"I screwed that up, too. I barely slept and I was tired all the time. I couldn't do it. I'm not 'Mom' material, I guess."

"No one said you had to do it all on your own. New mothers need a lot of help. Maybe I should have helped you more."

Molly turned to Emily, eyes wide. Probably

amazed anyone else would shoulder some of the blame. "You helped."

"Not enough, and I'm sorry about that."

Molly plopped down on her bed. "Is that the first time you did anything wrong?"

"You're kidding, right?"

"Sorry. Not trying to be a smart-ass. Dylan wanted me to do everything all on my own. And every time I asked him to help with housework, he'd call Violet. She'd run right over and practically make a list of everything I was doing wrong. Because of course, Dylan always did everything right."

"So you stopped asking him for help. You *should* have asked me."

Molly didn't look at Emily. "But I wanted you to think I could do something right. Without your help. Stupid, I know."

"No." Emily's heart cracked open a little bit. "It's not stupid at all."

"So what am I supposed to do now?" Molly rubbed at her eyes.

"You're going to march over to Dylan's and tell him you're back and you want to see Sierra."

"Or maybe I could keep showing up at the park. At least I get to see her that way. I pretty much have his schedule down."

"But what about the divorce?"

"We should probably get one."

"I mean," Emily said with a sigh, "what if Dylan tries to sue for sole custody?"

"Ha! I almost hope he tries it. He'll be walking funny for a while."

Emily shook her head. "You two should come to an agreement like reasonable adults."

"Good idea, but every time Dylan and I are together in a room there are no adults. No reasonable ones, anyway."

"Honestly? I think it would help if you just talked to him."

"What am I supposed to say? I'm sorry, Dylan, for the gazillionth time?"

"Tell him how you feel. How much it hurts not to be able to see her."

"He'll say it was my choice. And you know what? It was. My fault."

"But everybody deserves a second chance. What you're doing now isn't healthy. You can't just go dancing and pretend you don't care. I know what I'm talking about. For six months I barely left the house. And weren't you the one who told me that I need to stop hanging out with the geriatric set?"

"Yeah."

"I've done my share of hiding from my life. It doesn't work. And now I'm doing something with it."

"Flying is a crazy kind of something."

"I know you said I was nuts to try this, but if I

can do that crazy thing, you can talk to Dylan. He can't be any scarier than flying a plane, can he?"

"Guess not. But he's not going to listen to me. I just know it."

"You've got to at least try."

Molly nodded but didn't speak.

And something told Emily that this whole matter was far from over.

CHAPTER EIGHT

THE FOLLOWING WEEK, Dad finally got himself home.

"He's here! Daddy, Daddy!" Molly yelled, and Emily marched out of the dining room to see her sister run down the steps, taking them two at a time.

Emily wished she could do that, but she'd face-plant if she even tried. "Slow down."

Dad had been in Texas three weeks this time. Molly always missed him most of all, and Emily tried to miss him. She really did. Unfortunately, Emily resented that he hadn't been supportive of any of her ventures to date, calling them her *I Love Lucy* moments. She knew it was love and concern talking, but he had shot down every one of her business ideas even before they'd gotten far off the ground.

He couldn't see Emily was at least making an effort at accomplishing something significant in her life. She'd been the one to go to college, while Molly insisted it would be a waste of good money on her. While Dad adored Molly, he didn't expect much from her. A big mistake because Emily was convinced Molly had a lot more ability than she wanted anyone to recognize. If only he would expect more from her, she might actually deliver it.

Tonight Emily expected she would probably get a whole heap of that judgment from him because she'd been taking flying lessons for two weeks. Even if she'd used her own savings to pay for them in advance, Grammy had asked where she'd been spending her afternoons and Emily couldn't lie.

So there was probably little coincidence Dad had made his way back home shortly after Grammy heard about the lessons. He would probably forbid her from continuing, since he never approved of anything Emily wanted to do on her own. She was ready for this, and had been for a while. Dad couldn't tell her what to do. Not anymore. She was done with Doormat Emily.

"Hey, Dad," Emily said as he walked in the front door, Molly's arms wrapped around him like she was the bread and Dad was the peanut butter.

"My Emily-girl." At least he hadn't called her his favorite nickname for her: Lucy. "Thank God you're safe on the ground. Where you belong."

Grammy spoke from behind Emily. "Decided to come home? Won't lie, we've missed you around here."

"Hey, Mother. Sorry I didn't come last week,

but we bought two hundred more head of cattle. That ought to increase the net worth of Parker Inc. Don't you think, Trouble?" Dad ruffled Molly's hair like she was ten, and in his eyes she probably was, even if she now had a baby of her own.

"That's right, son. That's what we need. More cows." Grammy disappeared into the kitchen.

He made his way to his brown leather recliner in the living room and collapsed into it. "I'd like to know what you're thinking, Emily."

"That's what I said," Molly chimed in. "It's not safe. Of all your schemes, Em, this one has got to be the nuttiest."

So they were going to slide right into it. "You must be so tired. Why not go upstairs and change? Take a shower?"

"Lord love a duck, I am tired," Dad said. "Hey, sugar, why don't you go get me a beer? That ought to relax me."

Of course, *sugar* meant Molly. "Be right back."

Dad scratched his ear and glanced at Emily. "Did you get this idea from a late-night infomercial or something?"

One time. One time she ordered a real estate course from a late-night infomercial and she would never live it down. "No!"

"Where did this confounded idea come from?" He accepted the beer from Molly, who then pulled up the ottoman so she could sit closer to him.

Actually, the idea had been Rachel's at first.

But Emily was going to take credit for this one. Now it was her turn to explain the history behind it, and she could only hope Dad would find some pride in her then. She was, after all, following in the footsteps of a Parker. His family line.

"We've been doing the family tree and it turns out one of your relatives, my great-great-grandmother, Emily Parker, was a pilot."

"Is that right? Sounds like a nutcase to me. And here your mother thought she named you Emily after her favorite author, Emily Brontë. I wish she was here right now so I could tell her she mistakenly named you after one of my relatives. All the people she hated. What a kick!"

Molly laughed, but Emily didn't think it was funny. "I'm doing well. The teacher said so just yesterday."

That wasn't quite the truth. He'd kind of lost his temper a little bit when she touched a button she wasn't supposed to. One having to do with landing gear, before it was time. Mostly, he was a bit nicer though she seemed to bore him. He never flirted with her anymore. But the point was, she'd made progress on her flight hours and was that much closer to getting her license.

"What if you have an accident?" Molly asked.

"Flying is statistically safer than driving." Emily had learned that, among other things.

"But when your engine dies, you can pull over to the side of the road. In a plane, it's more like

'Sayonara, baby! Hope you got a parachute.'" Molly laughed.

Dad laughed, too. Naturally.

"At least I'm trying to do something with my life." She shot a glare in Molly's direction.

"Who says I'm not trying to do something with my life?"

"Now, don't you girls start fighting. Didn't come home for none of that. Emily, I'm glad you've had your fun, but it has to stop now. Just go over there and tell that teacher of yours you're done." He waved a hand in the air. "Mother needs you around here anyway."

"I never let it interfere with my job. Just ask Grammy. I'm the one who does most of the work around here." She could manage to keep a few balls in the air, thank you very much. And flying would not be the one to go.

"Well, I won't have it. What will people say? A real American man keeps his daughters safe!" Dad pounded his fist while his face colored to an interesting shade of red.

Emily would need to tread carefully now, because there was no point in upsetting him. His cholesterol and blood pressure were through the roof, and he refused to stop eating red meat. Said that would be unpatriotic. "Calm down. You know I love America. And also red meat."

"Stop making Daddy sick!" Molly said. "The doctor said he can't get upset."

"I'm fine, sugar." He patted Molly's hand. "Don't you worry none. Your sister has good sense. She'll come around, won't you, Emily, now? Where's dinner? Mother?"

Emily smiled and said nothing, because saying the truth would mean Dad's blood pressure would blow past the two hundreds. This might not be the best time to assert her newfound rebel streak and let him know she'd do what she wanted to regardless of his input.

She wasn't the young girl who listened to her father, no matter what he said. Even when it didn't make sense. Even when he hadn't let her go out with Luke Eilers, the handsomest boy in high school, because he came from a family of no-good un-American vegans. The horrors.

No, best to keep quiet and do what she wanted anyway.

If she'd learned nothing else from Molly, she'd certainly learned that.

CHAPTER NINE

EMILY WAS GRATEFUL for flying lessons. Dad had been home for a week now, and she hadn't had any trouble sneaking around yet, even if Molly did seem to suspect. Every afternoon Molly drilled Emily on where she was going then followed her out the door, where she'd stand, arms folded, shaking her head.

Molly was usually at her best when Dad was home, but lately she seemed jumpier than normal. She'd been back to the Silver Saddle many times now, without Emily, and even though Molly had said she missed Sierra, it certainly didn't look that way. It seemed lately that Molly's biggest concern was finding the party.

Sooner or later, Emily would have to talk to her again. She'd never seen Molly so afraid, but it seemed as if fear of failing again with Sierra had rooted her into a bad pattern.

In a bit of a contrast, this time it was Emily who had no fear. She was too busy making history to be afraid.

Flying lessons also involved sitting close to

Mr. Studley, while listening to the deep sexy timbre of his voice in her earpiece. So it was no coincidence that coming to the small airport three times a week was the highlight of her week. It also didn't hurt that he seemed to feel guilty about his attitude, even though he hadn't officially apologized. He also hadn't mentioned the date again.

For now, they had a silent agreement. He would teach; she would listen.

She wanted to ace this test and get on with the rest of her day in a hurry. She still had a full day ahead of her. Trish had already phoned twice with changes. This wedding was going to consume Emily's days and evenings even if it was a whole year away. She also had Ashley and Billy's wedding coming up, and already several more brides had called about the wedding packages.

"Are you listening?" He was always doing that—convinced she wasn't paying attention, like she was somehow going to break his precious plane.

And even though he made it hard to focus, she'd studied for the test today and thought she was ready. She saluted. "Yes, sir."

"Cut it out."

He didn't like it when she saluted him; pretty much why she did it.

"Okay, Miss Earhart. You know what to do. Pretend I'm not here."

"That's hard to do when you keep talking." She stared at the cleft in his chin, which she swore deepened when he was serious.

Today she was taking a quiz. In order to get her license, she'd eventually have to pass a test with her certified instructor, the hunk sitting next to her, and even though she was still several flight hours away from that point, she'd convinced Stone to give her a quiz. Just to make sure she was on track.

Besides, a quiz would only boost her self-confidence. She'd never had less than an A on a test she'd studied for.

"Here are my last words. The test begins…" He looked at his wristwatch. "Now."

I can do this. I'm the descendant of one of the first female pilots. A mover and a shaker. It's just taken me a while to find that out, but from now on, the sky's the limit. Ha. Quite literally.

While she couldn't help but shoot occasional glances in Stone's direction, she went through the flight-check procedures on her own and began taxiing down the runway. Even though he wouldn't literally grade her, this was a test in every sense of the word. A test to prove she'd been listening and not staring at his hard body. A test that would prove she was the new, bold Emily.

And then she was taking off. Just like he'd taught her, flying, on her own. Stone wasn't saying a word, his facial expression so unreadable she couldn't actually be sure he wasn't resting his baby blues underneath those *Top Gun* shades. He had the logbook on his lap, but he hadn't so much as lifted his pencil. Maybe she bored him. She had half a mind to entertain him with an unexpected turn instead of the precise directions he'd outlined beforehand.

Then again, that was Stone: cool as a cucumber. And she was mushy like a ripe banana. Good for banana nut bread but not much else. *Oh, come on, I can do this. I will not let this plane, this vast expanse of sky, intimidate me.* Hands down, taking flying lessons was the wildest thing she'd ever done. Mission accomplished.

One look at Stone and her nerves steadied a bit, like he'd loaned her some of his steel. Maybe, with any luck, it would rub off on her. She landed the way he'd taught her, the way she'd seen him do. And even if her heart beat in her eardrums, they were all in one piece.

Stone finally lifted his pencil and started to jot down some notes. "I'm impressed. You didn't ask me one question."

"You mean I could have? I thought I wasn't supposed to ask." That was what she got for following someone else's rules.

"That doesn't usually stop people. The point is, you didn't need to ask." He looked up from his notes, his eyes peeking out from over his sunglasses.

"How did I do?"

"You taxied too fast. Again."

"Oh, right. I'm sorry. I just get so excited." Or deathly afraid.

"And you missed a couple of steps on your preflight check."

Damn it all. "So—if you were grading me, what would you give me?"

"I told you, there's no grade. And this isn't the real test. You do remember that."

"But you could give me one. You know you could. If you wanted. I won't stop you."

He grinned. "So you want a grade?"

"Yep. What can I say? I've always been the teacher's pet." So far she'd been nothing but the consummate professional student, and now she was flirting. She blamed it on the flying. It had turned out to be some kind of aphrodisiac.

"Okay, you asked for it. You get a C plus." He continued to write down notes as if he hadn't just metaphorically slapped her face.

"A C? You're kidding, right?" She'd had one C in school and cried about it for a week. "I am not a C student."

"I said a C *plus*."

"C, C plus, what's the difference?"

"You're an average pilot right now. You'll get better."

"I'm in a hurry."

"Yeah, and I want to know why."

There was the matter of the alumni's newsletter, and she'd hoped to get in the next issue. It would be so impressive to be able to report she'd become a licensed pilot, and the tie-in to her namesake would make a nice little human-interest story. But she didn't think Stone would like that answer. "I'm not getting any younger."

Now he stared at her as if she had two heads. He was forever giving her that look, as if she confounded him down to the depths of his blue eyes. "Right."

"Why do you always look at me like that?"

"How am I looking at you?"

"Like I'm some odd human species you can't quite figure out. Like you don't understand a word I'm saying."

"Hmm. That isn't too far from the truth."

She slapped his shoulder. "Oh, c'mon. You know I'm your favorite female student."

"You're my only female student."

"Look at that. I guess that makes me the favorite."

"Don't push it, Parker."

She climbed out of the plane and followed him into the hangar, but only steps before the door she stopped in her tracks. She'd passed the test today. Unofficially, yes, and with a C. Her least favorite way of passing. But still, she'd passed. She was going to get her pilot's license. Soon, if she kept this up.

"Are you going to pass out again?" He opened the hangar door and paused, searching her eyes, his brow furrowed.

No fainting today. Not at all. This was a banner day for Emily Parker. "I passed."

"It wasn't a test. But yeah, if it had been. I passed you."

"But I'm going to be a pilot! Soon!" She shouted and ran toward him, almost surprising herself by grabbing his neck and planting a kiss on his lips. Apparently flying also gave her courage, because she'd wanted to do that for a while, too.

Good Lord, he smelled so good. Like a combination of leather and musk. Stone made her forget from time to time that she'd given up men. His surly gazes and hard body could make a girl forget all kinds of things.

In the next moment, Stone's arms came around her waist to pull her closer. "That was nice, but an apple would have been fine."

"An apple?" she stammered.

"Teacher, apple?" He held her practically pinned against him, arms tight around her waist, hands lingering a bit lower.

Okay, so she'd just forgotten a simple connection between apple and teacher. Her brain was officially on hiatus. "I lost my head for a minute. I'll bring you an apple tomorrow."

He looked like he would kiss her then, but the hot look in his eyes told her it would be nothing simple. She could almost taste his breath as he leaned in close, and she reviewed the reasons why she should forget about her plan to give up men. Molly was right. It wouldn't have lasted anyway.

Then his lips were on hers, and she nearly lost her footing when he deepened the kiss. His arms remained tight around her like he was claiming her for his own. And then it was over.

"Sorry," he said, pulling away. "I didn't mean to do that."

Emily tried to regain her balance because he'd nearly kissed the breath right out of her. *Wow*, was all she could think. *Wow*. Similar to the one-word thought she'd had the first night she'd seen him, only now he'd proved he could do a lot more than dance and enhance a wall. He could also kiss a girl like his life depended on it.

How exactly did one fall on another person's lips like that? She wasn't the picture of grace, but she'd never done it. "What did you do? Fall on my lips?"

He gave her "the look" again. "No, but that's something you might do."

"My kiss wasn't an accident. I might be a klutz, but even I'm not that bad."

"That wasn't a kiss. It was a peck. Mine was a kiss."

She couldn't argue that fact, or the indignation she felt coming on front and center. He didn't want her. Fine, she could accept that. He'd changed his mind, like most men. The same way she'd temporarily forgotten her vow to be done with men. But if anything, that smug look on Stone's face was a good reminder.

CHAPTER TEN

IN THE PAST two weeks, Stone had come to realize Emily Parker, despite her stripper-like body and Cupid's bow lips, was a nice girl. Possibly too nice, at least for him. He'd heard all about the family ranch, converted to an events place when her father decided to buy cheaper land in Texas for his new cattle ranch. Heard all about her grandmother, who'd raised Emily and her sister. Molly, who had a baby and put the *T* in *Trouble*. Mostly he'd become aware of her life history because Emily liked to talk. She was also quite obviously the force in her family, holding everyone together.

She wasn't any man's temporary girl, not by a long shot. Which was why he hadn't brought up the date again. Seemed a little too dangerous, even for a guy who courted danger. He missed his daily adrenaline fix, sure, but this wouldn't so much be an adrenaline rush as it would be sheer insanity. And although some of his air force buddies would disagree, he wasn't a fan of insanity.

He was a big fan of hot sex with equally hot and willing women. Dirty, hard and fast. Temporary worked. Temporary filled a need. Once in a while he'd been unfortunate enough to hook up with a woman who didn't understand the temporary nature of anything he could offer. Those goodbyes had been bitter, verging on hostile, and had never sat well with him. He'd been called heartless. Cruel. Cold-blooded. Unable to love and be loved.

That last one, at least, was a hundred percent false. His first love was the air force and always would be. And he'd loved his father, his AF friends. He of course loved his mother, and possibly Sarah if she'd stop being a pain in the ass. But women? He had no use for them for the most part. He understood that made him an asshole.

But while here in Fortune, he'd kept a low profile on the dating scene. As in nonexistent. And man, it had been so long, but it wasn't like he had much free time. This was best, anyway. No women who would later talk all over this small town about James Mcallister's heartless son. He hadn't been laid in eight solid months, which killed him. Emily wasn't going to break that streak.

And, he'd like to think, he could at least be a better man than someone who would follow through on that kiss. On that date. Yeah, he hadn't forgotten.

She'd given as good as she got in that kiss, reminding him of all the things he'd wanted to do to her since the first night he'd laid eyes on her. Thoughts he hadn't allowed himself to have since he started teaching her. But now, the look on her face. This was bad, because it mattered that her eyes were turning several shades of green, filled with hurt and something that looked a bit like shame. He had to fix this.

He followed her through the hangar, enjoying the view. Her hips were swinging in a particularly enticing way, probably because she was pissed.

"Hey, Emily. How was your flight today?" Jedd asked as they walked past him.

"Great, but Stone had an accident," Emily said with a bite in her words.

"Emily—" Stone warned.

"What happened to the plane?" Jedd ran outside, presumably to check for damage.

Stone would have stopped him, but he had his own kind of damage control. He followed Emily's stomps in the direction of his office, where she always kept her purse. She couldn't leave here without that. So she'd have to deal with him.

She passed by Cassie's desk, straight into his office, where she slammed the door. He was only a step behind her, but Cassie took the opportunity to throw him a pointed look. "What did you do now?"

He ignored the comment, let himself in his office and shut the door again. Emily had found her purse and was rifling through its compartments.

Her cheeks were flushed when she turned to him. "Look, it's okay. You changed your mind. I get it."

She continued to struggle with that blasted purse, and now it annoyed him since she used it like a shield to keep her distance from him.

He took the purse out of her hands and set it down on his desk. "I didn't make a mistake. I wanted to kiss you. I'm sorry because I may have gotten a bit carried away. My fault." He put a hand on his chest to demonstrate he meant it. Hormones not listening again.

She lifted a shoulder. "It's all right. You can kiss me like that again."

"Yeah?" He wanted to, right here and now.

And so much more. Something about her made him forget for a minute that he was a stranger in this town. She reminded him of his former overwhelming need not to hesitate. To plunge headfirst into dangerous territory. She, most unfortunately for him, seemed to serve as a reminder of who he was at the core. Not his father's son, but his own man.

But for right here, right now, he had to remember that first and foremost he was his father's son for all practical purposes. Mr. Good Guy, in the flesh. And Mr. Good Guy didn't seduce women like Emily.

"I mean, but only if you want to." She stared at his lips and set his groin on fire.

Mr. Good Guy was about to go on hiatus.

He didn't need another invitation as he drew her into his arms. She sighed as she leaned into his kiss and threaded her fingers through his hair, sucking the marrow right out of him. After several minutes, he pulled away because if he didn't stop now, they'd both be in trouble.

"I think we've established we both like to kiss each other." He sat behind his desk where she, and the rest of his staff, would be spared from witnessing the bulge in his pants.

Her lips looked bruised, her cheeks a flushed pink color that made him want her even more. "But this is probably not a good idea, right?"

He thought about the fact he had no real plans to stay in this town after he'd taken care of his father's affairs. He didn't do permanent or white picket fences, and Emily wouldn't want a fling.

No, this wasn't a good idea, but the hell with it. "What are you doing tonight?"

"I was beginning to think you forgot about our deal."

"Not a chance."

"Where are you taking me?"

"It's a surprise."

"I don't like surprises. We never established parameters for our one date, you know."

"Parameters?"

"Guidelines."

"You want guidelines?"

"Sure. Is this a coffeehouse date or a dinner date? Is it denim or silk? Should I—" At this, for some reason, she blushed. "I mean, throw me a bone. Where are we going and what will we be doing?"

"Wouldn't you like to know?"

"I would."

"I've got nothing. You'll have to wait and see. I'll pick you up around five."

"You don't know where I live."

"Your address is on all the forms you filled out. Remember?"

"Okay. But it's complicated. You need to go up the road and when you see the red barn, turn right. You'll see a large Victorian house. That's not where I live. I have the loft, which is a few yards away above the garage."

"I've flown an F-16. I think I can find you."

She nodded a little uncertainly but then smiled, turned and walked right into his dad's metal filing cabinet.

He stood. "You okay?"

"I'm fine." She rubbed her right shoulder, which seemed to have gotten the worst of it. She opened the door to his office and turned back to him. "Wait—what should I wear?"

"Casual—and that's all you get. No more questions."

EMILY DROVE HOME, wondering what she'd signed up for. He'd said casual. Casual pants or casual dress? Casual country or casual Fifth Avenue? At home, Emily showered and okay, waxed (one could never be too careful, but yeah, it wasn't going to happen) and tried on several different shades of lipstick and eye shadow. Green looked too pretentious on her eyelids and blue way too slutty.

She went with brown, her standby. Safe. Reliable. Every color of lipstick she owned made her look like a madame, so she decided to go with the clear gloss. She tore through her dressers and closet, discarding dresses, tops and slacks. Nothing seemed quite right. There were at least a hundred different levels of casual, and she'd gone through every one of them in the past two hours. When she thought she might have a coronary over the decision whether to wear a dress or jeans, she had to finally remind herself this was a "casual" date. Whatever that meant. Jeans it was.

At times like these, the loft did lend privacy, as she didn't have Grammy there to wonder why she was methodically going through everything she owned. Or Molly, with her keen observation for all things men-related, zeroing in on the fact she was nervous. About a man.

What am I doing? Oh yeah, I agreed to one date. But Stone was not her type. She'd stayed miles away from the handsome men. Because she wanted and needed control, she'd dated the kind

of man who was stable and secure, safe and—
and look where that got me. It got her Greg. Reliable Greg, who color coded everything in his closet and had every detail of their lives planned down to the days of the week they'd make love.

That was why it had been so humiliating to find him with Nika.

It wasn't even a scheduled day for sex. It was a Monday, and Greg always required a good night's sleep for his early Tuesday morning meetings at work. So when she'd brought him an early dinner that afternoon, so he could get his much-needed rest, she'd been shocked to find him on the kitchen floor with Nika—who was cleaning a lot more than the sink that day.

Even now, Emily couldn't push the image out of her mind. No way would she ever unsee that. She'd run out on both of them, without even so much as an "excuse me for interrupting," and informed her family the wedding was off. Eventually, Rachel had wrenched the whole sordid story out of Emily and been kind enough not to say "I told you so."

Now, Emily sighed and pulled out her laptop, ready to do some last-minute work before going out. It was her job to run every marketing tool for their family business. She alone kept the website and social media updated and the blog she couldn't seem to get herself to update on a regular basis. She posted some tweets and status updates, reminded everyone of their new wedding events package and checked their events schedule for the next month.

Emily's cell phone rang. Rachel. They hadn't talked much in the past week. "Hey. Everything okay?"

"We got an ultrasound, and it's a boy!" Rachel squealed into the phone. "There's no hiding that little pecker. Mr. Hot Stuff is so happy."

"Oh, honey, congratulations!" Emily bit back the envy that coursed through her. If things had turned out differently, Emily might have been pregnant as well. But pregnant with the spawn of Satan. It was probably better this way.

"So what's new with you? I've been so busy I feel like we haven't talked in weeks. How close are you to getting your pilot's license?"

"You wouldn't believe it. You know the guy you wanted me to ask out at the coffee shop? He's the pilot!"

Rachel giggled into the phone. "Isn't that something?"

If Emily hadn't known Rachel since the ninth grade, she might not have heard the teasing tone in her friend's voice. "What's so funny?"

"I might as well confess. I knew he was the pilot, because I was at the airport a couple of months ago to sell them some advertising space."

"But you're a reporter."

"At a small-town paper. We do a little bit of everything. When I took a look at that man, I knew he'd be someone who could give you a wild time. Lessons or not."

Okay, so she'd been thinking about it. A lot. Maybe it was time to try something different. She'd bet a lifetime supply of chocolate that Stone didn't have designated days of the week for making love. More like whenever the spirit moved him, which she pictured was often.

"I wish you'd told me."

"Why? Then you would have let it stop you from taking lessons, with your silly dry-spell idea. So? Have you, uh, you know, yet?"

"No, we haven't 'you know' yet. Have I known him for six months?"

"Right. What was I thinking? Emily's Rules. What a shame. I had him checked out anyway. If I'm going to play matchmaker for my best friend, I'm going to make sure the man isn't a convicted rapist. Or an ax murderer. He's neither, by the way."

Stone, an ax murderer. He was scary, but not that kind of scary. "Good to know I'm safe." Although *safe* was a relative term.

"I didn't say that. He sure doesn't look safe, at least not on paper."

Emily worried a nail between her teeth. "So what else did you learn about him?"

"He's your basic war hero. Not your type,

right? I'm thinking the man takes too many risks. You know, for God and country."

"You're not funny." There wasn't anything wrong with taking control when it came to romance. That was why she'd invented Emily's Rules.

"And there's also Pilots and Paws. Yeah, he flies dogs from kill shelters around the country to their forever homes. So, he's basically Superman."

"We had a fund-raiser for them here once."

"What's he like? He didn't talk much when I met him. I mostly talked to his office manager. He's a man of few words, I'm guessing."

"You're right. I thought I bored him, until today." Except that she'd made the first move, no matter what he said. Mostly because she'd lost her head for a minute.

"What happened today?"

"I kissed him." It was a peck but it counted. She was counting it.

Rachel squealed. "You are serious about this wild-woman thing. Girl, you haven't kissed a guy first since Jimmy Duvell in the tenth grade."

Leave it to Rachel to remember, and darned if she wasn't right about that. The memories came flooding back. "And he threw up right after I did."

"He'd eaten too many nachos."

It was most probably the real reason she'd

avoided kissing a guy first. This time it had worked out so much better.

"So, how was it?" Rachel asked. "Kissing a pilot? I used to have a fantasy about that. I still have the hat."

Emily now had to push one other unwanted image out of her head. "It was—" *Hot. Sexy. Scary. Wild.* "Amazing."

There were protesting male sounds in the background, and Emily recognized Jake's voice. "Gotta go. Hot Stuff keeps reminding me I'm already pregnant, so we might as well take advantage. He's got a point."

"See you later." Emily hung up with a frown. She loved her friend, but she never could understand Rachel's obsession with sex. Or Molly's, for that matter. Sex was nice, pleasant, sure, and she'd enjoyed it, too. Being held so close by the man you loved and feeling good about the orgasmic glow all over his face. For her, there'd never been any firecrackers, sunbursts, stars exploding behind her eyes or song lyrics, for that matter. Not any orgasms, either. She figured sex was just not her thing. It would be nice if it was and, on some level, she kept hoping.

Her cell phone buzzed again. Trish this time. Emily was nearly afraid to pick it up. A few days ago Emily had picked up the phone at 1:00 a.m., thinking it had to be an emergency and that someone was dead, but it was only Trish, unable to sleep and wanting to change her wedding flowers from red roses to orange daylilies.

For the wedding which was one year away!

"Hey, Trish."

"Oh, my God, I just came up with the greatest idea! Doves!"

Emily pulled out the five-page wedding "manifesto" Trish had emailed to make a note. "Dove chocolate?"

"No, silly. I want beautiful white doves released at the end of our ceremony! It's perfect. You have a ranch and all that wide-open space, and so we'll just release those beautiful creatures into the bright sky. Two of them, a male and a female. I don't know how to check their anatomy but I'll leave that to you. Like me and Jimmy, if we were doves, flying into the future. Our destiny together. Isn't that romantic?"

Emily swallowed. "Doves? Would you maybe settle for a couple of chickens?"

Trish burst out into peals of laughter. "Oh, you are a kick! I will say that you know how to make me laugh. But this is serious. My wedding day, remember?"

"I know. The day to end all days." And if that was beginning to take on a worrisome, nuclear-holocaust-like tone, that one would be Trish's fault.

Emily hung up with Trish and started researching doves online. She started off with "why doves are a bad idea at a wedding." She needed ammunition.

A few hours and twenty Google searches later, Emily's doorbell rang. She froze. That would be Stone, and she wasn't quite ready for him. Would she ever be? Stone was outside her little loft, where she'd never had a man before. The thought of it two weeks ago had made Grammy laugh. Because Emily had been entirely too predictable all her life, that was why. But that too was going to change. The doorbell rang again and she shoved a bag of Cheetos under a couch pillow then lunged for the door.

"Wait. I'm coming!" She threw open the door to *Top Gun*–shades Stone. That was always a good look for him.

"Without me?" He flashed his illegal grin.

She had no idea what he was talking about. "Huh?"

"Never mind," he said. "Are you going to let me in?"

"Of course." She moved aside then glanced at her jeans and suddenly began to question everything. She should have asked where they were going—surprises were not acceptable for people who were going on a first date.

"I could have used a little more direction on how to dress. There are at least one hundred different levels of casual, and if you were a woman, you'd know that. And did I mention I don't like surprises?"

"You look great," Stone said, appraising her clothing, even though he lingered a little too long on her northern parts. "Perfect."

He was checking out her home, a place which she'd thought of as temporary a year ago. But she was still here. While the loft was small, basically a studio apartment with a small kitchenette, Grammy had countrified it for Emily, putting Southern hospitality touches—including yellow curtains and rooster touches everywhere. It wasn't exactly what Emily would have chosen, but it hadn't mattered at the time. Now all she could see was a place she'd lived in for a year which had turned out to be more of a hiding place than she'd realized. A fort in which she'd figuratively pulled up a drawbridge and hibernated.

For one year.

Stone took it all in and, as far as Emily could tell, wasn't making any judgments. "Cozy."

"When I moved back home, my grandmother thought I might like a little privacy."

He glanced at her bed, and Emily felt a tingle go up her spine. The worst thing about a studio apartment was having one's bed in the room like it was part of the decor. She hadn't had this problem since her college days. This was so awkward. *Yeah, there's my bed. I sleep in it. And yes, always alone. Always.*

What did one do with a man like Stone? "Um, would you like something to drink?"

"I'm good. We should go."

Emily grabbed her purse. "Right. Where again?"

"Nice try." With one hand on her back, he steered her to the door.

Within a few minutes, they were in his long-bed truck driving to who-knew-where to do who-knew-what. "Any hint for me?"

"There will be food," he offered, giving her a sideways glance.

"Oh, good. I like food. Thanks for being specific." She relaxed a little, until he got on the freeway. There were plenty of eating establishments nearby, but they were obviously going somewhere else. Like, out of the area. She swallowed again, and turned to him. "How far is this place? How long will we be gone?"

"Do you trust me? You do know I'm bringing you back," Stone said with a smile tugging at his lips.

"Of course I trust you." If becoming airborne with him didn't demonstrate trust, then she didn't know what did.

"Good, because I don't know if I trust myself."

He did have an air about him at times, not that she didn't trust him to do his job. No, far from it. But at times a hard veil passed over those normally kind eyes, and she wouldn't ever want to get on his bad side.

"What's that supposed to mean?"

"Maybe I'll keep you."

He was kidding now. Flirting even. And the sexual innuendo from earlier had just hit her.

Sex jokes. She wasn't any good at them, but she understood flirting. "You may keep me, but will you know what to do with me?"

"I'd know what to do with you."

Of this she had no doubt. It was in the way he kissed her, in the certain way he held her that told her he knew very well what he was doing. What's more, he'd do it slowly and methodically. "Yes, you implied that the first night you met me."

The light teasing tone in his voice changed to something quite a bit more subdued. "I should apologize for that."

"For what?" She had a feeling she knew what he meant. He'd been very forward that night, not that she wasn't used to getting hit on at the bar.

"You know what. I'm surprised, actually, that you didn't slap me silly that night."

"I wanted to." She laughed a little, because he looked so humbled that she wanted to lighten the mood.

"What can I say? I was alone, and I saw what I wanted. So I reacted like a horny teenager. In other words, I let my hormones rule the day."

Emily let that settle in—he'd seen what he wanted. *Her.* "You're not the first man to let your hormones do the thinking."

"You make that easy."

"Well thanks, soldier."

"Airman," he said with a wince.

"Right, sorry."

What she wanted to do was ask more about the lawsuit, about his sister, everything. But this probably wasn't the right time. Eventually he took an exit off the freeway in Sunnyvale past Moffett Field and soon after pulled into a parking lot with a sign that read Air Borne Bar & Grill.

"Here we are."

CHAPTER ELEVEN

A MAN CAVE. He'd brought her to a man cave.

The place looked small from the outside, like there should be a neon cocktail sign hanging at its entrance. But as they walked inside, the size of it surprised her. It was shaped like a hangar. One end had a bar and the other end the grill. Big-screen televisions hung from every wall, interspersed with pictures of planes. Small-scale replicas of B-52 bombers and other planes hung from the rafters. A lone pool table stood nearly hidden in a corner.

"Um, am I the only woman here?" Emily scanned the room and fought the urge to cling to him. For cover. All the testosterone in here was bound to cause some kind of explosion.

He slipped off his shades. "Nah, but you might be the only Greenie here."

"Greenie?"

"Noob, rookie, fledgie."

He kept throwing out nonsense words. From the look on his face, he found comfort in this place. The planes of his face had relaxed somewhat, and his eyes weren't filled with that constant edge. Less than a minute after they'd walked in, they were surrounded by three large and buffed men.

"Oh, damn, it's Stone," one of them said. "I thought you'd be long gone by now. Isn't this the longest you've ever been grounded? Must be driving you crazy."

"Who said I'm grounded?" Stone asked the man he introduced to her as "Crash," leaving Emily to wonder how many of them had earned him that nickname.

"Don't forget he's running the aviation school," another man said while he practically wrestled a grown man to the ground.

Stone made introductions all around. Emily would have to remember Crash, Dave, Matt and someone they called NFG for some odd reason.

"This is Emily Parker. She's going to be a pilot," Stone said.

Emily sucked in a breath at being introduced that way from a man who apparently did have faith in her. He believed in her abilities, even if she still doubted them. She was now in the midst of what she assumed must be other air force pilots and, for the first time, noticed a few women sitting at a table nearby.

"You're letting this guy teach you? *This* stupid guy? I'll teach you everything you need to know, babe," the one named Dave said.

Stone put an arm around her, and she moved even closer to him. "She doesn't need to learn how to crash and burn."

"That's right. You'll take care of her, won't you, Stone?" the youngest-looking man said.

"Shut up, NFG," Matt said.

"Why do they call him NFG?" Emily whispered.

"He's the new guy and I'll let you figure out the rest," Stone said as a waitress ushered them to a table at the grill. The men, thankfully, didn't follow. Instead, they issued catcalls as they walked away.

The place smelled like onions, garlic, French fries and other enticing smells that were making her stomach do leaps in anticipation. This time his hand rode a bit lower on her back.

"Do you come here a lot?"

He nodded. "It's owned by a couple of retired air force pilots. Kind of a gathering place for those on leave, grounded between assignments."

The whole thing reminded her of the temporary nature of this date. One date. She hadn't forgotten that. "So…about your dad. I used to see him here and there at the diner and around town. I didn't know him well."

Stone smiled, something he should do a lot more often, and Emily went a little limp. "My dad was like my best friend. The flight school was his dream. And before he died, he just asked me to stick around until I could sell it to someone who would keep it going. He wanted me to keep it open so his employees wouldn't be out of a job. What can I say, he was a good guy."

"You were close."

"He raised me. My parents divorced when my sister and I were young, about ten, and their custody arrangement was I would live with my father and my sister with my mother."

"How do you break up a family like that?" Of all the crazy child custody arrangements she'd ever heard, this one was the craziest.

"Look, it's not like they each picked a favorite kid. Sometimes I think that's what Sarah believes. It's just not true. Our father used to take her fishing every summer until she was about thirteen. She stopped visiting after that. Her choice." Stone shrugged. "It worked for us."

Until now, she wanted to say. No wonder they hated each other. They had no real connection. "So—did you ever see your mom and sister?"

"Saw my mother on the occasional holiday, and summers. But as we became teenagers, neither one of us was much interested in wasting a summer away from our friends. They couldn't force it at that point. Honestly, it felt a little disloyal to ask to spend time with my mother. My dad was always there for me. It was enough."

"Have you tried talking to your sister?"

"I would talk, if I had anything to say. So far all she wants to bring up are lies."

"Lies?"

"Emily, I'd *really* rather not talk about this," Stone said.

"Sorry. I can't imagine not having my sister, even if she is a spoiled brat sometimes."

They ordered hamburgers and fries when their waitress arrived, and then Stone turned the tables on Emily. "What about your parents? You talk about Molly, your dad and your grandmother. Not your mom."

Jessica Lynn. Everyone had called her Jessie. Every time Dad said her name, his entire body seemed to cave in on itself. He still carried both the hurt and hate in about equal measures, even after seventeen years. Blamed the doctors. Blamed the hospital. "She died when Molly was three and I was about eleven."

Stone met her eyes and took her hand. "That's rough."

There weren't many photos of Mama left, because one day Grammy had put them all away after she'd found Dad crying. "It was hardest on Molly. She cried every night for three months. Now she doesn't even remember her."

Stone wasn't letting go of her hand right now. "Do you play pool?"

Emily looked in the direction of the pool table a few feet away. There seemed to be a bunch of sweaty men over there. "Maybe I've played once or twice. Why?"

"Let's play a game after we eat."

After Stone had paid for their meal, resisting her attempts to go dutch, she was rethinking the pool idea. She hadn't played in a while, and what she remembered about it was suddenly coming back to her in waves. A klutz and a pool table? Surely Stone hadn't thought this all the way through. The last time she'd nearly impaled a man when he'd come too close during her attempts at a shot.

But he talked the men into letting them have a turn. This was worse because now they had an audience.

"Yeah, I got hustled, too. He doesn't look like he plays pool," the guy they called NFG said.

"Why don't you just shut up and watch. Maybe you'll learn something," Crash said.

"Hey, genius. Stop your damned cussing, a lady is present." This from a woman who had sidled up to watch. She was beautiful in a hard way, hair pulled back so tight it made her eyebrows arch.

"Excuse me for living," Matt said.

"You're excused," she said, putting her arm around Matt.

Emily's hands shook by then. She had to come up with a way out of this. Maybe she could feign illness. She could say she was allergic to chalk. "I'm having second thoughts."

Stone was chalking up and turned to the small crowd. "Would you all just leave now? You're cramping my style."

"Ah, man," Crash said.

"Let's all play darts," the woman said. "I don't know how. Would you teach me, Matt?"

"Oh, hell yeah," Matt said, leading the way.

The woman walked away but not before throwing a smile in Stone's direction.

"Something tells me Matt is about to get hustled," Stone said.

"And that's probably the least of his problems," Emily answered.

Stone laughed. A hearty deep sound she'd never heard out of him before. "This game is more fun if there's a wager on it."

"I don't gamble, though. Sir." She started to relax now it was just the two of them.

"Not money. Something more interesting." He eyed her with a wickedly seductive glint in his eyes, and she nearly felt her womb leap in anticipation.

"Fine. If I win, you'll dance with me right here in front of your buddies. A country song." She waved in the direction of the jukebox. He'd already demonstrated he could dance, but something told her these boys didn't know it.

Stone scowled. "Agreed. And if I win, you'll—I should probably think this over. Carefully."

"Why don't we just call it a game now? You and I both know you're going to win. And as for me, we'll be lucky if I don't accidentally injure you."

"You're taking all the fun out of this. I need to earn it."

"All right, Mr. Show-Off. Earn it."

"If I win, I get one more date."

Emily swallowed. One more date with him wouldn't feel like losing, but she kept her mouth shut and watched as he made the next of several shots easily and effortlessly.

But then he missed a shot Emily thought he should have easily made and handed her the pool stick. "Your turn. And don't hurt me with that stick."

"Then watch yourself." Emily leaned down and began her halfhearted attempt at a shot. Major joke. She hadn't had nearly enough alcohol to pull this off.

But suddenly Stone's hard body was behind her, adjusting her shot. Oh my, she liked his assistance very much. It was by far the best part of the game. He leaned in close over her shoulder, one arm on her waist adjusting her stance and the other aligning the direction of the shot.

"Don't shoot until I move. I might want to have children one day," Stone whispered in her ear.

She laughed, waited and took the shot. Made it. Didn't even kill anyone in the process.

A few more shots and they were nearly tied. Not that she could have made any of the shots without him, which was strange. Maybe he didn't care about that second date after all. She tried not to think of that as she enjoyed the feel of his body against hers every time he lined up her shot. She took another shot and was suddenly ahead, but when it was his turn, he caught up handily and tied the game. "We could call it, or we can keep going."

"I say neither one of us wins."

"I'll tell you what. I'll dance with you."

This she did not expect. "You will? Right here?"

"But to my song choice. It's only fair. You get what you want, but I get to pick the song. Compromise."

"Whatever." So she wouldn't be dancing the two-step tonight. He'd probably play some kind of hard rock song, something neither one of them could dance to. She followed him to the jukebox, where she stood on tiptoes and tried to look over his shoulder.

"No peeking."

"You know, country music is sexy."

He grunted. "Yeah, right. I'll show you sexy."

She waited for the pulsing guitar riffs but instead, a familiar song wafted through the speak-

ers. Not country, not at all. But "Let's Get it On,"
Marvin Gaye.

The man had nerve, she'd give him that. Yep,
nerves of steel, and she was Play-Doh.

Yet it was impossible to resist when he grinned
and spread his arms apart, an invitation. "Let's
dance, baby."

She went into his arms, the new familiarity
between them making it a whole lot easier than
the first time they'd slow-danced when she was
caught somewhere between shock and arousal.

"Tell me why you like country music." Stone
grinned, and something pinged deep in her belly.
Did he realize what that smile did to women?
What it did to her?

"It tells a story, and I love stories."

"Even sad ones, when a man loses his cow and
his woman the same day?"

She smacked his shoulder. "If you must know,
I had a short-lived country music career."

"No kidding."

"But that didn't work out because I have terrible stage fright. So I tried to write a book instead."

"Didn't work out?" He sounded genuinely interested, and she wasn't quite used to that.

"Well, no. But maybe I wasn't meant to be a
writer. I'm a people person. So then I went into
real estate."

"Everyone needs to live somewhere."

"But it's hard to sell a house because buying a house is a life-changing decision. That's such a major commitment. I always had these men call me and tell me they wanted to buy a house. I'd take them around for weeks, even go out to dinner with them, but they all said eventually that buying a house was too big of a decision and they bailed." She figured soon enough that she was no salesperson because she couldn't seem to close the deal, as her boss used to say.

Stone narrowed his eyes. "Yeah. So—any women clients?"

She had to think about it for a minute. Her advertising had generated mostly calls from male clients. "None that I can think of. I put up a large billboard by the freeway and I had plenty of calls."

Stone cocked his head at her, again like he was studying some kind of specimen he couldn't figure out.

"You're looking at me like that again."

"Sorry." One finger of his hand caressed her arm from her wrist up to her elbow, and she shivered a little.

"Now I have a question. You said I'm an average student. Do you mean that?"

"For now, but I'm not done with you. Not even close." The sexy timbre of his voice matched with the passion in his eyes almost undid her. He was definitely not talking about her lessons right now.

"You gave me a C plus. Why the plus?"

"I couldn't keep my feelings out of it." He leaned down even closer, till only a single breath seemed to separate them, a smile in those blue eyes.

Emily swallowed. *What am I doing? This is one date.* There should be no kissing involved, but that was all a little too late now, wasn't it? All these thoughts were running through her head as she stared into his eyes, right before he lowered his mouth to claim hers. He had a way of kissing that made her want to give up breathing so she could kiss longer, harder. Oxygen was overrated anyway.

A ping rushed through her like an electrical shock, and she broke from the kiss to stare into eyes that didn't flinch from hers. "Tell me. When are you reenlisting?"

"It's that obvious?"

She glanced around the room. "You miss this. You're going back, aren't you? Just as soon as you sell the school."

His hands lowered to her hips, and he held her there, pulling her up against him. "I did tell you I'm a short-timer around here. I had to separate from the air force, but as soon as I get everything settled here, I'll reapply. If they need pilots, they'll take me back. If not, there are other things I can do."

"You don't like teaching?"

"I like it fine. But I'm here to save Jedd's job, and Cassie's, even if she doesn't want me to. Look, Emily this was just one date and we can stop any time you want to—"

But maybe he was exactly what she needed right now. "I'm good."

"Yes, you are." He lowered his head to kiss her again. And again. And again.

A tingle went down her spine and headed south. Her skin felt too tight and the back of her knees were already sweaty. The way this man kissed only confirmed that sex was highly overrated. She much preferred kissing. His kind of kissing, deep and probing kisses that were more than foreplay. Much better than sex.

He stopped and studied her for a minute too long.

"Do that again," Emily said.

So he did.

CHAPTER TWELVE

THAT'S WHAT I GET for playing with fire.

Stone had wanted to bring Emily here because she was, after all, his student and it sounded like something a good teacher might do. Something Dad might have done, go ahead and introduce her to other pilots. He was still feeling his way around this whole teacher-student relationship, and the kiss this afternoon hadn't helped. Emily wasn't making it easy, kissing the way she did.

Probably had been a mistake to pick her up at her place. The last thing he'd needed to see was her bed in the middle of the small room, which smelled so much like her—warm hints of vanilla and honey. It didn't help that she was dressed casually, because he imagined Emily's curves couldn't even be hidden underneath a tent.

She was being a good sport about his song choice to the king of make-out music. While he pulled her in close, he tried to not tease himself. It turned out he was able to mostly ignore the expressions of the idiots that had congregated to watch.

Matt was blowing kisses in his direction and Crash was grinding. NFG stood there with a sad puppy dog expression on his face, and damned if he didn't look like he was about to cry.

"Do you want to get out of here?" Stone asked when the song ended.

"Yes," she said. "Let's go to your place."

"Are you sure?"

She rolled her eyes. "I want to see where you live. I'm not going to sleep with you."

"Okay. But, for the record, I don't think we'd do much sleeping." He tugged on Emily's hand, managed to extricate them from his idiot friends without too much effort and drove home.

Home. To his father's house, basically. Because no matter how he sliced it, he was a tenant there. Not for much longer.

He offered her a hand getting out of his truck. "Watch where you step. There are a couple of stones loose in the walkway. Need to fix that."

He led the way up the front porch stoop but before he unlocked the door, he turned to Emily. She deserved a warning. "There's a dog."

"You have a dog?" Now her eyebrows lifted. Why were people so amazed by that?

"Used to be Dad's dog. And it's more like I have a roommate." How to explain Dad's dog had mistakenly assumed he was a human being? He rang the doorbell to scare Winston. It would give Stone a little more time.

"Is your dog going to open the door for us?" Emily said from behind him.

"No, but that would be cool." He let himself in the front door and turned on the light in the hallway entrance.

"Where's your dog?" Emily turned to him, eyes narrowed. "Do you really have one?"

"Don't let the silence fool you. Brace yourself. Stay behind me." As per the usual, after a slight pause, once Winston realized the doorbell sounds had ended, he came around the corner and launched in guerilla warfare attack mode.

"Down, Winston, down." Stone stood in front of Emily, taking the worst of it. He was able to fend off Winston's French kiss attempts and finally wrestled him into a sitting position.

"Wow, you're a big dog." Emily emerged from behind to pet Winston's head.

"See what I mean?" He hoped to gain some sympathy for his plight.

"He's adorable."

And Winston was behaving himself for the first time since Stone could remember. Winston managed to sit, albeit on Stone's foot, and panted, his tongue hanging out. "It's a trick. I don't trust him."

"Oh, c'mon," Emily laughed. "He's sweet."

"Don't turn your back on him." Stone walked farther into the house, turning on lights as he went.

"Aw. He just wants a little love."

But Stone hadn't been in the kitchen ten seconds when he heard a tiny squeak from Emily. He turned to see her lying flat on her back, Winston on top of her, paws firmly planted on her chest.

"Ooooof," Emily said, probably due to oxygen deprivation.

He rushed back to pry all ninety pounds of Winston off Emily. Who needed a workout when he had Winston? "Are you all right? Any vital parts missing?"

Emily cracked a smile and regained her footing. "Nothing major. Maybe my pride. I thought dogs liked me."

"You think this means he doesn't like you? Hell, this is his mating call." Holding her hand, he led her into the family room and helped her step over the gate he'd placed to block Winston from the room.

"I admit I didn't picture you owning a dog." Emily sat on the couch and scanned the room. He was suddenly hyperaware of the plaid couch, the decor that screamed aviation/fishing/hunting aficionado. Family photos scattered throughout—all of it his father's touches. Soon he'd have to pack every one of his Dad's belongings up and do who knew what with them. Maybe Sarah wanted a framed picture of dogs playing cards.

He couldn't cart any of it along. Not suitable for someone who traveled light.

"I don't own him. He owns me." Might as well state the facts as he knew them. "It's my dad's dog. My dad loved him. I still don't know why."

"And you won't get rid of him."

"No." Though he thought of it often enough. But in the end, he figured both he and Winston had a lot in common except for the fur and the fleas. Winston even had big balls. As if to prove it, he rolled over on his back, spread-eagled, and showed them off for Emily.

Dad should have neutered the big guy. "You want him? He comes with his own bowl."

"He's welcome to visit me anytime. Pookie is used to hanging out with big dogs." Emily turned in a semicircle, taking a good look at the room. "This house—it's your father's house, isn't it?"

"Yep. How'd you guess?"

"Wild guess. It's not you. It's too homey and lived-in."

"Thanks," he said, though he knew exactly what she meant. For the past few years he'd lived with what he could carry in a bag. Mementos, photos, furniture—they were all more anchors, making it hard to pick up and leave at a moment's notice when new orders came through.

"I mean, you're neat and compartmentalized. I expected to see sharp corners and lots of steel to match your nerves." She smiled and tossed her hair.

Was that a mating call? If not, it should be. In some countries, he was sure that it was. He still wanted a handful of that hair in his hands. It needed to be moved to get to the neck he wanted to lick.

"You want to see me lose it then dance with me again to Marvin Gaye. Right here. While we're alone." It was an invitation, or maybe a dare.

Emily stayed rooted in her spot, making it easier when he closed the distance between them and pulled her against his chest. He told himself this was okay. He was only playing, only teasing. Testing boundaries. He was a guy, after all. Sue him.

She didn't speak when he moved the hair from her neck and kissed the tender spot under her ear, then licked it. In fact, she went so far as to moan, a little sound that coming out of her meant he must be doing something right. And she did her magic again, fingers threaded in his hair, pressing even closer. Yeah, this was so much better than talking. Talking was for chumps.

Emily pulled away and he saw a look that meant only one thing to him. He was about to get lucky.

"Look at the time. I've got to go," Emily said. "You can take me home now."

She might as well have doused him with a pail of ice cold water. Had he misread her signals that badly? She tried to turn away from him, but he reached for her elbow and stopped her. An explanation would be nice. "Why?"

"I'm so sorry—but I can't do this right now."

Idiot. Thinking with the little head again. "You don't have to do anything you don't want to do." He ran his fingers down her arm to assure her he wasn't the Big Bad Wolf. When he reached her hand, he squeezed it.

"That's not the problem. What *I* want to do is the problem. I'm afraid I'm not the girl you think I am." She shook her head. "Or the girl I thought I was. I mean, the girl I thought I could be."

If only he could speak her language. "Explain."

"I don't know what this is, this thing between us." Emily squeezed his hand back.

"It's called chemistry."

"This is too much for me. You're too much for me. And besides that, this was supposed to be one date. One. I think we're forgetting that."

"Right." Which meant that again, he'd let her mess with his head. She was right. One date.

She took another step back. "Because that's what we agreed."

He didn't speak for a moment, just let go of her hand. "We did agree on that."

"You're my teacher."

"You're my student."

"Exactly." A hint of a smile curled her lips.

"And then there's the kissing. We should stop that."

Emily's expression became serious, and she seemed to consider it. "Probably."

Oh, hell yeah, he was in so much trouble.

CHAPTER THIRTEEN

STONE DIDN'T SEEM at all upset on the drive back to the ranch, choosing to joke with her about NFG and his other friends at the bar. Surprising, because she'd expected some sulking. Didn't all men pitch a fit when they didn't get sex? The first time she turned Greg down because she hadn't known him the prerequisite six months, he'd sulked all evening, barely speaking to her. When she'd finally broken down just shy of six months, she should have been the one to sulk. She'd been with two men in her entire life, both in heavily committed relationships. Sex was just part of the deal when you loved someone, but most of the time she could take it or leave it.

Stone walked her to the door of her loft, despite her protests.

"I can't let you in. It's already dark outside."

He cocked his head again as if she'd spoken in another language. "I've got to go anyway. Early day tomorrow."

"Okay. I had a great time."

He didn't say anything for a minute, just kind of studied her. "Good."

He walked back down the loft steps and got into his truck without even glancing back once. One date. They'd agreed. Another one would be nice but not part of the deal.

The lights were on in the kitchen of the big house, which meant someone, probably Molly, might still be up and about. She was the last person Emily wanted to see, but she didn't want to be alone right now, either.

Inside her loft, Emily pulled out her cell phone and dialed Rachel's number. She picked up after the second ring. "What's up?"

"I've done something really stupid."

"Oh, my gawd. Am I going to be on *Dateline*? You finally snapped, didn't you? What did you do to Nika?"

"No, stupid. I just got back from my date with Stone. The thing is, if I hadn't gotten out of there when I did—I think I was about to jump his bones." She was apparently just as much of a hussy as Molly. Emily was supposed to be the sensible one. Why keep hoping sex could be fun when it obviously wasn't her cup of tea?

"Wait. You were going to have sex with him when you haven't even known him for six months? But Emily, that's Rule Number One. Followed by, if I do recall, making sure to ask about his dental records."

"It says a lot about a person who takes care of their teeth."

"Yes, of course." If Emily wasn't mistaken, Rachel, who had long regarded Emily's rules as over-the-top cautious, had just snickered into the phone. "So what happened?"

"I had him take me home before I proved what a hussy I am." And it hadn't been easy, either. She'd forced herself to not look back so she couldn't be tempted to change her mind. The things he'd done to her had set every nerve on fire.

"If I'm not mistaken, that makes twice you've run out on his man."

Emily groaned. *That would be three times.* "It was one date. He and I agreed."

"You're going to give the man a complex." Rachel laughed, followed by a yawn. "Listen, I've got to get to sleep. But I suggest you get your little heinie back over there and tell him you had a fever and got temporarily delirious, or something."

"I can't do that."

"Why?"

"I'm—I think I'm scared." More like terrified. What kind of a wild woman was she? Answer: not even an average wild woman. At best, she was subpar.

"You know what, honey? I don't wonder that you're scared. I think this might be the first time in your life that you've had this kind of chemistry with a man. Isn't it?"

Certainly not with Greg. He'd had a paint-by-numbers routine, and she'd slid right into it. Never even questioned whether it was good enough or not. A good girl didn't need anything exciting, anyway. "You're right."

"Naturally. Now good night." Rachel hung up.

It was true. She'd never had a man make her pulse race, cause her to shiver at his touch and turn her on like he'd just pressed a button. But why choose the one man who had an expiration date on his time here?

Because I don't think I deserve to be happy?

Emily walked over to the main house and up the porch steps. If Grammy were the one still up, a hug and some hot chocolate would help. Everything seemed so out of control lately. She'd been grasping at straws ever since she'd come home. She wasn't supposed to be living at home at twenty-eight. She should be happily married to someone and starting a family. Instead she was taking flying lessons and tempted to jump into bed with a man she hardly knew. A man who scared her because he was so good at making her feel out of control.

She opened the front door and followed the sound of Grammy's voice to the kitchen.

"I want the plaque to have my favorite Bible verse on it, John 3:16. If there's room, it should say below my name, 'She loved her family.' Yes, and my birthday is April 16, 1936. Date of death? Of course I don't have that yet. Yes, it's for me. Weren't you listening? What do you mean call back when I'm dead? Let me talk to your supervisor, young man! Hello? Hello? Why, he hung up on me. Well, of all the nerve."

Why hadn't Emily noticed it before? There could be no other explanation for Grammy's sudden fascination with making her own funeral arrangements. Grammy was dying.

It would be just like her to not want to worry anyone with the little matter of her fatal illness. "What's going on?"

"Oh, just some young man who doesn't understand preparation, either." Grammy sat at the kitchen table, the phone nearby, a rolled up parchment to her right. Probably the family tree.

Emily reached down and encircled Grammy's shoulders, enveloping her in a hug. "Why didn't you tell me?"

"I did tell you. You saw the cremation vase. It's definitely going in the dining room. I don't care what your father says. Goodness, Emily, why are you crying?"

"I don't know what I'll do without you." Emily couldn't stop the tears from flowing. Grammy had always been there, and the world wouldn't spin the same without her.

Grammy stood and pulled Emily into her arms.

"Sit down, honey. You look like you need some hot chocolate. I'm not going anywhere for a while. I'm the healthiest eighty-year-old Dr. Lewis has ever seen."

"Then I don't understand." Emily wiped her tears with a napkin and took a breath on a sob. "You're suddenly obsessed with your death. I mean, you've never talked about this before. Why now?"

Grammy took the milk from the refrigerator and poured it into a pan, then lit the gas stove. "It's all the genealogy research. Made me start thinking about all these relatives, and the lives they led. You're not the only one that wants to leave this place better than they found it. It's important that you all remember me, and that I tried."

"I could never forget you." Emily hiccupped through her tears.

"Maybe, but I might never get to know your children. Not that I want you to rush out and get married. You take your time and do it right." She reached over and rubbed Emily's back.

"I thought I'd be married by now, maybe with a baby on the way."

"Things work out in their own time and not before," Grammy said as she stirred the milk.

"But at this rate, I might not have my first baby before I'm thirty." That used to be her marker, but she might have to move it back now.

Rachel was one person who didn't think a person's life could be planned out like a schedule of events in a day timer, and maybe she was right. The most important thing was to get it right, and if nothing else, the fiasco with Greg had taught Emily that.

"It's not a race."

"I know. What I need to do is take my mind off it. That's what I'm trying to do." So far it wasn't working too well.

Emily got up to mix the cocoa and sugar because that part had always been her job. She had the precise measurements memorized by now, given the ritual of homemade hot chocolate was nearly as old as she was. She'd sat at this very table on many a night when missing Mama had driven her out of a sound sleep. Grammy always thought chocolate made everything better, and she was right most of the time.

Emily topped their mugs of hot chocolate with a dollop of whipped cream. It was confession time. "I haven't quit my flying lessons. I just thought you should know."

Grammy didn't look surprised and nodded. The woman knew everything, it would seem. "Ah, chocolate. It makes everything go down a little bit smoother."

"I'm sorry I didn't tell you, but I was afraid Dad would find out."

Grammy scowled and waved her hand dismissively. "Your father is an idiot. The way he treats Molly like a small child makes me want to hurl."

Hurl?

"And he's never supported all your efforts the way he should have. I'm sure it's because he worries so. After he lost Jessie, he didn't want to let you girls out of his sight for a time. Even I worry about you flying, so it's not illogical for him to be concerned. But I do wish he would support you more. Give better attention to all you're trying to accomplish. It's something, Emily."

"I don't need his attention. I just need him to stay out of my way."

"You're serious about this, aren't you? Is it the flying you want to do, or do you just want to upset your father? I mean, I wouldn't blame you."

"I want to do this." Why was it so hard to believe that she wanted to do this for herself? She'd always done what was expected of her, and that hadn't gotten her anywhere.

Not with her father, and not with Greg.

"I have some news, Emily. And you shouldn't let it upset you." Grammy took a big gulp of her hot chocolate. "Hmm, that's good."

"I shouldn't let it upset me?" Did anything good begin with that kind of an introduction?

"Mistakes are made, even by experts."

Dear God. "But you said you aren't dying."

"Oh, not that expert. I completely trust Dr. Lewis." She smoothed the tablecloth.

"Then which expert?"

Grammy made a face. "Julia."

"Your friend Julia?" The Pink Ladies' resident genealogy expert, Daughter of the American Revolution Julia. "What happened?"

"Think about how common a last name Parker is."

"Yeah?"

"And then you add in Emily." Grammy shot Emily a significant look. Significant because her eyes were bulging a little bit. "I'm not surprised it happened."

"I don't know what you're saying. Why don't you just spit it out?"

She held up a hand. "So, you're not actually related to the Emily Parker who was a licensed pilot. Julia called today to tell me."

"What? But—"

"Poor Julia is mortified, but it was a simple mistake. A common last name, no? And when you think of it, this is a good thing. Don't be too upset with Julia. She would have come over to tell you herself, but I thought the news would be best coming from me."

Emily didn't speak for several minutes. Surprising how she'd let this belief color her vision for the past few weeks. Like the real estate. The writing. The country music. Another leaf tossed around by the wind and this particular leaf had flown out the window. She was chasing her tail most of the time.

"Oh. A little disappointing but not the end of the world, I guess." Now she'd still have to find out about her real namesake, that ever-elusive woman. Unless it didn't matter.

Grammy patted her hand. "It doesn't mean you can't still get your pilot's license. Be the first Emily Parker in our family to do it."

Later that night in her loft, Emily couldn't sleep. She drew the covers up then shoved them back down. Finally tossed them off her bed and let them fall in a heap. Tonight her past and future had shifted. Been rewritten. It didn't matter and yet it did. She'd allowed a piece of paper, a page in history, to influence her future. But it hadn't been her past.

Could it still be her future?

Her mind kept coming back to Stone. She hadn't meant to lead him on, but when his kisses had made her spine tingle in little pulses and shocks of desire, she had realized that she wasn't a wild woman after all. Not yet, anyway. And there were still rules. She'd put them in place for good reason.

Stone was leaving as soon as he could. He'd made that clear. And Emily had never in her life had sex without a commitment. Commitment was the only reason she ever had sex. It was the duty of a steady girlfriend. The whole thing was unthinkable. And yet…

She wanted to stop being so afraid. To live out her life full tilt. Becoming a pilot had been part of that plan. Check. But there was still something missing. If she had to put her finger on the pulse of what was missing, she might have to call it joy.

Rules. Hmm. Emily sat up in bed, an idea forming. She went to her desk and fished for a pen and paper, which she brought back to bed with her. What this Emily Parker needed were some new ground rules.

Emily's New Rules for Being a Wild Woman (and not losing my heart in the process)

Wear protection.
No spending the night together.
No asking for a second time.
No kissing.

She'd have to think about the "no kissing" rule. Sure, it might sound crazy, and she'd already kissed Stone. But that was part of the problem. The man kissed liked nobody's business, and kissing was such a tender gesture, especially when accompanied with making love.

Just sex. That's all she wanted from the man. It was time to find out what all the fuss was about.

CHAPTER FOURTEEN

MOLLY COULDN'T BELIEVE her luck. She'd driven by
the park on Friday afternoon, only to find Sierra
being pushed in the bucket swing by a woman
who was probably the babysitter. Dylan nowhere
to be found. It was the middle of the day on a
weekday, so it made sense that the park was filled
with nothing but mothers and their young children. In other words, Molly had hit the jackpot.

If she could hold her baby, the world would
right itself again and stop shifting off its axis.
She'd smell Sierra's soft baby powder smell, and
Molly's heart would resume its natural rhythm.
These hit-or-miss park days weren't going to be
enough. Now Dylan would be looking for her,
which would make it harder to watch her baby.
Yes and, by the way, *her baby* because that's exactly what Sierra was. Hers. And she didn't remember signing any papers giving her up, either,
even though Dylan was probably wishing she had
right about now.

She didn't even have to hide today, but she
still pulled the baseball cap on and tucked her

hair inside. She sat on the bench for a few minutes, making sure this woman knew what she was doing. Dylan shouldn't just let anybody watch their baby. But she had to admit the woman was attentive to Sierra.

Emily said that Molly should talk to Dylan. Explain. Pour out all the feels. Except that had always been so hard for her to do. Emily was right, of course, that eventually Molly would have to face Dylan and explain why she'd left. But first she had to figure it out for herself.

For now, this was just easier.

"She's really cute," Molly said as she walked over to them. Sierra was now playing in the sandbox with a bucket and shovel. Other mothers seemed to be talking to each other, so it seemed only natural that she would engage in conversation, too.

"She's a sweetheart." The woman had long straight brown hair tied in a tight ponytail and didn't seem like Dylan's type. Maybe she really was the babysitter.

"Is she your only child?" Molly wanted to test the waters and make sure this woman, whoever she was, wasn't going to lay claim to Sierra.

"No, she's not mine. I'm helping my next-door neighbor out today. My kids are already in school all day."

"I'm Molly." She only occasionally glanced

in Sierra's direction to avoid seeming like some creepy stalker-type.

"Sandy," the woman said with a smile. "And this is Sierra." She patted her tuft of red curls and Sierra smiled at her.

Molly felt a wave of love kick her in the chest with such power that she had to sit for a minute. She crouched down next to Sierra. "A beautiful baby."

"Where are your kids?" Sandy asked.

Of course she would want to know that. How many women randomly dropped by the park to check out the babies? Freaky types who were looking to steal a baby, that's who. Molly gave Sandy points for asking, but she managed to come up with a plausible lie. "My boys are right over there, playing with their friends."

Sandy looked in the direction of a gaggle of boys playing on the slide nearby and smiled. "Boys. Same here. I have three. Never had myself a little girl and we're done now. That's why it's so much fun to watch her."

"Yeah, I bet."

"How about you?" Sandy asked, while she handed Sierra another shovel. Sierra took it and put it in her mouth.

Molly sucked a breath in and resisted taking the shovel away. "What about me?"

"I mean, are you going to try for a little girl

someday?" Sandy asked, taking the shovel out of Sierra's mouth.

I already have one. "No. Not me. I'm divorcing my husband," Molly lied.

"I'm sorry."

"Don't be. He's a real jerk." Molly wanted to use another more accurate word, but there were children nearby.

"A lot of that going around. My neighbor, Sierra's daddy, is about to start divorce proceedings, too."

"He is?" *That rat. He's trying to blindside me.*

"He'll get full custody of Sierra. Isn't that right, sweetie?" Sandy cooed to Sierra, who squealed.

"No!" Sierra said.

"Isn't it funny how everything is no at this age?" Sandy laughed.

Molly felt her insides churn. What she had to do was run home and tell Daddy or maybe call a lawyer, but she couldn't seem to move away from Sierra. There was a good chance she might be able to hold her for a few minutes.

Suddenly, from behind them by the slides, an honest to goodness shriek of pain caused every mother in the park to look in its direction. Even Molly. A little boy came tearing toward them.

"Is he yours?" Sandy looked at Molly.

"No," Molly said with her heart in her throat. Pretty soon everyone would figure out all of these boys were accounted for and not one of them was hers. Then good luck getting this babysitter to ever trust her again.

The boy ran past them, holding his hand. All his friends ran with him toward a woman whose face had turned many different shades of terrified. The mother.

"I'm a nurse. I better go see if I can help. Would you keep an eye on Sierra for a minute?" Sandy walked a few feet away to help the mother and son.

Molly gazed at Sierra, who had not missed any of this commotion. Her face, in fact, reflected everything Molly felt inside: stiff puckered out bottom lip, quivering chin, tears welling in her eyes. It seemed only natural to pick her up and give her some comfort.

"It's okay, baby. It's okay," Molly said, as much to Sierra as to herself. Just as she'd thought it might, her breaths came easier, and her heart felt too large in her chest. She smelled her little baby hair smell. Johnson's baby shampoo. Molly used to wash Sierra's hair with the same shampoo and now wondered if she still hated getting her hair wet.

Sierra continued to sniffle and look in the direction of the mayhem and the crying. She pointed in the direction of the little boy and said, "Owie."

Then she looked at Molly like she was some kind of shiny bright thing she'd never seen before. She reached up and tugged on her baseball cap. "This hat," she said.

"That's right. This is my hat," Molly said. "You're a smart girl, aren't you?"

"Yay," Sierra said and clapped her hands together. "Yay, baby."

Molly closed her eyes and hugged Sierra tight. "My baby. I'm your mommy," she whispered.

Sandy walked back toward them. Apparently the commotion had died down, not that Molly had noticed until now.

"Bee sting," Sandy said. "Luckily I carry a first-aid kit in my bag."

From the way that kid was wailing, she would have guessed he'd lost an arm. "Is he all right?"

"He'll be fine. I see that somebody likes you," Sandy smiled. "Isn't she the friendliest baby you've ever met?"

"She is." Molly smiled and held her tight one last time before handing her baby over.

"It was nice meeting you," Sandy said. "Maybe I'll see you and your boys again sometime. I've got to get Sierra back for a nap. Dylan keeps her to a pretty tight schedule."

"I'll bet he does," Molly said. *A schedule I'm about to blow up into a thousand little shiny pieces.*

STONE HADN'T BEEN ABLE to push off the meeting any longer. He stared at the almost-stranger across the wide oak conference table in his attorney's office. A stranger who looked like him. No doubt, at least physically speaking, they'd both come from the same gene pool. Sarah had the same blue eyes. Her hair was dark like his, and she wore it in a bun that made her look like a librarian.

He hadn't seen Sarah in years and thought the attorney's office was possibly not the best place for a family reunion.

Stone's lawyer was the first to speak. "We thought this meeting might be a good idea." He had an annoying click in the back of his throat that punctuated the end of his sentences.

Stone didn't speak. Good idea or not, he resented the hell out of being here. Matt was right in that they should be able to do this without lawyers. But Sarah had hired one, which forced him to hire Mark. A man he'd love to fire right about now.

"Thank you for arranging this," Sarah said. "I haven't been able to have an adult conversation with my brother."

Conversation? Weren't the lawyers going to fix this? Weren't they on the clock? What good were they, anyway? Right now he didn't want to talk to anyone, but Sarah least of all.

"I suggest we give you two a few minutes alone, to talk things out. No lawyers. After all, sometimes we get in the way." Sarah's lawyer had long red fingernails she liked to tap on the glass table. Between her taps and Mark's clicks, it would be a small miracle if Stone could sit still for longer than five minutes.

"Don't worry, we're off the clock." *Click, click.* Mark stood.

Within a few minutes, Stone was sitting alone in a glass-walled conference room with his sister. The stranger who looked like him.

She turned to him. "I'll talk, since you don't seem to be fond of words."

Nice. He'd give her that. She got the first shot in. "Go ahead."

"By the way, our mother's doing fine."

"We email regularly." There were even a few phone calls here and there, not that he'd been a big talker. Point being, he hadn't felt abandoned by his mother, and he couldn't understand why Sarah had felt abandoned by Dad.

"She tells me. But I don't know anything about your life for the last few years, except that you're former air force."

"What else is there?"

She pushed her glasses back up on her nose. "I want to know why this school is so important. Why you won't just take the better offer. I'm guessing you're not exactly a high roller."

"Simple. Money isn't everything to me. Carrying out his wishes is all that matters."

"So interesting that those wishes weren't in the will."

She had to point that out. "It doesn't matter. I know what he wanted. He wanted for his employees to be able to keep their jobs. The buyer I have lined up wants to keep the school open, and he can do it. Why do you have a problem with that?"

She hesitated for a minute. "I think what he would really want is for both of us to do the best we can. And that means going with the better offer."

"The better offer means that someone is going to close the airport. That means a lot of people will lose their jobs. There's no other regional airport like this for miles. And the last thing this area needs is another strip mall." He hoped he looked as disgusted as he felt.

"What do you care? It's not like you're going to settle down and live here. I wouldn't even know that if Matt hadn't told me. You're going to take off as soon as this is all resolved. Aren't you?"

"It doesn't mean I don't care what happens to the people in this town. At this airport. They were Dad's friends, coworkers."

"Those people can find other jobs."

Yeah. He didn't like Sarah. In fact, he could fill the room with all the reasons he didn't much like her. "Is that all you care about? The money? Do you even know or care what mattered to him?"

"Maybe I would if he'd taken the time to get to know me. But he abandoned me and my mother."

Yeah, he couldn't sit here and listen to this crap. "Shut up, Sarah. That's a bold-faced lie. You obviously don't remember him."

"Exactly. And that's the problem. Why don't I?"

"Your choice." But for one minute, a sense of understanding passed over him. Until he'd joined the service, he'd always been a loner. Sure, there had been times he'd envied the larger families on the block—the mother who managed to be home every day after school, the kids who had enough family members to play a game of touch football at a moment's notice. But he'd found his extended family with his comrades in arms. Maybe Sarah had never found that.

"It isn't that he didn't want to be in your life. He always tried to do the right thing. The honorable thing. This must have seemed like it at the time."

Their parents hadn't managed to make marriage work any more than fifty percent of the population could. Most of his AF buddies came home to broken relationships and kids that didn't know who they were. Marriage was one big crapshoot and not worth the risk.

In a way, Stone already had the only family he'd ever need.

"I'm not surprised you would defend him," Sarah said with contempt in her voice.

Stone spoke between clenched teeth. "You

were the one who stopped coming to see him after that last summer."

"You mean the summer when no one wanted me?"

"Not true. You spent half your visit in the bathroom!"

"Dad barely talked to me after I told him I didn't want to go fishing. Just stared at me like I was some kind of alien creature he'd never seen before."

Or in other words, a teenage girl with attitude. And a nose ring, if he recalled. Did she really expect their father to know how to treat her? He'd had zero experience with teenage daughters and Sarah had gone from cute girl to hormonal teenager in one short year.

This wasn't going to work. Not like he hadn't seen it coming. Time to bail.

She pointed at her chest. "I'm his flesh and blood. He wasn't there for me."

"Look, Sarah, I get that you have daddy issues. Believe me. But this has nothing to do with me."

"It has everything to do with you. You could have called us. Why wouldn't you tell us he was dying? You think his ex-wife and daughter might have liked to know? Wasn't it any of our business?" She stood, hand on her hips.

He stood up and joined her. "I followed his wishes."

"But you didn't have to listen to him. You

should have picked up the phone and looked us up. Told us he was dying. Did you ever think maybe our mother wanted to say a final goodbye to the man she once loved? That maybe I wanted to say goodbye to my father?"

And there it went again. The now-familiar tightness in his chest.

"Look, you can take it out on me. That's fine. Just don't blame it on him. You're right, I could have called you. But I didn't." He made his way to the door. "All I'm asking is for you to let me sell the flight school to the buyer who won't change everything about it. It's what Dad wanted, if that matters to you."

"I don't know if I can do that. It's not fair. This whole thing is just not—fair."

"Fair is the weather."

He left her standing in the conference room. In a perfect world, they might have grown up together straight into adulthood and had deeper and lasting family ties. A bond or connection that went beyond mere biology. But it wasn't there anymore, and seemed it never could be now.

"Wait. Mr. Mcallister," Sarah's lawyer called out.

He chose not to listen but kept walking out the double-glass doors and outside into the bright California sun. It wasn't until he reached his truck that he allowed himself to take a good solid breath of air.

Shit.

He'd lost his temper again and the meeting had accomplished exactly what he'd expected. They'd made negative-point-five progress. Sarah possessed the gift of making him feel like an asshole when he was trying to be a good guy.

Or in other words, she managed to see right through him.

It wasn't that he hadn't picked up the phone half a dozen times and thought about contacting Sarah or his mother. Sure, Dad had asked him not to do it, but maybe he wasn't in the best condition to make those choices. Maybe he should have vetoed his wishes and done the right thing. But in the end, Stone had settled into the familiarity of following orders up the chain of command. He'd been asked, not ordered, but the wishes were clear. It wasn't up to him to decide if they made sense or if anyone would regret them. Tough decisions were made dozens of times a day, and the one thing he realized was he'd never make everyone happy.

So why was he allowing the guilt to eat him alive?

Sarah would continue to fight him and if she did for much longer, he wouldn't blame his buyer for backing out. What would happen to the airport then and all the small businesses that depended on it?

Yeah, he cared. He wasn't sure when that happened. Stone slid the key in his ignition and got the hell out of the office suite's parking lot. He needed to blow off some steam.

Today was a clear day, the kind of day Dad would have loved to fly. He used to say aviation wasn't so much a profession as it was a disease. Stone hadn't always understood what Dad meant, but he did now. He wasn't at all sure he could go a day without flying. These days it didn't seem to matter so much that it wasn't a jet.

But now he wondered what Dad would think about Sarah wanting to go with the highest bidder. Hell, maybe wherever he was right now he didn't give a shit. Might even say "do what you think is best." But Jedd had a baby on the way, and he needed the job. Stone also couldn't accept an entire airport being gone. The Air Museum, gone. The Shortstop Snack Shack gone. All because land in these parts had reached the kind of high value some people only dreamed about.

But dammit, money wasn't everything.

He walked through the airport hangar, toward the back and his office. He caught sight of Jedd over by the Snack Shack getting coffee and waved. No Cassie, though. Probably on her two-hour lunch break. Would be nice if every now and again she'd help him save her job.

Stone opened the door to his office to find Emily sitting behind his desk. She swiveled then got up rather suddenly, like she'd been caught in the act of pretending to be the boss. When she rose, he got a better view of what she wore, and what a view it was—a short red clingy dress which showed a lot of curvy leg. His favorite kind of dress. The type that made him grateful for his twenty-twenty vision, even if he preferred X-ray vision at the moment.

He allowed his imagination to take a little tour inside that dress. "Hey. It's not your lesson day, is it? You might be a little overdressed."

She walked around from behind his desk. "I came by to see you because I've been thinking."

"Uh-oh."

She reached up and smacked his shoulder. "Smart-ass."

"Okay, what's up?" Admittedly, she always had his attention, but now she also had his curiosity. Their one-date deal was done, and she'd made it clear there would be no others. Okay by him. All right, even if it wasn't okay, he had to admit she was right. He hardly needed the distraction, and she'd proven to be one hell of a distraction.

She moved oddly around him, like circling her prey. "Would you consider a second date?"

He grabbed her wrist and pulled her in. "Why?"

She seemed to enjoy that, pressing in even closer. "I'm having second thoughts."

This he understood. He was familiar with women who came on to him, who made it clear exactly what they wanted. Even if Emily wasn't too convincing, it helped that he wanted to believe her. And except for the fact she was behaving out of character, almost like she was reciting a script from a porn movie, he might.

"Want to tell me what the hell is going on?"

She wrinkled her nose. "I'm not sure you'll understand."

"Try."

Then she surprised him by backing up and walking back to his desk to fish something out of her purse. "Let's get some ground rules down first."

"Rules?"

"Emily's Rules." She smiled. "I'd like another date."

One more date didn't make a relationship. He could handle that. Sure he could. "Are you asking me out on a date? Again?"

"Hang on. There's a little more to this." She blushed and flapped that piece of paper in the air. "I want one night with you. One night of wild, passionate sex."

He couldn't have heard that right. "What?"

She glanced at her list. "I've thought a lot about it. Do you want to see my list?"

"Try and stop me." He stepped forward to grab the paper, but she snatched it out of his hands.

"Patience. I'll read them off. And don't say anything until I'm done." She held up her index finger. "Number one—use protection. And don't look at me like that. It's a valid concern." She cleared her throat. "Number two—no spending the night. Number three—no asking for a second night. And the last one is no kissing." She put her list away and turned to study him. "Are these rules acceptable to you?"

"No *kissing*?"

"I like the way you kiss me, and well, I think it would be too much. The sex should cover it."

The sex should cover it? "Is that right?" He stepped away from his desk and closed the distance between them. "Do I have any input on these rules?"

She shook her head. "Nope. This is the only way I'll do this. Are you game?"

Was he game? The only way he could possibly not be game was if he couldn't fog up a mirror. And yet. "Emily. This isn't what you want."

"Yes, it is."

"Yeah. No, I don't think so." He walked back to his desk. "You're not the type. Don't try to be."

"Ouch. So are you turning me down?" Funny, she appeared confused. She apparently hadn't considered he wouldn't want this.

Neither had he. "Not exactly."

"I mean, don't you want to? I thought all men wanted a one-night stand."

"First, thanks for lumping me in with all men. Second, you're not one-night-stand material. And besides that, the idea of a one-night stand is someone you'll never see again. I'm your teacher."

"So I don't know all the correct terminology. You tell me what to call it."

"Crazy."

She shoved her hands on her hips. "I'm not kidding."

"Neither am I."

"Look, we had one date. I agreed to that. Why can't you agree to this?"

He closed his eyes and studied the inside of his eyelids. "No. If you still want this in a few days, maybe we can revisit."

"You make it sound like it's some kind of transaction."

He quirked an eyebrow. "Who has a set of rules written down? I'm surprised you don't want a notary to sign off on this. This *is* a transaction. Yours, apparently."

"When you put it that way." She frowned. "Maybe I'm overthinking this."

"You think?" He flipped his calendar closed and sat down. "Want to tell me what happened?"

"This has nothing to do with it, but a couple of days ago I found out I'm not actually related to the Emily Parker that was the first licensed pilot in California." The words left her in a whoosh.

"Uh-huh. That's too bad. I'm not related to any pilots in history, either."

She sat in the chair by his desk. "I know, you think this is silly and stupid."

He leaned across his desk. "No, hey I—"

"I thought the connection could be something special. But it's not a big deal. It just happened to lead me to something that I love. That I want." She studied him. "Flying, I mean."

"Right."

"I still want my license. I'm not giving up."

"Good."

"I just also want this." She traced her finger along the damn piece of paper like it was a road map.

But she was missing the point. He had a few years on her and he'd guess a whole hell of a lot more experience, and there was one thing he could tell for certain. Nothing between the two of them would ever be easy or light or contained by a set of rules, written down or otherwise. He had a feeling that together they'd be fiery and explosive. Two of his favorite things. But since he'd come to town, he'd been James Mcallister's son. Not many had taken the time to get to know him, nor had he let them. Too many, Cassie and Jedd included, assumed he was a good man like his father. Of course, they'd be wrong, but that didn't mean Stone shouldn't try. It was what he'd been doing for the past six months.

Trying to be the kind of man his father had been. A man like Dad would have probably already found a way to smooth things over with Sarah by now. Found a way to compromise in that lawyer's office instead of losing his temper and walking out.

Taking Emily up on this insanity, much as he wanted it, would be a dickhead move. And he wasn't going to be that guy. Not with this girl, and not here in his father's town.

He was going to do the right thing, dammit, even if it killed him.

"Go home, Emily."

CHAPTER FIFTEEN

THREE DAYS LATER, Fire Chief Jake was on his forty-eight hours on, which meant Rachel wanted company. So Emily had rented every romantic comedy she could find because tonight she wanted to laugh. She wanted to watch a girl strike out again and again with the man of her dreams but wind up with him in the end. Happily ever after. The End.

Emily had just finished telling Rachel that Stone had turned her down. She'd found the one man in America that didn't want uncomplicated no-strings-attached sex. Not with her anyway. Rachel had cleared her throat and asked for more details, as if she hadn't heard them all the first time.

"Don't make me say it all over again. Please." It had been humiliating enough to live through. She'd never thrown herself at a guy like that, just to experience a flat-out rejection. This was what she got for trying something new. Something daring.

Go home, Emily.

"You have to admit, though, you and this guy. I mean, what else can go wrong? Don't answer that. Seriously, you may have just met the only guy in the state who would turn down a deal like that." Rachel reached for another chocolate chip cookie and took a bite. "Which means this is worse than I thought."

"How could it get any worse?" It wasn't like Stone could be Mr. Right. He was Mr. Right Now. And Mr. Right Now didn't want to deliver the goods.

"No, I mean he must really like you."

Emily reached for a cookie and dunked it in the milk. "Sure he does. That's why he didn't want to hook up with me."

"No, it's why he doesn't."

"You're not making any sense. Maybe it's the pregnancy hormones. I swear your baby is sucking out all your brain power."

Rachel nodded, held up a finger and took a gulp of milk. "He's trying to not be an asshole."

"Well, he failed!" She'd worn her sexiest come-hither dress and he'd told her to go home.

"It's a good thing. Don't worry. He'll come around." Rachel flipped the TV on and slid the DVD in.

"He'd better hurry before I change my mind. I don't want to wait. I want to get this over with!"

Rachel nearly spat out her milk. "No. You don't. This is the fun part. The chase."

"I don't want a chase. I've got my rules, and I'm ready. And after the other night, I thought he was game. But no." She sat back and groaned. "I don't even know *why* I like him."

"Probably because you took one look at him. And then there is the man-in-uniform thing. And the Pilots and Paws thing."

"Yeah." Emily stayed silent for a moment, thinking about Stone. With him, it wasn't just one thing, like a hard body. It was the eyes, the smile, everything lined up and put together right where it should be. It was a wonder he didn't have women lined up for miles. Then again, maybe he did. What did she know about her teacher? He sat next to her and grunted, occasionally smiled his dimpled smile and kissed her like he had a graduate degree in the sport.

Rachel, remote control in hand, pointed it at Emily. "And another thing, Em. Your rules."

"What about them?"

"Get rid of them."

"Absolutely not. The rules are good. Why? Is there something missing from it?" Emily resisted the urge to pull it out of her purse and see if she'd missed something vital. But no, she'd thought of everything.

"A list is for grocery shopping. I mean, I'm glad you're changing up your old rules, but why not go for broke and throw all rules out the window?"

"Oh, no, I couldn't do that." Rules for dating

made her feel safe. They gave order to her world. Why didn't anyone get that?

"I guess you're not quite ready for no rules." Rachel pressed Play.

Within moments, the credits to *When Harry Met Sally* rolled across the big-screen TV.

"But if you want to step outside of your comfort zone, you need to lose the rules."

"Next you'll be telling me I should just do what feels good."

"What I'd like to see you do is stop trying to control everything. Some things just have to happen, like love. Follow your heart."

"Fine, but you sound like a greeting card commercial."

"You've tried to control too much, Em. Even your anger. And your no-kissing rule? That can't be healthy. When you see Greg tomorrow night, I want you to tell him off right in front of the entire restaurant."

Greg had called and said he needed to see her again. It was important. He had a big request to make, and he'd sounded small and weak on the phone. She guessed things hadn't worked out with Nika. She'd probably dumped him and found a new NFL boyfriend.

Her plans were to wait for him to beg her to come back to him and then she'd get up and tell him exactly what a jerk he'd been. "I will. I can't wait to see his face when I tell him off."

"He'll never see it coming. The fool. Maybe you should let me go with you. Just to make sure you don't do anything stupid."

"No need. I've got this."

"Make sure you wear the little black dress so he remembers what he left behind—what he's never going to have again." Rachel paused and threw Emily a significant look. "He's never going to have it again, right?"

"You have to ask me that?"

"Just checking."

They'd been yacking so long the movie was already at the scene in the restaurant. Sally was carrying on like she was having the best sex of her life, right across the booth from Harry.

"See that?" Rachel turned to Emily, a sly grin on her face. "I never have to fake it."

The camera zeroed in on the wise older woman who told the waiter she wanted whatever Sally was having.

So did Emily.

THE NEXT EVENING, Emily launched Operation Make Ex-Fiancé Regret It. The operation involved thong underwear, a push-up bra and that little black dress. It involved a straightening iron to tame her wild waves into submission, which took the better part of an hour. And finally, it involved cherry red Here Come My Lips lipstick.

She'd practically worn herself out by the time

six rolled around and she popped into the main house to let Grammy know she was off. "Don't wait up."

"What have you done to your hair?" Grammy asked from the kitchen sink. "It looks so—limp."

"I prefer the words sleek and stylish."

Grammy shook her head. "I happen to love your natural wave. And I haven't seen you wear that dress since your engagement party."

"Exactly," Emily said, trying on her sexiest smile.

"Why are you smiling like that? You look like a shark. What's gotten into you?"

She hadn't told Grammy because she might not understand. Hadn't Grammy always taught her to be kind and forgiving? Some people couldn't help the fact their gene pool had gifted them with an extra-mean chromosome in their DNA strand. Poor souls. Some people couldn't be helped. Just bless them and carry on.

Grammy meant well, but maybe that was how Emily had eventually wound up being a doormat.

"Nothing. I'm just going to meet an old friend for dinner and drinks."

That was her story, and she'd stick to it. If Grammy was to find out Emily was on her way to meet Greg, she'd probably call a Pink Ladies' intervention.

The Ladera was crowded for a Monday night, and the host said Greg had a table in the back. She followed the host. Greg stood as she approached. Oh, the look on Greg's face. Where was her camera?

"Emily."

Emily stopped moving. Seated next to Greg was Nika, smiling. No, this had not been part of the plan. Emily was supposed to sit through dinner with her ex-fiancé, look good and tell him about how she'd moved on with her life. Or rather, had taken steps to move on with her life. Not watch these two lovebirds sit in front of her, mocking her with their wacked-out kitchen-floor happiness.

Damn you, Greg. Emily considered turning and walking out of the restaurant, but all eyes seemed to be on her. Greg made a move to pull a chair out for her, but the host beat him to it.

"Thank you," Emily said, pulling her dress down.

At least Nika looked matronly tonight, wearing a white tent of a dress that probably gave enough room for her bump. Unfortunately, she was glowing. "Thank you for coming."

"Yes, thank you," Greg added, taking Nika's hand.

How are the hemorrhoids, Nika? Oh, never mind, one of them is sitting right next to you.

The waiter interrupted, at her side with a wineglass. "From the gentleman seated behind you."

Emily turned to see a young man smiling in

her direction. "Isn't that nice." She mouthed a thank you in his direction and held up the glass in a silent toast. She couldn't drink and drive, but maybe a sip wouldn't hurt. Especially since she wanted an entire bottle at the moment.

"You look beautiful, Emily," Nika said.

"That dress is something else," Greg said with a sour expression.

Score one for Emily. No doubt he remembered the dress. "I haven't worn it in a while. But to be honest, it's no longer a good fit. Why am I here, Greg?"

"We want your forgiveness. Both Nika and I do." He turned to Nika, who nodded. "My psychiatrist says I won't be able to move on until you forgive me. Us."

Great. Just great. "Okay, so you're getting married, having a baby *and* you want my forgiveness? Isn't that a little greedy?"

"Emily, you upset baby." Nika glanced at her stomach and patted it with one hand. She sniffed and swiped at her dry eyes. *Faker.* "If I'm having good healthy baby, must make peace. Doctor says so. Right, honey bunches?"

Greg nodded. "What happened wasn't right, and we know that. How can anyone's happiness begin based on someone else's pain?"

"I am shamed," Ms. Waterworks said, her shoulders shaking.

Emily was about to tell her she ought to be

when Greg set down his water glass and put a protective arm around Nika. "It's okay."

Even a waiter nearby filling water glasses pulled out a folded handkerchief and handed it to Nika. This was not going well. Couldn't the jilted fiancée get a little sympathy in this room?

"Don't cry," Emily ordered. *That's not fair. I should be the one crying. I don't have a fiancé, and I certainly don't have a bun in the oven.*

"I betray my friend," Nika said through her sniffles. "My only American friend."

Emily took another sip of the Chardonnay, noting the rim of the glass was now wearing some of her she-devil lipstick.

"Emily doesn't have a hateful bone in her body. She isn't shaming you, honey bunches," Greg said with a moony-eyed look.

Wait till I get going, Emily wanted to say, but she took another glance at Greg. He had a helpless lovesick teenager look on his face. Had he ever looked at Emily like that? He'd often said sweet and loving things like "you're way out of my league" and "how did I ever wind up with you?" But when it came to "I love you," Greg often tripped over his words. Emily had thought it adorable at the time.

"My whole family is shamed of me," Nika continued. "And not one will come to wedding."

"Visa trouble?"

"They say now I'm capitalist whore."

"I thought it was pig."

"For me, they say whore."

"It's my fault. This whole thing is my fault." Greg waved a hand in the air as if he would dismiss any other possibility.

"I couldn't agree more." Emily cast a significant look in his direction.

Nika seemed to ignore that comment and dabbed at her eyes. "Baby first is not traditional Russian Orthodox."

Neither, Emily assumed, was the kitchen floor, but that hadn't stopped Nika.

"It means a lot you forgive. I don't have right, but you come to my wedding?" Nika asked.

Brain freeze. Speechless. Words would be nice right now. Ones that could convey shock and disgust. Oh, and outrage. That was a good one. But no, wait. She had to be kidding.

Say something. "Um, what?"

"Please." Nika's brown eyes pinched, as if they would start fake leaking again.

"But—I—" It was true Nika didn't have any US friends. Women didn't trust her. Except for Emily, and look how well that had worked out. No. No way could she do this. Nika didn't deserve Emily's forgiveness. Going to the wedding was never going to happen.

The waiter appeared again at Emily's elbow with another glass of wine. "From the gentleman at the bar. He wants to know if you'll accept this drink from him."

"Thanks." Emily tried a smile in the direction of the man who, for the love of God, looked to be about her father's age.

"You certainly are popular tonight," Greg said.

"Some people like me, Greg. Because I'm nice. And loyal." And now she was beginning to sound like a dog.

"And there is the dress." Greg's mouth turned up in a smug smile. "I honestly thought this might be too difficult for you, and I warned Nika."

Too difficult?

Emily opened her mouth just as her phone buzzed. Rachel.

How's it going? Remember, you are Emily Parker, wild woman!

Yes, she was, so why was she having such trouble telling these two off?

"Oh boy." Emily stared at her phone.

"What is it?" Nika said.

"An emergency. Sorry, I have to go."

"Seriously? What kind of emergency could an event planner have?" Greg said.

He had never respected her work. As far as he'd been concerned, she just booked events and everything else magically happened.

"There's a *sale* on doves, if you must know! And if I don't get mine tonight it might be too late." She stood, ignoring Greg's confused look.

"I'll call you!" Nika said as Emily walked away.

If either Molly or Rachel could see her now, they'd probably give her thirty lashings for sheer stupidity. Speaking of doormats. Emily could have created a scene, splashed water on pregnant Nika and hot coffee in Greg's lap. And then when Nika cried real tears and not that horrible reality TV–level acting, well, Emily would just harden her heart and walk out the door with her head held high.

Unfortunately, her hot little dress wasn't made for driving in a truck, and Emily felt the cool breeze of night air hit her ass as she climbed in, pulling down on the hem of her dress to preserve her dignity. She stuck her key in the ignition and then hit the steering wheel with her fist so hard her horn went off. A man a few cars away jumped and when his eyes fixated on her, he gave her a dirty look.

Emily honked again then rolled down her window as he passed nearby. "That's right. I honked my horn. Do you want to do something about it?"

The man quirked an eyebrow at her before he hurried into the restaurant.

That felt kind of nice. Powerful. And a little stupid. But maybe crazy stupid was what she needed tonight because she was certainly dressed for it. Rachel was right in that Emily needed to loosen up a little bit. Let go a teensy bit. Emily started up the truck and headed toward the Silver Saddle. She hadn't been back there since the night she and Molly caused a bar fight, but at least Molly wouldn't be there tonight. She'd gone to San Francisco for a night out on the town with a friend. Maybe it was time for the other Parker girl to make an appearance. Show everyone how much living she'd been doing these days. Flying the friendly skies. No more hiding in the shadows.

Greg was getting married, and it was amazing how much that didn't bother her. It was all she could do to call up her righteous indignation. But the baby. That bothered her. She'd wanted kids. A lot. And now Greg and Nika, who'd done such a bad thing, were ahead of her on that end. It wasn't fair.

But it wasn't a race, as Grammy liked to say.

The parking lot was practically empty, a few straggler cars belonging to some other sad and lonely people who had found themselves with nowhere to go on a weeknight. She could go home to her prison loft, but she'd been in that cage too long. The world had kept revolving without her, traitor that it was.

Time to rejoin the merry-go-round.

Jimmy was behind the bar. "Hey, you. Haven't seen you for a while. What's up?"

Emily took pains to properly sit on the stool

and not let everyone in the bar see half her ass. "I've been around."

"Heard you're taking flying lessons." Jimmy winked.

"Yep, that's right. Soon enough I'll be a pilot and I can take all of you on a ride."

"Not me." Jimmy slid a Coke toward Emily. "I hate heights."

Emily pushed the Coke back. "Let me have a tequila shot."

"But it's not Saturday night." Jimmy deadpanned.

She was that predictable. "I'm trying something new on for size." She fished in her purse and laid a twenty dollar bill on the bar. "Keep 'em coming."

He poured a shot and slid it in her direction. "Weekday drinking? You are getting adventurous. You're giving me your keys, I hope you know."

"Yep. And you need to talk to Trish. She's becoming one of those Bridezillas."

"Oh, shit. What now?"

"She wants doves released after the ceremony! Doves! That's so sad. Do you know what's going to happen to them after you release them and they fly away? Death, that's what! I won't kill animals at weddings! We could do a chicken because at least they won't go far. And speaking of chickens, you shouldn't be one, Jimmy. Go up in the plane with me. Maybe you can impress Trish the Bridezilla."

"By going up in one of those teeny tiny planes? What the hell for?"

"Because you might like it," said a smooth and deep voice behind Emily.

That kind of voice made her shimmy and shine. Emily turned to see Stone. Of course. That voice should be bottled and sold as an aphrodisiac. For all she knew, he haunted this place every night since she'd met him here. Picked up a girl or two or three. Ones that didn't have rules. She gave him the once-over, her gaze drifting over the hard body dressed in jeans and a Henley shirt.

"I had to fly once on a small commercial plane and dry heaved into a bag the entire time. I don't call that fun." Jimmy went to take care of another customer.

Stone eased up on the stool next to Emily. "Hey."

Emily scooted her body as far away from him as she could, without falling off her stool. "Look who it is. The guy who turned me down. You're all this night needed."

"Bad day?"

"Try bad year."

"Want to tell me about it?"

"Heck no." She slammed her shot.

"That bad?" His eyebrow quirked up.

She, Emily Parker, was making men's eyebrows quirk up. Two in one night. *Oh, hell yeah.*

"I did something stupid."

"Find someone else to take you up on The Rules already?" He grinned. "Because *that* would be stupid."

"No! Listen, mister, I don't go around offering those terms to just anyone."

"That's encouraging. So what did you do?" His eyes narrowed. "Is this about your ex?"

"Of course you know about that. People in this town talk too much."

"They do." He nodded.

"Fine. Everyone in town already knows, so you might as well, too. He cheated on me. With my friend. The cleaning lady." It was the first time she'd said the words out loud to a man. When a man chooses any other woman over his fiancée, what does that say about the fiancée? That she wasn't anything special. Not worth keeping.

"The cleaning lady."

"She's Russian. Gorgeous model-type, about six feet. Huge gazongas. I mean, if you like that kind of thing."

"You must have trusted him a lot. Unless he's in the very small male population that doesn't appreciate huge gazongas."

"I got her the job! She wanted to stay in the country, and I was her only friend. I should have seen it coming. I'm an idiot."

"You're not the idiot. The guy sounds like an ass. So does she."

"I'm too nice. That's the problem."

Jimmy came back and poured her another shot.

"Is that what he said?" Stone pushed the second shot away from her.

She pulled it back. Slammed it. "He didn't have to. Do you know I think I actually said 'sorry' when I interrupted them? On the kitchen floor, of all places." These shots had turned out to be some kind of truth serum.

"The kitchen floor?"

She rolled her eyes. "Why? Doesn't that sound erotic enough?"

He lifted a shoulder. "The kitchen table, maybe. It would have to be sturdy though."

Dang, apparently the man had given it some thought. "Molly would have burned the house down. Anyway, that's why I've been changing. No more Miss Doormat."

"I like you the way you are. And here's the thing. I don't see you as all that perfect."

She sat up straighter. "Are you here to cheer me up or insult me?"

He cleared his throat. "Let's start with your sense of balance. Every time we're up in the plane, I'm grateful the cockpit is klutz-proof."

"Ha! You're funny."

Jimmy poured her another shot. Stone waved him off.

"You're not drinking?" Emily said.

"Nah. Never know if somebody might need a ride." He slid her a look. A look that said he was talking about her.

"I already asked you for a ride. You said no. Remember?"

He grunted. "Yeah."

Emily heard some whooping in the back corner of the bar. Sounded almost like—but it couldn't be. This night might finally be taking a turn. "Hey, Jimmy, don't tell me Bertha's back."

"She is, indeed." Jimmy smiled and brought her over another draft.

Stone gave him a dirty look and Jimmy lifted a shoulder.

"Three years, and she's finally back up and running. Good ol' Bertha."

"Bertha?" Stone asked.

"The mechanical bull in the corner." Emily had been on Bertha once. She'd made it four seconds before being thrown off. The record was ninety, held by none other than Jimmy. Bertha was fierce. Bertha was ruthless.

And Bertha would be Emily's tonight.

Emily climbed off the stool and rubbed her hands together. "I think I'm up for another chance at her."

"Tonight?" Jimmy asked. "But you're not exactly dressed—and the last time you tried—"

She waved him off and kept walking toward

the back of the bar. "I can't let a little thing like what I'm wearing stop me. I've let too many things stop me in the past. Oh, it's too fast. Oh, I might fall. Oh, what if I break a nail?"

"What if you break your arm?" Stone was at her elbow.

She stopped in her tracks and turned to him, pointing to his chest. "This is one of the many things you don't know about me. I have strong bones. I drink lots of milk. And I won't break an arm."

"You've had three tequila shots tonight, so this isn't a good idea. You have trouble with your balance on a good day."

Maybe, just maybe she could win Bertha over tonight. She could feel it in her bones. Tonight was her night. Because things couldn't possibly get any worse. It was all uphill from here, and Bertha would see her through. They'd do this together. Two women who'd been through the ringer. Broken, even, but put back together again better than ever.

The only thing she had to do was figure out how to, uh, straddle the beast and keep her dignity. This would be tricky but, with a little luck, she could manage. Maybe make it to twenty seconds this time.

Because tonight, anything was possible.

CHAPTER SIXTEEN

STONE WAS RELIEVED to find mats all around this beast everyone called Bertha. No stranger to mechanical bulls, he'd ridden one in Texas five years ago for sixty seconds and beat the evening's high score. But he hadn't been drinking.

He wasn't even sure why he was here, except he'd felt out of sorts all day, gone back to his father's house and packed up more stuff. He'd finally become sick of staring at the same four walls, Winston following him from room to room with moony eyes. Yeah, Stone got it. Winston missed Dad and Stone was a piss-poor substitute. At eight, he made the decision to wander into the bar on the chance he might find Emily here because, let's face it, with her there was never a dull moment. This example being much of what he'd come to expect from her. Times ten.

Her hair was limp tonight, and she wore a skintight black dress riding up her thighs. That dress made him sweat. The dress got an A-plus, if he were grading. Which he wasn't. Instead, somehow, he found himself in the rather ridiculous position of trying to talk Emily out of riding a bull named Bertha.

Who the hell named a bull Bertha?

Emily now waited in line for her turn with the bull, which he would refuse to call Bertha. Rider after rider, all men, were thrown off within a few seconds. Stone stayed right behind her. If he couldn't stop her, at least he'd be nearby for damage control. He only wished he had a first-aid kit with him. Something told him this wouldn't be pretty.

"You sure about this?"

"Oh, yeah, airman." She saluted, he was sure, simply because she knew how much it annoyed him. "You just stand back and watch."

"Listen, let me tell you a few quick things about falling. There's a right way and a wrong way. If you fall to the—"

"Oh, look, it's my turn!"

He resisted the urge to throw her over his shoulder and haul her out of there because she was a grown woman. A grown woman with a great ass, and he might as well enjoy the show like everyone else would be doing.

Emily kicked off her high-heeled shoes and climbed the bull. One deliciously curvy leg came down on either side, the dress riding up high. Stone tried not to salivate, but, man, it had been a long time, and he'd had that exact leg recently pressed up against him. The leg looked even better than it had felt. He needed to seriously reconsider this nice-guy scenario and go ahead and take Emily up on her offer.

That dress was now up to her cheeky ass, sitting tight and covering just enough. Emily kept pulling it down in the front, which made it ride slightly up the back. Every time it did, one of the men in the small group surrounding the bull groaned a little.

And this all before the ride had even started.

"You ready?" The operator asked.

"Hell, yeah!" Emily turned to them. "Let 'er rip. Hey, guys, I bet I beat Jimmy's record tonight. Wanna make a bet?"

"What's Jimmy's record?" Stone asked the guy closest to him.

"Ninety seconds," the guy said, shaking his head. "Not gonna happen."

Jimmy had made his way out from behind the bar and now stood at Stone's elbow. "Should you be doing this right now?"

"He's just afraid I'm gonna take his record. Right, guys?" Emily said.

"Yeah," the small crowd echoed, obviously more concerned with watching Emily gyrating on that bull than the honest truth.

The bull started moving, slowly at first, but within a second, it was moving as fast as any bucking bronco. Emily hung on, to her credit, her blond hair tossed about in waves around her head.

But not for long.

Stone didn't time her, but his educated guess would be three seconds. Emily flew off the bull and landed on the mat, her world-class ass sticking straight up in the air. Mooning the entire group of men.

For a second, there was nothing but dead silence and slackened jaws.

Stone turned to the group of men. "If any of you says a word about this to anyone, I'll personally kick your collective asses."

"That goes double for me," Jimmy said.

Stone moved quickly after that and squatted at her side, simultaneously blocking everyone else's view and helping to pull her dress down. "You okay?"

"I did it!" Emily squealed as he helped her up. She pushed hair out of her eyes."

"You did great!" one of the guys called out, earning cheers from the group.

"And you're done." Stone hauled her up in his arms.

"Wait. I was thinking I might go again."

"No." He proceeded to walk through the bar with her in his arms, earning no small amount of attention from the patrons. Jimmy had gone ahead of them and opened the door.

"What do you think? Shouldn't I go again? I'm feeling lucky," Emily said to Jimmy.

"I don't think so, hon. Better quit while you're ahead." He handed Emily's purse to her.

If by "ahead" Jimmy meant still in one piece with a comforting lack of bloodletting, Stone would have to agree.

She squirmed in his arms. "Way to ruin my night, guys. I guess I need a ride home."

"You think?" Stone carried her outside, managed to shift her weight so he could open the passenger door to his truck, lift her in and latch her seat belt.

When he came around to the driver's side, Emily studied him. "Dang, you're so bossy. You don't need to take me home. Jimmy can do it."

Stone put the key in the ignition and turned to her. "I'll do it."

"Of course you will, you party pooper." She stuck her feet up on the dashboard.

He pulled out of the parking lot. "What the hell is going on with you, anyway? Riding the bull when you have trouble walking and chewing gum?"

"I'm trying something new."

But she didn't fool him. There was sadness in those eyes that he hadn't seen there before. She definitely wasn't telling him something. He'd bet it had to do with the ex-fiancé, and if it had to do with that asshole, Stone wasn't sure he wanted to hear about it anyway.

Emily popped on the radio, changing his preprogrammed stations until she got to the country channel. "Oh, I love this song!"

She proceeded to sing off-key to "You Should Have Kissed Me" and pointed a finger in his direction every time the song hit the refrain. He didn't like country music when it was sung in tune, let alone Emily's rendition. Hopefully she sang better when she was sober or he was fairly certain it wasn't stage fright that had ended her country music career.

Finally he reached her ranch, pulled up near the loft and came around to open the door for her.

"Thanks for my ride, sailor. I'll take it from here."

"You don't have any shoes." He stared at her feet.

"What happened to my shoes?" She wiggled one foot.

"I forgot to get those for you."

"That's what happens when you hurry. You forget things. Let that be a lesson to you."

"Sue me. I wanted to get you out of there before you tried to do that again." He pulled her up out of the seat and walked up the stairs to her loft.

"I can walk barefoot. I was raised on a ranch." But she smiled at him, batting her eyelashes. "You want to come in?"

He did, and he didn't. Coming inside meant it would be open season on teasing him, he had a good feeling. And he wasn't even going to kiss a tipsy Emily, much less make love to her.

He set her down just outside her front door. "It's dark. Thought I couldn't."

"Oh, I did away with all those old rules!" She opened the front door. "I have a new set. You coming?"

Not likely, Stone thought. Still, he strode inside and shut the door. He took another glance at his surroundings. Cozy. Girly to the core. And yes, there was the bed in the same small room. Why he chose to torture himself this way he'd never know. He should turn around and walk out of there right now. He should say good-night, sleep tight and see ya tomorrow. But he couldn't do any of those things because he was a glutton for punishment, Emily-style. Besides, Dad's house was beginning to feel like one never-ending project. He'd start to paint a wall and discover a hole behind a picture frame that needed to be repaired first. Every project led to another one, and every corner of the house reminded him of Dad.

At the same time, Stone refused to believe he had problems. He realized what real-world problems were, and fixing up an outdated and cluttered house for sale was not one of them. Neither was dealing with a pissed-off family member. These were minuscule baby problems.

On the other hand. Emily.

She was a bit of a problem for him. He'd started

to understand that the pull she had on him was a little different. Of course, there was the unbridled lust she brought out of him, but there was something else, too. Something he couldn't quite quantify or figure out. He liked her. That much was clear. A whole hell of a lot. She made him laugh. Helped him to forget for a little while.

"I'll be right back," she said now, taking off behind the closed door he assumed was the bathroom.

Great. He could only hope she didn't come out of there with fewer clothes on than when she went in, or all bets were off. He was a human being, and no saint. While he waited, he grabbed a seat next to a stuffed animal. He reached to move it and the thing squeaked and moved. It was not stuffed. Not at all.

Emily swung the door open and came out, fully clothed, though, it didn't help much. The thin pajama pants hugged her bottom and the tank top stretched across her breasts. "You met Pookie?"

"*Pookie?* Does he usually stalk unsuspecting men? Sit still and pretend to be stuffed?"

"You thought *she* was a stuffed animal?" She picked up the ball of fur, and the dog licked her face. "Pookie used to sleep outside with the other dogs, but she's gotten too old. She doesn't even move much these days, poor baby. Too much effort. I'm letting her inside with me from now on."

"I think she appreciates it."

Emily carried the dog like a football in one hand and went toward the fridge. "You want something to drink?"

"I'm fine. I should probably—"

"Go?" she turned to him, a water bottle in her hand. "I'm not drunk, you know."

"You're not perfectly sober, either." He stood.

She set the dog down on her bed and came toward him. "Don't go."

When she reached him, she put her arms around his waist, and it was natural to pull her even closer. "It isn't that I don't want to stay. It's just—"

"My rules?" She gazed at him, and something in his heart pinched.

"You can do better than me."

"What if I don't want better? What if you're what I want? Right here, right now."

He swallowed hard, not at all used to refusing that kind of blatant invitation. Taking what he wanted. Right on this couch, consequences be damned. Not like he hadn't done it before, time and time again, barely apologizing to the women as he walked out the door. They were all grown-ups, and adults fully aware of the temporary nature.

But this was different. He wasn't sure how, when or why he had begun to want more than no-strings sex. "Do you trust me? Because maybe you shouldn't."

"I'm not sure why, but I do. I think it's your eyes." She pulled on his hand and sat on the couch. "And I don't want to be alone right now. Can't you just stay with me a little while?"

He sat again, instinctively drawing his arms around her. She sighed and nestled in. Cuddling. Who would have ever thought he'd have the patience for this?

"This is nice," Emily said, her head on his chest. "So nice."

"Yeah." Could she feel his heart as it raced at Mach levels? What would be nice would be to show her what he could do with his tongue.

Within a few minutes, Emily made a sweet sound in the back of her throat and her breaths had become slow and even. She was dozing on him. The girl trusted him so much she fell asleep in his arms, when he didn't think he could trust himself. This time, instead of the direct line to his groin, the surge of electricity happened a little too close to his heart for comfort.

Shit, he was in such trouble.

CHAPTER SEVENTEEN

STONE COULDN'T AVOID the walls any longer. He had to paint. The Realtor he and Sarah had agreed on would put the for-sale sign up this week, and no one wanted a house that was stuck in early eighties decor.

Last week at Builder's Emporium, the clerk had recommended something called Dakota Loam. He didn't have the foggiest idea whether it was the so-called trendy earth-tone decor the clerk had said it was, because it looked like brown to him. Spending the past ten years in military housing meant he didn't pay much attention to the color scheme of his surroundings. It didn't matter when it was all so temporary.

This, on the other hand, didn't feel temporary. These were Dad's walls. It felt like he should take great care with the color he put on these walls.

He trudged into the family room, carrying the gallon of paint. "It's just you and me, wall. Let's get it on."

A couple of hours later, he had taped the room and laid plastic over the worn carpet. Another thing to replace; although, the Realtor believed they could sell the house without replacing it. He stirred the stick in the thick paint and then heard a knock on the front door. With any luck, Crash and Matt had gotten a clue and would be here to help him, maybe even with a beer or two.

But no, when he opened the door, who should be on the other side of it but the woman who wanted everything. "What now?"

Sarah pushed by him, the old Mcallister temper being the one thing she'd inherited from dear old Dad. "I'm done playing it your way. He was my father, too."

"Fine, come on in. Don't let me stop you. As you can see, the place is lovely. Thinking maybe I'll bring *Better Homes and Gardens* in here for a spread." He waved his arm.

"What the hell is that?" Sarah pointed past him toward the kitchen floor.

When Winston slept in the hallway, he looked like a huge and dirty heap of a throw rug. "That's Dad's dog. Winston."

"That's a dog?" She walked closer to Winston and bent down as if to inspect him.

Winston lifted his head but took one look at Sarah, got up and lumbered into the back bedroom. Probably he was a whole lot smarter than Stone had ever given him credit for.

"What is it you want? A tour of the place?" Did these look like the digs of a man who hoarded gold bullion? What the hell was wrong with his money-grubbing sister?

"That might be nice."

He ignored that and marched back to his ready-as-ever wall because he was no damned museum docent.

Sarah followed him. She stared at him, then at the wall. "You're painting?"

"It needs it." He picked up the roller and laid it in the paint. "The whole house does. There's a lot to be done around here."

"Don't let me stop you or anything."

"Wasn't going to."

She let out a deep sigh, the kind women gave when they wanted your attention but wouldn't say why. The kind that usually meant you were about to get an earful, like it or not. "I've decided I want to help you get the house sellable. Are you going to let me?"

"Do I have a choice?" He slathered on the first coat. Brown. What the hell. Since when did they call brown Dakota Loam? He'd been right in the first place. This room would probably be way too dark now. Damn.

"I wish you would talk to me."

"I am talking."

"In tiny three-word sentences. About stupid stuff. I want to talk about the big stuff, like how Mom and Dad made a big mistake. Whoever heard of such a child arrangement? Splitting up a family the way they did was criminal."

Stone stiffened. Had his sister just called their parents criminals? Hell, no. She hadn't. As usual, civilians threw the word criminal around so much it lost its real meaning. "Criminal."

"Yeah. I've never heard of anyone else splitting up the kids in a divorce—you take one, I'll take the other. You needed a mother, and I needed a father. We were both ripped off."

"Got it." He didn't disagree or agree. It was all damn water under the bridge.

And this color was way too dark.

"Why won't you talk to me? Don't you feel cheated, too?"

He dropped the roller. "Cheated? Hell, no."

"Okay. So you didn't miss having a mother. But I want to know more about my dad. I want to know about this town and why he moved here. What he thought about me, if he ever thought about me, and how he loved his children. Or I should say, his son."

And now she was crying in his family room. He didn't do crying women. When a woman cried, he was usually watching her back as she walked out the door. He lifted a hand as if that could stop her. "Don't."

Sarah plopped down on the couch. "I'm sorry. I'm not after anything. You called me to the reading of the will, like all I should want was my share. Like I wouldn't have wanted to say good-bye to him first. Mom told me to hire the lawyer, and hell, after you both treated me the way you did I decided why the hell not? But I'm sick of fighting with you. You can sell the flight school to your buyer. I only wanted to remember him since I didn't get to say goodbye."

Stone reached for a box of tissues he'd bought to wipe up Winston's constant slobbering and handed it to Sarah. He didn't know whether he could trust her. She'd so quickly changed her mind after giving him such grief. "What do you want to know?"

"Everything." She pointed toward the wall with her tissue. "And by the way, that color is going to be way too dark for this room."

Damn.

A COUPLE OF HOURS LATER, Stone had just hopped out of the shower when he heard someone pull up outside. Was Sarah back again?

I am done with the crying for one day. First, he'd agreed to her choice of a lighter brown color for the walls. He'd gone back to the store and returned to find her waiting. Then he'd slathered the paint on while she watched from the sidelines, letting him know when he missed a spot.

Later, he'd let her go through boxes of photos and albums as she tried to revisit the past. It turned out his sister found a certain kind of joy in going through one man's junk that he couldn't quite understand. But if she was willing to help him in that regard, he couldn't very well argue, since it had taken him the better part of two months and he'd barely made a dent in it.

Why Sarah enjoyed torturing herself by wallowing in what could never be altered, he'd never understand. He'd finally given her all the photo albums and told her she could come by again anytime. Promised that yes, they'd talk again. If he'd known that was all she wanted, they could have both avoided some grief and lawyer bills.

And it was strange, having a sister again after all these years. The pictures were enlightening to him, too; though, he didn't share that with Sarah. He'd almost forgotten the trips they'd taken together in the earlier years. Camping trips to Yosemite National Park and Lake Tahoe. Disneyland. Sarah seemed to get more emotional with each photo, and all that emotion was way over the top.

He remembered his mother being the same way. She'd come to see him just before he'd shipped off to boot camp. Thrown herself at him, weeping and clutching. Cursed at his father for failing to stop Stone from signing up. He'd been disgusted at the time by her lack of self-control. It took him a few years to understand her position. Over the years, they'd kept in touch mostly via email. He understood that as a parent, she'd wanted to save him from some of what he'd seen and experienced. So did Dad, but he hadn't resorted to emotional tactics. Instead, he'd tried to win Stone over with logic. The only problem was that logic was in Stone's favor on all accounts. The air force was his best shot at an education.

And by God, he'd received one.

When the knocking persisted, Stone realized Sarah wasn't going away. Typical. But when Stone opened the door, Emily stood on the other side. He hadn't seen much of her since the night of the full mooning. The picture of her ass was still burned into his brain, and he doubted he would ever forget the image.

"Hi," she said. "Have you eaten yet? I brought you some dinner."

He took the packages from her and led her into the kitchen. "You didn't have to do that."

"I don't mind. I felt like Trail Dust tonight, and it's always too much food for me."

He opened one box to discover a full rack of ribs. "I can see why."

Winston chose that moment to lumber into the room, bowl in his jaws. Great. He'd forgotten to feed him dinner.

Emily laughed. "He's good at communicating, isn't he?"

"My bad." Stone pried the bowl out of Winston's jaws and stayed between Emily and Winston. "Watch yourself." The last thing he needed was a repeat of the last performance, with Emily lying on the floor out of breath.

The next time she lay anywhere breathless, it would be because of him, not the dog.

"I'm not afraid of him." Emily bent down to ruffle his head.

Winston lifted moony eyes in Emily's direction. Flirting.

"You should be. I think he likes you."

Stone fed Winston, then brought out paper plates, utensils and napkins.

Emily opened cartons of potato and macaroni salad and uncovered a loaf of baked bread. "Thank you, by the way."

"Why thank me? You brought the food."

She met his eyes. "For taking care of me last night."

"Ah." Great. Like he was supposed to be some kind of hero because he helped pull her dress down and carried her out of there. Not like he hadn't also taken a moment, okay, more than a moment, to enjoy the view. "Glad I could help."

She stopped serving to glance at him. "When I woke up the next morning on my couch, you were gone."

"Yeah. I didn't want to wake you to say goodbye." He sat on one of the stools at the counter and accepted his plate when she pushed it in his direction.

She stood on the other side of the counter and

they ate in silence for a few minutes, accompanied only by Winston's somewhat pitiful sighs and begging eyes. Because, even though he'd just eaten a bowl of dry dog food, Winston was no fool. He recognized the good stuff when he smelled it.

He jutted his chin toward Winston. "Does your dog do this?"

"No. Pookie has mastered the art of begging. But she's an old gal. She could teach you a thing or two, Winston." Emily pointed her fork at him. "Pookie sits next to me when I eat, right at my feet, her back to me."

"Playing hard to get?"

"Trying to act like she doesn't care whether or not she gets any scraps." She lifted a shoulder. "It works."

"You give in?"

"Of course. Dogs don't live long, so they might as well enjoy it. Good food is one of life's great pleasures." A small amount of barbeque sauce dripped down the side of Emily's mouth, and her tongue went out to flick it off. "Oops. This is messy."

That tongue action went straight to his groin, and he was reminded of another one of life's great pleasures. He didn't break eye contact with Emily as he slowly lowered his hand to Winston and handed him a rib bone. Winston reacted as though the rib bone might be his last meal on earth, nearly taking one of Stone's fingers with him. Stone knew, for a fact, Winston would lumber out of the room, taking that bone with him to enjoy his feast in private.

"You should at least make him work for it. Sit, or shake or lie down." Emily licked her lips again, like she understood what it did to him. "I taught Pookie how to lie down and play dead."

"That's Winston's only trick. He lies down and plays dead almost twenty-four-seven." He wiped his hands clean, stood and moved toward Emily.

Her eyes on him, she laughed a little louder than normal. "That doesn't count."

"Nervous?" He reached her side. "You have something—right here." One hand holding her chin, he leaned forward and licked her lips. "Mmm."

His hands pulling her in, her entire body responded to him. She dipped her finger in his mouth. "It's good, isn't it?"

He licked it dry then bit it. Yeah, he didn't know what the hell he was doing. He'd pretty much stopped thinking. Emily and that mouth. Those eyes. Her laugh. She'd robbed him of his last brain cell. She kissed him then, or he kissed her, he couldn't be sure who started it. It didn't matter because things moved quickly then—her grasping at the hem of his T-shirt and tugging it off, him cupping her ass and pulling her against his erection.

She licked and nipped at his collarbone, and he drew in a ragged breath. He pushed her up against the kitchen wall. "Is this what you want?" he whispered into her hair. Figured it might be a good time to ask, because soon they'd be past the point of no return. But if the way she moved in response to him was any indication, she was very much on board.

She pressed into his hardness, making his temperature shoot up into jungle-fever levels. "I want you. Now."

He lifted her arms above her head and pinned her against the wall. She made a small sound of pleasure somewhere between a moan and a squeak. That single needy sound pushed him to lick from her neck down her shoulder, moving her shirt and bra strap with his teeth. With one hand he reached under her shirt and bra, feeling breasts more plump and round than he had imagined. Rosy pink, achingly soft.

"Damn." He lifted up her shirt and shoved the bra cup to the side, his mouth covering one warm breast, sucking her nipple in hard. Her entire body tensed, and she arched into him, moaning.

He moved back to her mouth and kissed her, lingering there. Her body tensed, and he wasn't sure if it was because of the stupid rule he'd just broken. But when her fingers threaded in his hair, pulling him closer, it became clear the kissing wasn't a deal breaker. Good. He had to remind himself this was what she wanted from him. Hard. Rough. Fast. Even if what she inspired in him was something altogether different. An unquantifiable something he couldn't put his finger on, and might be best left unexamined. For the first time in a long while he wanted to feel something. A feeling that wasn't pain or regret, even if it was only temporary.

Don't think. Just feel. She tastes so good. Like home.

He pulled her jeans down. "Kick them off."

She did, stepped back and stood in front of him in nothing but her thong and bra, fleshy beautiful skin curving in all the right places. In case he had any lingering questions, she removed them with a few words. "I've never wanted anything or anyone as much as I want this."

"Come here." He tugged her to him and eyed the kitchen table.

She noticed, and her brows rose. "Really?"

"It's here."

"Yes," Emily said. "I don't want to wait another minute."

He pulled a condom from his pocket before he lowered his jeans and boxers. She moved to the table and backed up to it. Her eagerness worked for him, and he was rock hard as he slipped the condom on.

As much as he wanted to slide into her wet heat, he couldn't resist falling to his knees to take a taste of her warm sweetness, like honey on his tongue and lips. He couldn't get enough of her, flicking his tongue slowly in and out. Her body tightened, and she shuddered and bucked beneath his lips, saying his name on a moan as she came. He rose then, easing one of her legs around his waist and leaning her against the table. With one hard quick thrust, he was inside her, warm and wet and wondering if he might stay there forever. But this was just once, and he reminded himself of that fact. So, if it was once, he would enjoy it. Enjoy the hell out of it.

Emily's eyes were at half-mast, but he wanted her to see him. For reasons he couldn't explain, he wanted her to remember who made her feel this way. "Look at me."

Her green eyes darkened as she opened them. "You...you feel so good."

He couldn't say the same. He'd felt good before. This was better. This was a word that hadn't been invented yet. When Emily made a soft little sound in the back of her throat and when she tightened around him, he could no longer hold back.

With one last thrust, he groaned and followed her over.

CHAPTER EIGHTEEN

EVENTUALLY EMILY AND Stone made it to his bedroom, but she would never think of a kitchen table in quite the same way again. Now she fully understood what it felt like when the bedroom was too far away, when the need was so great the nearest surface would do. She'd received entrance into the Society of Satisfied Women, and she was likely never going to give up her membership card.

Once more, she found Stone could do something with amazing skill. She mentally checked off the list: he could fly a plane, hold his own on the dance floor, rescue a damsel in distress, play a mean game of billiards and make a girl's eyes roll to the back of her head. That last one was her favorite.

She hadn't been this breathless since Molly talked her into an Insanity workout session over a year ago. Emily hadn't been back to that gym since, but she couldn't say she didn't want to be back under, and on top of, Stone again.

She hadn't planned any of this when she'd

come by to bring him dinner. But then he'd licked the sauce off her lips. That had started off an avalanche of licking and touching that hadn't ended until he was inside her.

She stretched and took a good long look at him now, lying asleep beside her. His body might as well be a statue chiseled out of the perfect definition of a man. Defined pecs and washboard abs. The strong biceps of a working man, and two military tattoos—a flag on his right biceps and an eagle on his rib cage.

Poor thing did look exhausted. No wonder, since she'd worn him out by begging him to do it again. And again. In her mind, she'd quickly redefined that "once" didn't mean literally one time. It meant one session. Strange, because she'd never been quite so flexible with her rules. But this, again, was part of being a wild woman. Bending the rules, when it made sense.

Emily Parker, a wild woman. At last.

Emily lifted her head off the surprisingly soft pillow, and scanned the bedroom she'd been too busy to notice last night. A dresser, a lamp and a duffel bag near the closet gave off new meaning to sparse. The rest of his father's house might be packed to the gills, but Stone's room shouted "temporary." No pictures on the walls, either, save one framed photo of a plane.

Temporary or not, she would enjoy every moment of this, and her hand reached out to touch him one more time. But just before her hand reached his pec, he caught her wrist midair, causing her breath to catch.

One eye opened and assessed her.

"I was only going to touch you." Emily swallowed.

Both eyes now open, he released her wrist. "Go ahead."

She let her hand rest on his right pec and caress down to his abs before she smiled at him, losing her nerve to go any farther. She had a lot to learn, and taking the initiative wasn't in her bag of tricks. Stone wasn't smiling. The hungry look in his eyes made her think of being eaten alive. She felt like a bunny alone in the big, vast forest. Except a bunny probably wouldn't feel the intense and pleasant heat that ran a pathway straight from her heart down to her southern region, which she might as well rename the equator.

Her heart skipped a beat. Holy Helena, it looked like he would bite her now, like he'd once said he might. "Want to tell me what happened Monday night?"

"You know what? I should probably go."

Suddenly, he unceremoniously flipped her over on her back, lying on top of her like the rock of Gibraltar. "Nice try. Tell me."

She felt just a tad vulnerable in this position,

and she pushed against him. He didn't budge. "What do you want to know?"

"Whatever you want to tell me." He eased up off her, leaning on one elbow.

Nothing. It's too humiliating. "Nika. She's pregnant."

"That was fast."

"What bugs me the most is everyone else was right. And I was wrong."

"About what?"

"Nika. Rachel and Molly were suspicious. They said she was calculating and probably planning on marrying someone just so she could stay in the country. I thought they'd watched one too many movies. I didn't think that kind of thing happened in real life. Nika needed a job, so I thought she could work for Greg."

"So you got her the job, and then she slept with your fiancé."

"Ex-fiancé. She probably did me a favor. But I can still be mad about it."

"Right." He studied her for a long minute. "Except you don't act mad. Having dinner with them. It sounds like you're all friends again."

"She's pregnant. I'm trying to do the right thing. I *am* mad, though. Can't you tell?"

He didn't look like he believed her, his eyes narrowing slightly. "Why don't you show me how angry you are?"

"How?"

"I know exactly what you need."

He got out of bed, naked, completely confident about his body. He grabbed a pair of pants and pulled them on.

"Where are you going?"

"Get dressed and come with me."

Get dressed? She'd been ready for round four and if last time was any indication, she'd do even better this time. Because a few minutes ago, Sergeant Stone Mcallister had been, by all indications, for the first time since she'd met him, at her mercy. She saw it in his eyes when she touched him the right way and heard it in his voice when he groaned. For once in her life, reading had helped her with a man. *Thank you*, Cosmopolitan.

"I don't think what I need involves getting dressed." She let her eyes drift the length of him, even as he was pulling on his shirt.

He grinned, showing one of the dimples. "Just trust me."

"Um, most of my clothes are in the kitchen."

"Right." He was back within a few seconds with Emily's push-up bra and thong since, thank you Molly and Rachel, she'd had the presence of mind to wear sexy underwear to deliver dinner. Just because, according to Molly and Rachel, a woman should always be prepared.

"What about the rest of my clothes?" She'd

worn jeans and a tank top, too. She clipped her bra on and glanced at him to find him watching.

"One thing at a time. I think I'm going to enjoy watching you put those on as much as I enjoyed taking them off."

Once she was dressed, he took her hand and guided her through the house, through a doorway in the kitchen to the attached garage. The place seemed like an automobile mausoleum of sorts, filled with old road signs and an old Ford taking up most of the room. His hand slid over the hood of the car as he passed it. "Nineteen seventy-two. The days when the cars were the size of boats."

"Why do you think I need a car right now? Do you know me at all?"

He came so close she thought he might kiss her, but instead, he put two big hands solidly around her waist and turned her to a far corner of the garage.

"A punching bag?"

"I put this in here a few months ago, after I moved in to help my dad." He swung a fist into the bag and it swayed toward him. "The minute I heard about the misdiagnosis, and all that wasted time—"

"Misdiagnosis."

"Yeah, they thought he had irritable bowel syndrome when what he really had was colon cancer. And by the time he got the right diagnosis..."

"Too late," she finished his sentence. "I'm

sorry. So the bag was to help get out your frustrations?"

"Seemed like a good idea at the time. Better than knocking out the doctors. Or the wall."

Emily came up behind him and wrapped her arms around his waist. He'd shared more with her in those few minutes than he had in the month or so she'd known him.

"But what does this have to do with me?"

"You need this."

"Me? You've got to be kidding. I've never punched anything in my life. I was taught to use my words."

"Listen, I don't want to hear about any more nights like the other night on Bertha. And by the way, who calls a bull Bertha?"

"The previous owner named her. It was supposed to be funny."

"It's not." He touched the bag. "This is a lot safer for you than Bertha."

Aw, he was worried about her. Concerned she might go getting herself injured falling off Bertha. He had a solid point. "Don't worry. I won't do that again. You'd be there to stop me anyway. Right?"

He didn't make eye contact. "Yeah, I forgot to tell you. My sister has agreed to sell the flight school to my buyer. So, I should be all wrapped up in town pretty soon. The house goes on the market on Monday."

"Oh. Good." Now it all made sense. He was leaving, and she'd inspired such overwhelming confidence in the man that he thought he had to make sure she'd be all right without him.

"I still have some time. I just don't know how much."

"I'll be all right, you know." She'd never expected forever with him. He was supposed to be Mr. Right Now. And apparently he felt some guilt that maybe he'd taken advantage of poor, innocent Emily when she'd known exactly what she was getting into.

"I know."

But she wasn't sure he did, dammit. It was her idea to have no-strings sex and she'd done it. "This was my idea, if you remember."

"How could I forget?"

"And I don't need your stupid bag." She swiped at it with the back of her hand.

He glanced from the bag to her. "That was pathetic."

"I wasn't trying!"

"No kidding." He came up behind her. "Put your hands into fists and then swing."

"I can't do that." She pushed back into him, rubbing her butt into his groin. They were wasting valuable time in this dusty, drafty old garage.

He groaned. "Hit the damn bag, Emily. Pretend it's your ex. Or your former friend."

"My God, Stone, I can't hit a pregnant woman."

"It's a *bag*."

Emily gave him a long look. "Why do you want me to do this again?"

"I know a little bit about anger. And I think you've been angry for a while. With your ex, with your old friend, with yourself. Maybe even with me. Keeping it inside isn't going to help. Believe me."

He might be right. When Emily stayed in her loft all those months, Grammy left many an article sitting on the counter, wide open to the page she wanted Emily to read. One of the articles was titled "Anger and Depression in Women." The article had suggested women often traded anger for depression because girls had been mostly raised to believe anger was unacceptable. Emily had dismissed it all as pop psychology. Eventually, the fog had lifted, but in a way, she'd never dealt with the anger. Others had for her. Molly. Grammy. Rachel.

"This is going to help me get my anger out?" Emily stared at the bag. Maybe if it had worked for Stone, it could work for her.

"Yeah." To demonstrate, he gave the bag a punch.

"Like this?" She took a swing and missed.

He frowned. "Next time, try hitting the bag."

"I'm trying." She lifted up fists, feeling like a cross between Muhammad Ali and Cinderella. Her right hook missed the bag.

Stone looked at the bag, then Emily. "How are you doing this?"

"I told you. I don't hit." Although, this swinging felt pretty good. Freeing. Almost like hitting the horn accidentally and watching the stranger's surprised expression. There was a fire in her, and she felt it now. She just needed to connect with this bag, but it kept moving out of reach.

"Not like that, you don't." He came up behind her to position her hands, and yeah, maybe she enjoyed the closeness a little too much.

She relaxed her body into his.

"Hold your fists like this."

She held her fists in front of her chest and eyed him as he went behind the bag and held it in place. "You just need a little help to get the hang of it."

It worked. Emily swung and swung again, hearty punches into the bag, her breaths coming hard and fast. She pictured Greg falling down. She pictured Nika thanking Emily for getting her the job, cleaning the apartment and laughing about dorky and cute Greg with his color-coordinated ties and pocket protectors. "Engineers are definitely not my type. I like them big and strong," Nika had said with a wink. Nika telling Emily she wasn't interested in ever having children. Too expensive, she'd said. I want a beamer instead.

Bang! You're going down.

Nika lay flat on the ground.

Bad friend. Liar. "You're right. This is fun."

Relief flooded through her. She pictured Greg's face as she pummeled it. Greg's face, puzzled and questioning: *What's gotten into you, Emily? You're always so kind and reasonable. You mean there's a limit?*

Heck yeah, there's a limit. The nerve of you blindsiding me like that. I wanted you to be sorry. Instead, I wound up leaving that night a loser. Again. I hate your stupid face. I hate the way you make me feel. You were never right for me.

Oh.

"Are you okay?" Stone's voice broke through the haze.

Emily stopped swinging, her breathing heavy and ragged. She wiped sweat from her forehead. "Sure. Why do you ask?"

"You've been at it for a few minutes. Thought I'd lost you there." He grinned so wide both dimples appeared.

"Okay, you were right." She backed up, worn out and sweaty. "I needed that. It felt good."

He came around from the side of the bag. When his arms went around her waist, she leaned into him. "You feel good."

"So do you." She kissed him then, thinking no one had ever cared enough to show her how to deal with her feelings in any real and tangible way. Not talking it out, as she would have expected from any psychologist or girlfriend, but physically hashing it out. And it made sense. Stone was a man of action.

His arms slid up and back down her arms, and he seemed to study her. "Don't let me hurt you. Don't ever let anyone hurt you. Ever again."

"I don't know if that's possible. I—"

"Promise me." His hands tightened around her arms.

"Okay. I promise."

She kissed him again, tenderly, and then again not so tenderly, the only thought in her head being that she'd just made a promise only he could make her break.

CHAPTER NINETEEN

EMILY HANDED GRAMMY a tissue. Weddings always made her cry. Even this wedding, and that said something. The bride and groom had written their own vows, but apparently neither one of them had thought of first consulting a book. Or even a dictionary.

"I hella love you, Ashley," the groom said. "I swear I'll like, love you forever and all. For real, dude."

"Billy, when you, like, asked me to marry you, like, I couldn't believe it. But you're like my soul mate, so what could go wrong? I promise I'll like love you for always."

"Maybe the next wedding will be more romantic," Emily said from the back. The bar hadn't been set too high, after all.

Dad, for his part, had retreated to the big house and locked himself in his office, away from all the "lunatics" on his property. The night was cool and clear, and as they moved outdoors under the stars for the reception, the band began to set up on the makeshift stage.

"This must be hard for you. You should have reconsidered having a wedding this soon after, well, you know," Grammy said.

Emily put an arm around Grammy. "Don't worry about me. I might never get married."

She might adopt someday. Lots of kids needed homes. Should she ever get it into her head she had to somehow pass on the Parker genes (lovers of beef), she'd visit one of those sperm banks. Pretty sure someday they'd be on every corner, the way things were going. The First National Sperm Bank on one corner, The Sperm Credit Union on the other. With men like Greg being the marrying kind and men like Stone being the runaway kind, she figured a visit to a sperm bank was unavoidable.

"You don't believe that, sweetheart. You've been planning your wedding since you were eleven and used my white lace tablecloth for a veil." Grammy dabbed at her thick clumps of mascara.

"I'd rather marry that lace tablecloth." Emily was stronger now. Smarter. Not as easy to fool next time, should there be a next time. The jury was still out on that.

Molly appeared behind her. "Everything's ready at the buffet line."

Billy and Ashley walked out of the barn first, followed by their wedding party.

"Follow me." Molly led them to where the photographer waited to take photos.

Emily and Grammy stayed behind to direct the guests to the tables and buffet, where a long line had begun to form.

No time like the present. Hoping it wasn't completely tacky, Emily walked up to Ashley and congratulated her.

"So, where did you get your tattoos?" Emily dared to ask.

"Billy did my tattoos."

"Billy, your husband?"

"That's how we met, at the tattoo parlor. Why? Do you know someone who'd like a tattoo?"

Emily looked at the ground then met Ashley's gaze. "Yeah. Me."

To her credit, Ashley didn't appear shocked to find that straightlaced Emily Parker wanted a tattoo. "Hey, come by anytime and we'll do it free of charge."

Ashley was pulled away by the photographer, and Emily found Molly at her elbow. "You? A tattoo? It doesn't come off, you know."

"I know. That's the point." Emily was pretty certain she had a stupid smile on her face. It felt good. She'd get the tattoo she'd always wanted but was too worried to get. Of course, first she'd make sure the parlor followed all the health guidelines. Giving up a little control didn't mean she wouldn't be smart about it.

Now to decide between a butterfly and a dragonfly.

Emily hadn't spoken to Stone in a few days. Cassie said he'd been busy fixing the house, apparently spending time getting to know his sister and working out the sale of the flight school. Emily had met the new future owner, a nice man in his fifties, who planned on hiring an entire staff of instructors and expanding. Emily would have her choice of instructors, he'd assured her. But none of them would be Stone. The man who didn't want to hurt her. Didn't want anyone else to hurt her. But somehow, he alone made her heart ache. In a good way. In a way that reminded her she was alive and breathing, young and strong.

Most importantly, she had no regrets.

A few hours later, the wedding party was scattering and the hired help were cleaning up. Molly appeared at Emily's elbow, holding a bottle of champagne. "Sneaked this from the bar before they packed it all up. What do you say we have a drink?"

They walked down to the fence post and Emily kicked off her shoes, sat on the post, took a swallow of champagne and handed the bottle back to Molly. Despite her recent meltdown at the Silver Saddle, Emily wasn't a big drinker. But tonight, champagne seemed to be the right answer. She was celebrating, in a way.

Celebrating her new life.

With all traces of the wedding now gone, and with only the light from a full harvest moon, Emily thought about Stone. The few hours they'd had together, touching, feeling, forgetting the outside world existed, had been the best of her life. She did have one regret.

There wouldn't be a next time. He was leaving soon, and that was the deal. Besides, one more time with him and she'd be hooked.

"I think you have to admit I've been super patient," Molly said.

"About what?"

"You and the pilot guy. I know you had sex, Emily. I can see it in your face. In your eyes. You had great sex, and you haven't shared with me!" She pointed an accusatory finger.

"All right, we had sex. And—I didn't know it could be like that." But somehow, she couldn't bring herself to share any more with Molly. It was too special, too private. The memories made her cheeks grow hot, even in the cold night air.

"Once you've had great sex, you never go back." Molly took a gulp from the bottle and made no move to give it back.

Emily reached for the champagne and took a nice long swallow. The bubbles slid down her throat. "It was just the one time. We made a deal."

"What kind of a deal?" Molly tried to pry the bottle out of Emily's hands.

"I made a whole new set of rules." Emily didn't release her grip but took another sip.

"Your stupid rules again?"

"You might want to laugh, but it helped. Doing something crazy, but with rules. It gave order to my madness. And I realized something. Greg never made my heart shimmy and shine. It's not that I didn't love Greg, because I did. But I never loved him in that can't-eat-can't-sleep kind of way."

"But that's the best way!"

You're telling me. "At least I know that's what I want now. Even if it scares me."

"What you're talking about isn't being scared. It sounds like excitement. But it's all right to be scared sometimes," Molly said. "Even I am."

"You?"

"Don't look so shocked. There's only one thing that scares me now. Sierra is going to grow up and not know who I am. I'll be a stranger."

"You don't have to be."

"I've already missed so much. I don't want to miss any more." Molly chugged some champagne with a little too much gusto for Emily's taste.

"Then don't."

"I'm not. I just decided right now. I'm going to get Sierra back! And I don't care what it takes."

It was about time. "Good for you."

Emily jumped off the fence post rail and landed

on her knees, causing Molly to break out in giggles that rippled through the quiet of the night. A light was on in the kitchen of the main house, and Emily could picture Grammy doing the dishes by hand as she did nearly every night. Even if she had a state-of-the-art dishwasher.

Emily brushed off the damp grass from her knees and Dad's voice boomed, calling to them from the wraparound porch. "Molly! Emily! Where in tarnation are you girls?"

"Coming, Daddy," Molly shouted back.

Emily carried her black pumps and walked over the cool grass to the bottom of the porch steps, Molly following.

Dad, wearing his Stetson, looked like he'd swallowed poison. "Are they all gone now?"

"Yes, they're gone," Emily said.

"No more weddings. I told your grandmother, and now I'm telling you. It's one thing to put up with the parties and picnics. But I'll draw the line at marriage ceremonies. My ancestors didn't farm this land and raise cattle to have a bunch of no-account people have fun all over my land!" He waved his arm across the expanse of what was left of his land.

"Calm down, Daddy. Your blood pressure," Molly said.

"I'm leaving tomorrow, by the way." Dad took off his Stetson, scratched his head and put it back on.

"Tomorrow?" Molly whined. "But you just got here."

"Now, now, I've got a real cattle ranch to run in Texas. It ain't my fault the doggone eminent domain put the freeway through our land and took most of it."

They'd all heard that story a hundred times.

"Right." Molly kicked a blade of grass, a sure sign she wasn't a happy camper.

"And one more thing, Emily. I need you to stop them darn flying lessons and come back to your ever-lovin' senses. What's gotten into you, girl?"

Emily turned to Molly, prepared to slug her. But one look in Molly's wide eyes and she could see that, without a doubt, she hadn't been the one to tell.

"How did you know?"

"Everyone in town knows. I talked to Charlie, Jedd's grandfather. He told me Jedd can't stop talking about it. Says you come in five times a week sometimes. For all the tea in China, give me one good reason why."

Emily straightened. "I'm sorry you found out this way. But I'm not going to stop taking the lessons."

"What did you say?" Dad thundered into the night.

Molly, now standing next to Emily, elbowed her in the gut.

Emily rubbed the sore spot and ignored Molly.

Some things just needed to be said, and finally she had the guts to do it. "I'm going to keep flying, and I'll have my license soon. I'm good at it, and I won't stop now."

With that, Emily walked slowly up the steps and past a bewildered-looking Dad. Jaw slackened, he didn't look so much angry as confused.

"Don't worry, she's just kidding. I'll talk her out of it," Molly said as she followed up the steps.

Emily turned at the screen door. "I'm not changing my mind, and you all won't change it for me."

Both Molly and Dad followed Emily inside. Molly stood a few feet behind Dad and alternately took turns scowling, pointing at her heart and then pointing at Dad. Emily would have expected no less, but though she didn't want to give their father a heart attack, it was time to speak her mind. Long past time.

"What in all creation has happened to you, Emily?" Dad pushed his hat back, like a cowboy at the O.K. Corral.

"I'm twenty-eight, and you can't tell me what to do anymore. I'm good at flying, and I want to keep going until I have my license." All the breath rushed out of her at once, and she nearly wanted to turn and see who'd spoken because she could hardly believe those words had come out of her.

"What are you going to do with it when you get it?" Dad asked.

She took an uneven breath. "I don't know yet. Probably volunteer for Pilots and Paws. But you don't need to worry about me anymore."

"Well, I beg to differ, young lady. I'm your daddy and I'll always worry about you and your crazy fandangled ideas. This one being the latest in a mighty long line." He waved a hand in the air.

Emily prepared to go in for the kill. This had to be done, this had to be said and apparently she would be the only one to say it. "Maybe you need to stop worrying about *me* so much and start thinking about what you're doing with *your* life."

She thought Molly might have gasped, and Dad put a hand to his chest. "What I'm—what I'm doing with my life?"

"That's what I said. You forget that you have a family here, a ranch, too. Okay, so maybe it's not a cattle ranch anymore, like in its glory days, but it's home. Your home, Dad. Texas is *not* home." Man, she'd wanted to say that for a long time.

Now Molly nodded in agreement. "She's right."

He waved his arms around. "What in tarnation has come over all of you? I work, and I work, and I slave for this family. And this is the thanks I get. Do you think it's easy running a cattle ranch?"

Emily folded her arms. "No, but it's also not easy running this business without you. Grammy and I have been doing it for a while without your help."

"I never thought it was a good idea in the first place."

"Whether you think so or not, last year the revenue for all the events we did increased the net worth of Parker Inc. by thirty-five percent." Dang it, she was proud of the fact Grammy had found a different way to use the land. Their ranching days were long behind them, but that didn't mean they weren't still relevant.

"What do you want me to do? Everywhere you look, these vegans are trying to convince people red meat is gonna kill 'em. And we're still trying to recover from the Mad Cow days. Mad Cow, my ass. It was one cow!" Dad rubbed the back of his neck.

"So, we'll keep doing weddings as long as it makes sense. And another thing, too. I've been saving up for a long time. As much as I love that Grammy wanted me to have the loft, I'm moving out."

"Moving out? Again? Emily, that didn't work out so well last time. Don't tell me you're going back to that bozo, because I won't hear of it." He took his hat off and fanned himself with it.

"No, I'm not going back to Idiot Greg. But it's time to move on from here." She'd looked at the one-bedroom apartments in town, and there was a development in her price range.

"What about your grandmother? She needs your help," he continued.

"I'll be fine," Grammy said from the doorway to the kitchen. "It's time Emily did something for herself."

"I can help around here, too, Daddy," Molly said quietly from next to him. "I can do a lot more than you think I can."

Dad ruffled her hair. "Of course you can, sugar."

"I'm still going to work, it's just that I'm going to have actual regular work hours and the rest of the time when I'm not at work, I'm going to go home and do—other stuff," Emily said.

"Well, Mother, as long as this is all right with you," he said, sliding his arm around Molly.

Grammy put her arm around Emily. "It's more than all right."

CHAPTER TWENTY

MOLLY SUCKED IN a breath as she stared at the one-story gray house on Sycamore Lane. The house where Dylan and Sierra lived. Dylan's battered old green Ford Ranger sat in the driveway. She didn't even want to think about what they'd done in the backseat of that truck, because it might as well have been a thousand years ago.

Dylan wouldn't be expecting Molly. That would be because she hadn't called ahead. Why bother giving him a chance to say no? This way, she'd have the advantage. Shock and awe.

Pretty much what Emily had done two nights ago with Daddy. Molly still couldn't believe that, of all people, her perfect big sister had been the one to tell Daddy what no one else dared. He had to stop acting like his home was in Texas. Home had to be with his family, with his mother and his daughters. With his granddaughter.

Daddy had still left the next morning. But maybe, with any luck, all the things Emily said would make him think.

Before Sierra, Molly had believed her Daddy

was by far the best father in the entire world, or at least this continent. But in the end it was Dylan who had earned the title in Molly's book. He'd never walked away like she had, or pawned off the raising of her to his mother, as Daddy had to Grammy.

Emily always said that Daddy had made life too easy for Molly, and therefore never realized how much she could really do. Maybe that was a little bit true. At the park, she'd seen that Dylan hadn't picked Sierra up every time she fell.

Daddy had always rescued Molly, like she couldn't handle anything on her own. Eventually she'd believed him. Only Emily had thought she could do better. And Dylan.

Or at least, he used to believe in her.

Molly loved her father, but sooner or later he would have to realize she'd grown up when he wasn't looking. She had a baby of her own, and she'd just have to show him that she could handle Sierra. Handle Dylan.

Because Emily might be a first-class organizer, but she had no idea how to brush her teeth while simultaneously propping up a bottle for a baby with one elbow. Molly did. She could hold her baby while rocking and swaying like a palm tree's leaves in a tropical night breeze. She had memorized all the words to her favorite lullaby, could carry Sierra in a football hold like an NFL champ, and occasionally sleep with one eye open. So maybe she hadn't been a total disaster as a mother.

All right. Time to do this. Molly gathered her purse and her courage and marched to the front door. She held out her finger to push the doorbell and then pulled it back.

She didn't know why, but Dylan scared her a little bit. There was no reason for it, as he'd never so much as raised a hand to her. Not a hand, but he had that look. She used to call it the Drill Sergeant glare.

But dammit, there was no world in which Emily had more hutzpah than Molly did. She pushed the doorbell and then once more for good measure.

Footsteps sounded from inside as did her baby's deep belly laugh. Sierra used to laugh like that when they played peekaboo. Had Sierra outgrown peekaboo? What if Molly couldn't think of any new games to play with her?

And then Dylan's voice called out, "All right, all right, I'm coming."

When Dylan opened the door, Sierra in his arms, it didn't take two seconds before he'd given Molly the Drill Sergeant glare. "I might have expected this."

"Hi, Dylan. Hi, Sierra."

Sierra stuck her thumb in her mouth and smiled around it.

"What do you want?"

He wasn't going to make this easy, was he? "I want to see my baby."

"I thought we talked about this." Dylan didn't move from his spot as Door Guard.

"You talked about it. And here's the thing. That's not going to work for me." Molly wanted to take the snippy comment back as soon as it had left her mouth. Dylan held all the cards right now, and she needed to play nice.

Dylan sighed. "Let's not do this."

"Sorry. We're going to do this. I'm not going anywhere. Are you going to let me in or what?"

By some small miracle, Dylan hesitated only one second before he moved aside and nodded for Molly to come in. Once the door closed, he set Sierra down and she toddled off.

Molly tried to follow her baby girl, but Dylan grabbed her arm. "Wait."

Why was it that, against all odds, she still felt a shiver roll down her spine? Dammit. "Wait for what? I've been waiting. I'm done with it."

He let go of her arm. "Just don't—confuse her. Please."

Somebody stop the presses. Dylan had just said please. "I'd never do anything to hurt her. Is that what you think?"

"What I think—what I know is that you don't always think things all the way through."

Thank you, Dylan, for being right again. One

day she'd tell him how annoying it was. "I just want to hold her again."

What was it Emily said about letting Dylan know how much it hurt to be away from Sierra? But even now, her back tensed with self-righteous anger. She needed to take a deep breath and calm down. Dylan loved Sierra, too. He only wanted to protect her. The problem was, he seemed to think Sierra needed protecting from Molly.

She'd have to show him how wrong he was. When she turned into the living room, it was to see the most precious display on the planet. Sierra stood a few feet away at a little play kitchen, chewing on a plastic spoon.

Molly's hands shook a little bit. What if she messed this up, too? "She's gotten so big."

Dylan stood inches behind Molly. "This isn't some game we're playing. This is my daughter's life."

Molly whipped her head back. "She's mine, too. And I don't know what game you think I'm playing."

"We're not going to fight over her like she's the last slice of pie."

"I didn't say we were."

Dylan moved toward the couch. "This isn't a good idea if you're going to leave again."

Molly clenched and unclenched her fists. "I'm not. I made a mistake before."

He grunted. "Some mistake."

If only he'd had a clue of what she'd been through in those first few months. How tired she'd been every day. "You want to punish me for that, don't you?"

"You have no idea what I want to do." His voice was so cold it seemed like the temperature in the room lowered by several degrees.

But then he walked right over to Sierra and picked her up gently. "Sierra, this is your mommy."

Molly expected he would argue the point and want them to ease into the situation so as not to confuse Sierra. But the truth could never stop being the truth. Whether he liked it or not, she was Sierra's mother.

And so they were diving in, feetfirst. "Hi, Sierra."

Sierra wasn't impressed as she glanced at her and then laid her head on Dylan's shoulder. Apparently, the words, the moment, hadn't carried the same significance to Sierra.

"You realize she probably doesn't understand," Dylan said as though he thought he had to defend Sierra.

"Did she ever call someone else Mommy?" Finally, the question she'd been so afraid to voice for fear she'd rip Dylan to shreds when she heard the answer.

"Never," Dylan said hotly. "She tried to call my mother Mama once, but now it's Nana. Mommy is a brand-new name for her. But it might as well be 'Molly' or any other name for all she knows."

"Right." Molly let that settle in her stomach, currently residing at her feet. Her baby had no association with the word *mommy*.

Sierra wiggled out of Dylan's arms and toddled back to her play kitchen. Molly walked slowly to Sierra and dropped to her knees beside her, picked up a pot and spoon and started stirring. Sierra ignored her as she put a picture book in the oven and turned knobs willy-nilly. But in the next moment, Sierra stared at Molly, as if she'd just noticed a shiny new object, then took out the picture book and offered it to her. "Cake."

"Thank you," Molly said.

Dylan still hovered, like he thought she might steal Sierra.

Molly narrowed her eyes at him. "I'm not going to take her, you know."

Dylan scowled. "I know because I won't let you."

Maybe she deserved that, but she didn't like it when Dylan got all Alpha-man. "She's my baby, too, and don't you forget it."

"You gave birth to her."

Molly's throat burned with the words she held back. It probably wasn't good to cuss around babies. "I did a lot more than that. I took care of her the first few months, while you were out—"

"Earning a living?" he interrupted.

"You don't know how hard it was for me. I cried every day. She cried every day and I couldn't do anything to make her stop. I couldn't do anything right."

"So leaving? That was doing something right?"

"No." She bit her lower lip. "You were right when you said Daddy spoiled me. And the thing is…the problem is I never could figure out how to fix anything on my own. So I left it up to you. I knew you'd both be fine without me."

Sierra handed Molly a spoon and smiled. "Need 'poon."

Just like that they were both reoriented to their daughter. The reason they were here. The best thing they'd ever done together.

"Here," Dylan said, picking up another picture book. "She likes this story."

As if they'd been doing it all along, Sierra situated herself in Molly's lap, squirming until she got comfortable. Molly touched her baby's soft curls and opened the book. She read the title and wondered if Dylan had picked this one only to hurt Molly.

I'll Love You Forever. She remembered the story. Molly read the book, swallowing the golf ball in her throat so Dylan wouldn't know how much it hurt. This mother had stayed. This mother had never left her baby. Unlike Molly. Point taken, Dylan.

Never let them see you sweat. She wouldn't

let Dylan have the satisfaction. Molly kept reading, as Sierra alternately touched the pages and
sucked her thumb. Finally Molly closed the book
to find her baby asleep in her arms. As though
it was the most natural place in the world for her
to fall asleep because maybe, on some cellular
level, Sierra did remember.

"Sorry about that," Dylan said, not looking
the least bit sorry. "I forgot this book puts her
to sleep."

He came closer, as though he believed he had
a chance in hell of taking Sierra out of Molly's
arms.

"But I just got here." Molly pulled Sierra closer.
"I don't care if she's asleep."

"This is crazy. She doesn't even know you're
here now. You're basically visiting with me. Is
that what you want?"

"What I want is to jump into a time machine
and go back. I don't want to miss her first steps,
her first word. I want to take it all back." Now
the tears filled her eyes. Dammit. Sierra seemed
to have the same skill that Emily did at turning
Molly from an edgy cactus into a soft fluffy pillow. Had to be some kind of recessive gene on
the Parker side that had missed her.

"Even leaving me?" Dylan asked.

For the first time since she could remember,
Molly was speechless. What could she say? That
she wished he could still love her, if she hadn't

done something so horrible, so unforgiveable that whatever affection he'd had for her had died? That she realized he couldn't love her any more than she could love herself right now?

"Yeah, that's what I thought," Dylan said, a harsh edge in his voice.

"Go ahead and let me have it. You know you want to." Holding Sierra gave her a kind of peace she'd forgotten existed.

Dylan took the invitation. "What did you think would happen when you showed back up? Am I supposed to just open up my arms and forget everything?"

"I'm sorry." Molly realized in that moment it might have been the first time she'd said it to Dylan and meant it.

"I wish I could trust you, because I know Sierra needs her mother. But I don't believe you'll stay. I think you'll get your fill of playing with her and take off again."

"No, I won't. It's different now."

"How?"

"I don't know how, it just is. I didn't want to leave, but I just didn't know how to stay. I thought maybe someone else could raise her and do a better job than me. Like you. But I couldn't forget her. And then I realized that I didn't want someone else to raise her. Even if they could do it better than me." She hung her head. "I'm sorry if that sounds selfish."

"It is selfish. In a good way."

Silence passed between them, and Molly bent down to kiss Sierra's soft cheek.

Dylan stood. "Do you want to see her room? You can put her in the crib."

She wasn't sure she wanted to let go, but Dylan had offered to let her see Sierra's bedroom. This was progress. He wasn't going to fight her anymore. "Okay."

Dylan leaned down and took Sierra from her arms so Molly could stand up. She followed Dylan into a pink room, much like the room Molly had shared with Emily for years. Pink gingham curtains hung on the windows, rainbow colored letters on the wall spelled out Sierra, and a beautiful white canopy crib stood in the center of the room.

For the first six months of her life, Sierra had slept in a cradle beside their bed. Molly's side, of course, so Dylan could get his sleep. Back then Molly had wondered if there would ever be a time when Sierra would sleep in her own bedroom, and now here it was in living color. A little princess room. "She sleeps in here?"

"Most of the time. I know you didn't think it would ever happen, but she does sleep through the night now." Dylan skillfully let down the side rail with his knee and laid Sierra down.

"Does she try climbing out of here yet? Because Emily says I climbed out of my crib when I was one."

"I'm not surprised." Dylan almost cracked a smile. "She hasn't tried that yet."

It didn't seem possible, but he had nearly smiled. Molly loved Dylan's smile, a cross between an altar boy who'd snuck a taste of wine and a sailor on leave. The problem was he was downright sexy. He always had been. Too hard to resist. That one factor combined with the failure of birth control at a particularly passionate time had led to Sierra.

Outside her bedroom, Dylan stopped in the hallway and turned to Molly. "How are we going to do this?"

For one moment, all Molly could think about was all the places they'd made love—the backseat of his truck, the bed of his truck, in a sleeping bag outside under the stars, in the shower. Some of those locations required some creative positioning. *How are we going to do this?* Dylan had once asked.

"How are we going to do what?" Molly reached out to touch his beard. The one she didn't think he'd ever be able to grow. He'd done it. Just like he'd raised their daughter on his own for a year. Without Molly.

Dylan stopped her hand midair. A hot look appeared in his eyes, but it wasn't sexy. Not by a long shot. "What do you think you're doing?"

"Nothing. I'm sorry."

Dylan ran a hand through that thick honey-hued hair. "All right. This is what I suggest. For now, you can come over three times a week to watch Sierra."

Three times a week. She was the luckiest woman on the face of the planet. No more park visits. "I can? Thank you."

"But there's nothing going on between you and me. You get that, right?"

"Of course I do." Just for one moment, she'd thought, maybe. She'd been kidding herself, of course. Dylan wasn't all that forgiving.

Something they had in common.

"Because Sierra has no choice. You're her mother, right or wrong. But me? I'm a different story. You're not fooling me, Molly. Never again."

CHAPTER TWENTY-ONE

FOR THE FIRST TIME in her life, Emily had free rein to decorate. And while Greg had preferred off-white walls and window treatments and every shade of beige on the color wheel, Emily went for big splashes of color. She hung amethyst drapes in the family room of the duplex she now rented, and burnt orange in the bedroom. Rachel had helped Emily find the couch—a deep forest green which she accentuated with gold, red and choco-late brown pillows.

When Rachel had come over last week to see the finished look, she'd declared it a "beige-free zone" and wiped away a tear.

"What do you think, Pookie?"

Pookie lifted her head from her new miniature couch on the floor and sighed. Emily would take that as official doggy-sanctioned approval.

Dad had gone back to Texas after all, but he'd promised to come back sooner this time. Emily thought maybe her words had had some impact and made him think about the choices he'd made for his family. Molly definitely thought they had.

The only thing left on her list was filling out paperwork for her pilot's license. She'd been avoiding that. Stone had pulled her into his office yesterday, and while she'd wondered if he wanted to revisit her one-time rule, it seemed she was the only one who wanted to a second time.

He'd wanted to talk to her about applying for her pilot's license. "You're ready," he'd said, his blue eyes edgy. He looked tired, a new tightness around the corners of his eyes she hadn't noticed before. Lack of sleep? Guilt?

Maybe she didn't want to know. "I think maybe I need to log in more hours. I'm not sure."

"I am. You're ready." He'd told her to ask Cassie for the paperwork and to get the process started.

She hadn't. Not yet.

He'd been distant since they'd made love. Or had sex. She wasn't sure what to call it these days. Not that she'd had any yardstick against which to measure so-called casual sex. Because that's what it was. What it was supposed to be. She didn't know anymore, except that she'd assumed sex with no commitment would feel shameful. Wrong. This, somehow, didn't. She had to believe it was because of Stone. He'd managed to make it special, despite its temporary nature.

Experience, she had to assume.

Her cell phone rang. No caller ID. "Hello?"

"Emily. Thank God you answered," Greg said

from the other end. "I was afraid you'd blocked my number."

She had thought about it. "I'm glad you called. I can't make it to the wedding."

"No need. The wedding is off."

"What? Why?" This didn't make sense.

"One day I was at home sitting with Nika on the couch watching old *Ghost Whisperer* reruns, and I took a good long look at the couch. You picked it out, remember?"

Emily sighed. "I remember picking out the best-looking beige couch I could find for you."

"I started shaking. I planned on spending the rest of my life with you. We bought the couch, and I don't know what the hell happened after that. How did I wind up here? I'm going to be a dad. I'm not ready for that. Nika wants to buy every kind of designer baby shit they make. Infant Nikes for fifty dollars? When the kid can't even walk? What the hell is wrong with her? I can't handle it."

Emily could almost picture Greg on the other end, wiping the sweat off his wide forehead. She had a road map as to how they'd wound up here, but she didn't think Greg wanted to hear it.

"Listen, I can tell you really love her. You're just getting cold feet." This was generous of Emily, and she knew it, but she didn't love Greg anymore. She no longer wished he'd drop dead of a heart attack, choke on a peach pit or fall down an elevator shaft. He could just get on with his life and leave her out of it.

"That's it! I had cold feet with you. And if I'd had someone like you to talk me through it, I wouldn't have—"

"Wound up on the kitchen floor with Nika?" Funny, the image didn't make her cringe anymore. Actually, the entire thing was a little embarrassing for Greg and Nika. Nobody could look attractive in that...position.

"We'd be married by now, maybe with a little one on the way. Like we planned."

Thank God for clean kitchen floors then. "You *do* have a little one on the way."

Greg sighed. "But it was supposed to be with you, not Nika."

Poor Greg. What a sap. A realization hit her square between the eyes. "You would have walked out on me, too, wouldn't you?"

"No! If not for Nika, I know we would have worked it out."

"Maybe," Emily said. "But I don't think so. You want to know what your problem is?"

"I'm still in love with you?"

"You're a commitment-phobe masquerading as the marrying kind. That's because you're too chickenshit to tell women the truth." At least Stone had been honest with her.

"No, no, that's not it. It's you. You're the woman for me."

"You're too late."

"No, it can't be too late. It's never too late. I'm not married yet. You're not married."

"But I'm in love with someone else." Wait. Had she just said those words out loud? No problem, because she didn't mean them. Did she?

Don't think, don't worry. Just stay in the moment.

Maybe this was love. She couldn't stop thinking about him. Couldn't stop feeling slightly sick to her stomach. Either she was in love or fighting a virus.

Greg groaned. "Are you kidding me? Are you telling me there's no chance for us?"

Funny how puzzled he sounded. As if she'd been standing by waiting for him to make up his mind that he'd made a mistake. "Go talk to Nika. Work it out. It's time to stop running. Pull up your Pampers and deal with it."

"You're the most wonderful woman I've ever known," Greg said with a whimper. "And I blew it."

"And that's the perfect way to end this call. Goodbye, Greg. Have a nice life. Don't call me again." She clicked off, feeling a sense of finality course through her body. Closure. The last time she'd ever hear from Greg.

She breathed a sigh of relief and went to start dinner.

STONE HAMMERED THE last nail into the hardwood floor repair and stood back. Another room he could call complete. The for-sale sign had gone up, and a few buyers had come by. Not a whole hell of a lot of interest, though. Or offers. The Realtor had suggested some improvements to attract more buyers. Curbside appeal. Light and bright. Stone was trying like hell to sell a house he wasn't sure he wanted to let go.

But he had to. Sarah had come by to offer her own litany of suggestions. If it was up to her, apparently, the entire house would be gutted and they'd start over from scratch. While there was something to be said for that and starting over, time was running out. He'd been accepted back into the air force sooner than he could have hoped. His orders would come through any day, and he'd either have to accept or have a week to leave the air force. This time permanently.

Dad would understand. He'd always been proud of Stone's service. The air force had been his life since he'd been eighteen. So why did the whole idea of going back now feel like such a betrayal? He thought he'd fixed everything, and there was nothing left to do in this town.

As nighttime fell, he showered and climbed in his truck for a little drive-by recon. He drove by the Silver Saddle and didn't see Emily's truck.

Might be a good time to check out her new place. Convenient that she'd left her new address with Cassie.

He drove around the neighborhood, in full-on investigative mode. While all of Fortune was decidedly smack dab in the middle of Suburbia, USA, there were some less than desirable pockets of areas, too. As he pulled up to Emily's place, he was relieved to see her duplex was not in one of them.

The place was painted blue, with little pink and red flowers lining an outside window box. There was a small shared lawn in front, and through the window he saw movement inside the house. For a moment, he sat in the truck and watched. Waited for the logic to hit him. The moment when he'd turn around and go back home. He was supposed to be the one who excelled at detachment. Distance. If he'd caught anyone else in this position, he might use the word *stalker* and haul him out of the vehicle by the scruff of his neck. Tell him to stay the hell away from her.

What the hell was he doing? Sitting here, not working too well with the whole detachment thing. It occurred to him, for the first time since he'd landed here, he might be lonely. He wasn't one given to a lot of introspection, but facts were facts. He hadn't smiled since Dad's death. Until Emily. He'd gotten himself emotionally attached, dammit, and that might be a big problem because he was pretty certain she felt the same way.

Which made them both a couple of fools.

The front door opened and Emily followed her little dog outside. "Hurry up, Pookie. It's grass. You don't have to inspect it." Then she noticed him, sitting in his truck. *Busted.* She smiled, which didn't help the situation.

He got out of the truck, grabbing some paperwork. "I brought by some stuff you'll have to fill out for your pilot's license."

"Oh." Her smile fell. "Since you're here, do you want to come in?"

"Yeah." Sure he wanted to come in. Maybe what he needed was one more time to get her out of his system. Move on. Maybe it was what they both needed.

Emily picked up her dog and took the papers from Stone. She walked back inside, and he followed.

Stone was nearly assaulted by all the color. The room was a far cry from the countrified yellow rooster loft she'd lived in before. This fit her a lot better.

She turned to him. "What do you think?"

"You sure you have all the colors in here? I think you might have missed one or two."

Her smile was the brightest he'd seen it yet. "I decorated it all on my own. I never thought I would have this much color. But it feels good. Right."

This time there was no bed in the middle of the room beckoning, but that didn't mean he was thinking about it any less. "It's a safe neighborhood. I checked."

Her eyebrow quirked up. "Okay. Thanks for checking."

She flitted around the room, closing windows and drapes. Trying to keep busy, like she didn't know what to do with him. Again, it had become difficult not to smile. They'd already been so intimate he knew that her eyes darkened when she came, and still she was shy around him.

"Do you want something to drink? Eat?"

She finally walked close enough by him that he was able to grab her wrist and spin her into his arms. "Yeah. You. I want you."

He wanted his hands on her, everywhere, teasing and coaxing her to let go. To give in to him, to stop thinking and planning. To let go.

Her arms wrapped around his neck and pulled him closer still, and he felt her smile against his lips before he kissed her. Again and again. "But my kitchen table isn't sturdy enough."

She led him toward her bedroom between long and deep kisses, twisting and turning, both of them in such a hurry they nearly knocked her dog into next week.

"Oops. Sorry, Pookie," she said.

The smart dog scurried off and once inside her bedroom, Stone shut the door with his back.

He pulled back to look at her and met eyes so

raw and hot with passion he felt it down to the soles of his boots. "Look what you do to me."

Her palms slid up his chest and back down to the waistband of his jeans. He kissed her, and she returned hot openmouthed kisses that sent him into sensory overload. The kisses turned wilder, bolder, and she ripped off his shirt, buttons flying.

"Not so shy anymore, are you?" He felt a smile coming on.

Then he took over, his open mouth sliding to the side of her neck and to every inch of exposed and tender skin as he bent lower. And lower still. He pulled down her dress and took her nipple in his mouth and she gasped, arching and pulling him closer. He got greedy then. A moan escaped her when he kissed her again, wet and warm kisses that he tugged him under, making him hazy with lust. One hand slipped under her dress, tugging roughly at her thong. He needed this. Here. Now. Her.

He pushed her lightly, and she fell back onto her bed. He followed her down, burying his face in the side of her neck. His breathing had become hard and raspy, and a deep groan vibrated in his chest.

"You have too many clothes on." He resolved that in seconds flat, removing her thong and nudging her thighs open. "Mmm. Is this what you want? Do you like this?"

"Y-y-y-es. I'm so close. Stone."

He didn't need to hear any more.

She gasped and shuddered under him then became a little more demanding. "Please. Now—"

He enjoyed this new side of her. "Now what?" he teased.

"Get in me," she said on a whisper.

"Don't do that," he said, his thumb brushing her bottom lip. It felt like she was forever hiding from him, holding on to some part of herself that she wouldn't let him have. He didn't know why that mattered so much and it worried him that it did.

"Don't do what?"

"Get shy on me. Retreat." He kissed her again, and tongues tangling, gave her some of her own sweet taste.

Lifting himself up, he rolled on a condom then pushed inside her like she wanted. He gave her a moment to adjust to him then moved with slow even strokes, forcing himself to take it slow even if it killed him. And it just might.

"Faster." When she pressed a hand on his hips and met him thrust for thrust, urging him on, he was tempted to give her everything she wanted. And more.

"Not this time."

He took his time, watching her writhe under him, clutching the sheets, clutching him. When she trembled and cried out his name, he swallowed her moans with a kiss and kept moving inside her.

"Say it," he demanded, even as he realized he was about to ask for something crazy. But she did this to him, made him want more than he should have. Left him greedy for more. Always more.

"Say what?" she gasped.

"Say you're mine." He stared in her eyes, unflinching.

"I'm yours."

He didn't know if it was those words or her muscles clenching and milking him, but a groan ripped out of him as he came harder than he'd ever come before.

CHAPTER TWENTY-TWO

WHEN HE WOKE the next morning, Stone didn't say the first words that popped came into his mind. *I was wrong.* He'd been so certain having sex would have lost some of the thrill of that crazy balls-to-the-wall first time. Wasn't it always that way? It certainly had been that way for him in the past. Just not this time.

She was breathing softly next to him, her legs entangled with his.

"You okay?" He kissed her temple softly, surprised at the tenderness that stirred in him.

"No. Okay is not a big enough word for the way I feel."

He agreed. This was new. Different. And while he would rather have his balls roasted over a flaming hot fire than cop to it, he was a little bit worried. Maybe even a tad bit scared. The difference between him and Emily was that he and fear were well acquainted. Over the years, they'd developed a kind of truce. They didn't avoid each other. What was the damn point? Being an ever-present facet of his life meant he and fear would need to learn how to get along. And they had, for many years.

When he'd separated from the air force, he'd had a moment when he didn't think he could idly stand by and watch his father wither away from the strong man he'd once known into a skeleton of a man. But he'd managed that. And every single day that he tried to somehow take his father's place, there was that small fear that someone would find out he was a fraud.

And now he was forced to face the fact he was shit-faced crazy about this girl. This made leaving a real problem. One for which he had no viable solution, because he had to go back.

He'd be receiving his orders any day now, and she wasn't even aware he'd been accepted back. He had to tell her soon. But all he wanted was a few more minutes. A few more minutes to pretend that nothing else mattered but right here and right now with her. A few more minutes before maybe she'd start to see him like every other woman he'd left behind had. Because it mattered what Emily thought of him. It mattered too much.

"You know what I was thinking? Our first date was at a man cave."

"I should have done better than that." He kissed her shoulder. "In a way, though, you met my family that day."

"It was perfect. I love feeling like I'm one of the guys." She propped her chin on his chest.

"You could never be one of the guys, babe. I don't sleep with the guys." He let his hand dive under the covers, exploring. She shivered and the expression in her eyes grew soft.

"You know what I mean. Have you ever made love to another pilot before?"

What a dangerous question. *Women*. And what if his answer had been yes? As it so happened, he wouldn't be lying to say no. He wasn't even sure he'd ever made love before. Great sex? Yeah. But again, this was different.

"You're my first." Under the sheet, he tweaked her nipple. It hardened to a solid peak.

"Would you please stop doing that?" She put her hand over his, stopping the under-the-sheets play. "It makes it hard to concentrate."

"So it's working." He went for her neck, licking and nibbling.

She laughed, but then she moved and gave him better access. "Stone?"

"Yeah?"

"I've been kind of avoiding getting my license."

He stopped kissing and went up on one elbow. "I knew it. Why?"

She sat up, pulling the covers up to her neck. "I don't know. It just feels like—the end of something."

"It's not. It's the beginning."

"Doesn't feel that way. When I get my license, I guess I won't need you anymore."

"That's the idea."

"Aw, but I'll miss you sitting next to me pretending you don't give a shit."

She had him dialed, didn't she? "And I'll miss you sitting next to me, inappropriately saluting me."

She smiled shyly, and something tugged in his heart. "You're going to miss me, airman. Admit it."

She had no idea how much. He drew her back into his arms where it felt like she belonged. *Careful with that line of thinking.* Look where it had him so far. In her bed going against every standard he'd set up. He was supposed to be better than this. Stronger.

"You're a genius, babe. A damn genius."

EMILY DIDN'T WANT any of this to end. This whole setup, her idea entirely, wasn't working for her. She might as well have forgotten she had rules, for all the attention she'd paid to them lately. There wasn't supposed to even be a second time. But it also wasn't supposed to be this good. She wasn't supposed to be having all these feelings, but there they were. She had a real problem, and its name was Stone Mcallister.

She still didn't understand what made a man

like him tick and why he cared so much when he still had plans to walk away from it all.

"Seems like you're forgetting this is what you wanted," he finally said.

Okay, busted. She'd tried like hell to turn herself into some kind of wild woman overnight, but clearly she'd failed. She felt something for this man. A lot of somethings. This had all worked out completely different than what she'd planned.

"I suck at letting go and finding my inner bad girl."

"I was talking about your pilot's license."

"Oh, sure." She tried to recover. "That's what I meant, too."

"Yeah." He tugged on a lock of her hair. "For the record, the reason you can't find your inner bad girl is because she isn't in there."

Dang, she hated it when he was right. "Does that make you happy?"

He studied her. "My happiness isn't the issue."

"Why not?"

And just like that, he shut down. His eyes hooded and whatever she thought she'd seen in them before—love, tenderness, affection—was gone now. He was back to steel and sharp edges. Emily couldn't get past the thought that Stone had a guilt riding him that wouldn't let go. She only wished he'd think to share a small piece of it with her.

He pulled back, ignoring the question. "I

should probably go. I've already outstayed my welcome."

Right. She'd put that rule in place for a reason. Even if it had boomeranged on her.

He got out of bed and pulled on his boxers and jeans.

"You're enjoying this, aren't you?"

"I'm enjoying what?"

He buttoned his shirt and rolled the sleeves to his elbows.

Why were men so much sexier when they did that? She climbed out of bed, too, and searched for her bra and panties, pulling them on.

"You like that I made the no-strings rules and you get to benefit from them."

"Hey, don't blame me. I'm the one who thought it wasn't a good idea."

She pulled her dress back on. "Guess what? You get to be right. The whole thing was crazy. I can't do this. I tried, I really tried to be someone else, but I can't help it if I'm reasonable, reliable Emily."

"And you and I—we're not reasonable? We don't make sense?" He shoved his boots back on, looking slightly irritated.

"You said it. I didn't."

"I was always honest with you." He straightened to his full height. "I'm not a good long-term bet. The air force is my life, just like the ranch and your family is yours. I've tried, but I'm not half the man my father was."

"Why do you think you're not as good as your father was?"

"Let's not do this."

"I'm sorry, we're doing it."

He looked surprised, his eyebrow quirking again, but he didn't say a word.

"You care about this town, and not just because your father did. You didn't have to keep Winston, and life would have been easier if you didn't. You could have walked away from the school and let it go to the highest bidder, but you wanted to save their jobs. And you didn't have to keep flying for Pilots and Paws, but you did."

He looked at the ground, shaking his head. "Okay, that whole thing was—"

"Your father's pet project. Flying adopted dogs to their new homes. It's a good cause. And you're a good man. Just like your father was."

"The best thing you can say about me is that I'm loyal to the core to the few things I care about. But I won't hesitate to make the tough choices when I get a chance to make them. The ones no one else wants to make."

"That doesn't make you a horrible person."

"I'm not saying that I can't put up a good front, and I may have fooled everyone here. But if I had been able to do the right thing with you, I wouldn't be here right now. I would have had the strength to turn you down and stay away."

"You go on believing that if it makes you feel better. But not long ago you told me you thought I was angry, and you were right. I didn't think it was okay to feel that way for a long time so I kept in inside. Truthfully? I think you're still grieving."

"Look—"

"I know a little bit about losing a parent. I might have been a child when it happened, but I still thought there must have been something I could have done. For a while, I thought it was my fault. My fault she died because I hadn't kept my room clean, hadn't finished eating all my vegetables, hadn't been a good enough little girl. I think deep down you think you could have done more for him. I don't know what it is, but you're hanging on to something that's eating you up."

He shoved a hand through his hair. "I don't want to talk about this."

"Of course you don't. Because we're getting somewhere. I'm getting to the bottom of what makes you tick, and you don't like it." She stabbed a finger into his chest.

He stared her down then and even if she'd found new courage, that look in his eyes made her retreat. "Listen. We did what you wanted.

And maybe now we're finally out of each other's systems."

Ouch. "Out of my system? Is that what you think?"

"We've been dancing around each other since the first night we met. 'Just the sex' is what you said, if I remember right. And I'm guessing now we're done." He moved toward the front door.

Shit, he can be an asshole when he wants to be. "If that's what you want, we're done."

"It isn't about what I want. It's about what has to be done. Always. You belong here in Fortune with your family. And I belong with mine."

The air force, not his sister.

"Don't bother saying goodbye when you go."

For a moment, she thought she saw a flash of surprise or pain in his eyes. But then they shifted again back to the tired edginess she'd grown accustomed to recently. "If that's what you want."

"It's about what needs to be done." She shoved his words back at him.

"Yeah. And you're a quick study." He turned and walked out.

Emily stared at the door for a few minutes. Stone's truck door slammed shut. Pookie was at Emily's ankle, whimpering. Funny that she could hear anything at all with her heartbeat thudding in her ears. Emily understood hurt and loss. Even if her heart had been broken for the first time at eleven with the biggest loss of her life, she wasn't sure why this moment honestly felt like the first time.

"It's okay, Pookie." Emily picked up her little dog and buried her face in her fur. "We'll be all right. We always are."

CHAPTER TWENTY-THREE

NICE, IDIOT, VERY NICE.

He'd done it up right, practically twisting the knife in her back. *We're done.* Effectively telling her she'd been nothing but a quick and satisfying lay. It was what she thought she wanted, so it had become easy to throw it back in her face. Even if he knew better. It wasn't what she wanted. Not even what he wanted.

They'd both failed miserably at keeping it light. And he'd known from the moment she walked into his office that it wouldn't be easy. Having understood that, he'd still plunged in headfirst.

More like heart-first.

She was dangerous. Like a full-blown addiction. The giving of killer orgasms shouldn't give a girl insight into his mind, but she'd done it. Like a ninja she'd broken through his defenses and next she'd try to fix him. He didn't need her to fix him. If something was broken, he'd fix it himself.

Had always been that way, and always would be.

Of course, she was right, too, which severely

pissed him off. With all he'd had to deal with in the aftermath of Dad's death, Stone hadn't allowed himself any time to grieve. And while James Mcallister had always been his personal hero, he'd been forced to deal with the fact that his father made plenty of huge mistakes. And left Stone with the emotional mess to clean up.

Too bad he couldn't be angry with his old man right now, but if he could, he'd ask what the hell he'd been thinking. Sarah deserved a goodbye. He drove savagely through town, all rolled up now since it was past six on a Sunday night, and gripped the steering wheel till his knuckles were white. The truth was something he didn't want to face, but he was also not a coward.

No retreat. No surrender.

He pulled off the side of the road and went for his cell phone. "Hey."

"Stone?" Sarah answered. "Is everything all right?"

"No, it's not. It's shitty."

"What happened?"

He didn't know where to begin. "You were right. I should have—I should have called you and Mom. I should have ignored what Dad told me to do. Sometimes when people are sick, they don't always make the best decisions. And I—"

"It's okay—"

"Let me talk. I wish now I would have told you everything. He didn't want you to see him that way. It isn't easy to watch someone slowly wither away from a strong and able man to a living corpse. It was ugly. Painful. Hard to watch someone you love die and not be able to do a damn thing about it."

"Especially for you, I imagine." Her voice was soft.

"But no one has the right to take that choice away. He was wrong. You should have been told. Mom, too. She was married to the man for ten years. I'm sure she still cared about him."

"She used to say James Mcallister is the kind of man you never forget."

"Anyway, I'm sorry, Sarah. If it means anything to you now."

"More than you know."

He dragged a hand through his hair, pissed beyond words. He'd failed this mission. "Nah, it's not good enough. But it will have to do."

"It's life, Stone. None of us ever get out of this alive."

Stone choked on a laugh. "Is that supposed to be a joke?"

"Just one of the many crazy sayings I remember from Dad." She laughed.

"He was the king of them. I thought it sounded familiar. It's not any funnier coming out of your mouth."

"Can I ask you something? Are you really leaving town? Because, from what I've seen so far, you fit here. This is a small place, and everyone I meet seems to know you. Danny from the Emporium, the barista at The Drip and the waitress at the diner. They all say you're a good guy."

Yeah, he'd done a great job of playing the part. Saving the airport jobs. Flying for Pilots and Paws. For a while, at least, he'd succeeded in putting his own desires in the background knowing all along he'd be back to his life soon enough. But he'd just done the last thing he'd ever wanted to do. Hurt Emily.

"No. I can't stay. I'm going back to the air force."

"And—does *she* know that?"

How the hell did Sarah know? He thought about the fact that he already had firsthand experience with how the people in this town couldn't stop talking. "Yeah. She knows."

And on that note, Stone hung up with Sarah and drove home to get properly smashed.

THE NEXT MORNING, Stone woke up with patches of morning light sifting through the kitchen window. He was on the floor with Winston on his stomach, snoring. One eye open, Stone glanced around and zeroed in on his surroundings. Yep, he was on his kitchen floor where he'd fed Winston a bowl of food the previous night. While he ate, Stone had gulped down a thousand beers. Or so it seemed, if he were to judge by the Grand Canyon–like size of his headache.

He moved Winston off his stomach and pulled himself up, trying to get the brain in gear. *Emily.* Damn, he was such a pathetic, sad fool. He'd hurt her, lied to her and walked away. A real dickhead move on his part. He'd done a lot of stupid shit in his life, but he wasn't sure he could ever fix this.

The doorbell rang, and Winston rose from his slumber, skittering into the back room like his tail was on fire.

"You know what? I'm not going to make fun of you anymore. So you're afraid of doorbells. There are worse things."

Stone glanced at his watch. Nine in the morning.

He opened the door to find Sarah behind it. "Holy hell, what happened to you?"

You should see the other guy, he wanted to say. Instead he went for the truth. "Your kind has done her damage."

He waved her in, and she stepped inside. "A woman."

"Good guess." He walked back to the kitchen and she followed. "Want some coffee?"

"Thanks." Sarah found a place on one of the stools. "Um, so is this your girlfriend we're talking about?"

"I'm not talking about it." He put one heaping tablespoon after another into the coffee filter.

Sarah scowled. "Of course you're not. I wasn't sure you had one, that's all."

"I don't." The coffee would be extra-strong today, and he hoped Sarah wouldn't choke on it or anything.

"Ouch. Sorry."

"Yeah."

Sarah shifted in her stool. "You probably wonder why I'm here."

"You want to talk about Dad."

Sarah looked flustered for a minute, shaking her head and throwing up a hand. "No. Here's the thing. I've got an idea, and I don't want you to just reject it the minute you hear it. Think about it, give it some time. Let it sink in. It's not such a horrible idea once you get to know it."

Sarah was apparently working on her word count for the day. "Were you planning on telling me this idea sometime this century?"

"I was thinking, you know, why don't I just buy the house?"

He didn't picture Sarah as someone who would want to live in Fortune. "You want to buy Dad's house? Why the hell would you want that? You're aware it's a fixer-upper."

"I talked to my attorney. The way we'd do it is I would buy you out. We'd go with the price we set to sell it, which is fair, considering all the work it needs."

"You mean you're going to stay in Fortune?"

"Maybe. At least for a while."

He didn't hesitate. "If you're serious, I think it's a great idea."

"You do?" She looked surprised, like she thought he might prefer a stranger to have this house. Why would he want that when his sister could live here? Dad would have loved the idea.

"But you'll need to keep Winston, too." He cleared his throat. "He comes with the house."

"I'm more of a cat person, but okay. So we'll take the house off the market today. I'll call the Realtor, and we can work out the details." She pulled a cell phone out of her purse.

"Are you sure you want to live here? Didn't Mom want you to go back to Fort Collins?"

"This will give her an excuse to come out. You two can visit."

He'd like to see his mother again. He'd dropped in on her rarely over the years when he could, but it had been a long time. "She better come out soon or I'll miss her. I'm expecting orders." Winston had lumbered back into the kitchen, and sat on Stone's foot.

"Do you know when that will be?"

"Any day now."

"We'll make the most of the time we have left before you take off."

"It's been too long since we were all together."

Their odd custody arrangement hadn't been the brightest idea either of his parents had ever had, but something told him, like most people, they'd done the best they could. They'd also loved each other at one time, presumably. He understood now love wasn't ever easy. Sometimes good intentions paved the way to hell. Because he'd been unable to stay away from Emily, he'd done the last thing he wanted to do.

CHAPTER TWENTY-FOUR

LUANNE HINCKLE WAS a regular at The Hair-Em, but Molly didn't usually attend to her. It generally wasn't a good idea to work on Grammy's friends, but when Luanne showed up for a walk-in on Thursday, Molly was the only attendant available.

"I want periwinkle red," Luanne said, touching her short white curls. "I want to look just like Ann-Margret. Can you do that, sweetie?"

"Sure thing. Let me mix it up."

About thirty minutes later, Molly checked the color. As close to Ann-Margret as any mere mortal could attempt.

"Let's get you shampooed." Molly walked Luanne over to the bowl bassinet and ran the water until it was warm. The worst part of this job had to be the shampoos. She often wished people would walk in with wet hair and just let her do the cutting and styling. That was her real talent.

It certainly wasn't entertaining her daughter, as the past few times she'd been to visit Sierra, she'd cried every time Dylan walked out of the room. Dylan, for his part, was about as warm to

Molly as a Frosty Freeze shake. But, as Grammy and Emily reminded her often, Molly had to be patient.

"Honey, any chance Emily's done working on herself yet and might go out with my grandson The Doctor?" Luanne asked, eyes closed as the water ran through her hair.

Molly tried not to snicker at the way Luanne talked about her grandson The Doctor like it was some kind of new invention everyone should try at least once. Emily was working on herself, all right—working on achieving multiple orgasms if the spring in her step and the pink in her cheeks were any indication. And the man responsible for those orgasms was someone who looked like he could be the spokesperson for them.

For the first time since Molly could remember, it would seem Emily was having a whole lot more fun than Molly. That was okay. For now. "I don't think so, but you'd have to ask her."

"I will next time I see her. But she's missed the last few genealogical meetings. It's been an ugly thing. Julia took over the computer searches now, too. It feels like a dictatorship. Honestly."

"Uh-huh." Molly concentrated on massaging Luanne's scalp. This was always a good time to work out some of her tension.

"Ouch. Not so hard, dear. And how's that little baby girl of yours?"

Just like that, Molly eased up on her scalp. Her

baby girl. She had a smile that made Molly go a little weak. "She's so smart. She talks a lot. I'm actually starting to understand some of it, too."

"Baby talk. Only Mommy and Daddy understand it."

"And Grandma," Conchita added from the shampoo sink next to Molly's.

Speaking of which, she had to get Sierra over to visit Grammy sometime soon. Both she and Emily wanted to spend more time with Sierra. So far Molly hadn't left the house with her, not even to take her to the park. Dylan and his rules. But unless she was kidding herself, he did seem a little more relaxed around her these days. Occasionally she'd glance his way to catch him staring at her before he'd quickly looked away.

"How often are you getting that baby, Molly?" Conchita asked, pouring conditioner in her hands.

"Three times a week. I'm seeing her this afternoon." Molly patted Luanne's hair and wrapped it in a towel.

"Why only three times a week?" Conchita asked. "You're that baby's mother."

"I'm letting Dylan call the shots for now," Molly said. "Soon enough, I'll be able to watch her while he works."

"What kind of nonsense is this?" Conchita scowled. "You mean you're not even good enough to babysit? He has to be there when you visit her? Like supervised visits?"

Conchita didn't know the details. Didn't know the full story. But apparently, because she had a hundred grandchildren, she considered herself an authority.

"They're not supervised. He leaves the room and sometimes works in the garage or in the backyard. I'm alone with her a lot."

"She's your daughter. You're not the babysitter," Conchita said.

She had a point. So far Molly hadn't made any mistakes, and damn it, she'd been the one to take care of Sierra on her own for six months. She could take care of her own daughter, thank you very much.

"You're right. I'm going to talk to him about this."

SIERRA DIDN'T USUALLY want to be held unless it was bedtime, or if she wanted to reach the window so she could watch Dylan at work in the backyard.

Molly picked her up and Sierra pointed to the window. Her little legs kicked in joy. "Daddy, Daddy, Daddy."

Most of the time, Molly couldn't blame Sierra. Like today. Dylan was working on pruning the apple tree and had pushed up a ladder to get to the tallest branches. He'd pulled his shirt off, and the sweat glistened on his back, making his muscles stand out. He was all man, that one, and he didn't make it easy for Molly to forget it. Almost like he threw it in her face, sometimes—making her regret she'd left.

Today they were going to talk about their little arrangement, one way or another. But when she'd arrived this afternoon, it was clear Dylan had mapped out the day as usual. So she'd played with Sierra and fed her a peanut butter sandwich. Watched *Beauty and the Beast* with her and tried to distract her from the windows. But Sierra, it would seem, couldn't be dissuaded too long from seeing her daddy. It didn't help that he was in the backyard, one of her favorite places on earth.

Molly opened the window. "She wants you, Dylan." So did she, for that matter, not that he cared.

"Hi, Daddy! Hi! Me out," Sierra squealed.

"Not now, sweetie. Keep her inside, Molly. I've got too many tools lying around. She could get hurt."

"All right." Molly shut the window and put Sierra down, who whined. "Let's go see if there are any more of those cookies."

It would have been so much easier had she been allowed to take her daughter out of the house. The park would do it, for sure. But she wasn't allowed to take Sierra anywhere. Even though it had been two weeks since she'd started coming over. Sierra still wasn't calling her Mommy, even though Molly encouraged her frequently.

Molly had her speech prepared. She'd tell Dylan that while she appreciated everything his mother had done for Sierra in the past few months, Violet's babysitting services would no longer be required. Violet could take a backseat now and be grandma for a while. As long as Molly started out by acknowledging the way Dylan's family had pitched in, the rest might be well received. It sounded like something Emily would approve of, so it had to be good.

An hour later, Molly had read every book in Sierra's bedroom, and Dylan still hadn't come inside. "Let's see what your daddy is doing."

Molly wandered over to the window, where she saw Dylan on the ground, appearing to inspect his leg. But the way he sat on the ground, one of his ankles crooked, didn't look natural. Molly opened the window. "Hey, Dylan? Are you almost done?"

"Call 9-1-1. I broke my ankle." Dylan said the words easily, but they caused a cataclysm in Molly's heart.

She picked up Sierra and rushed out the back door, phone in hand. "What happened? What did you do? Did you climb up there and fall down?"

"Calm down. You're upsetting Sierra," Dylan said, his face ashen gray. His pant leg was covered in blood. "Don't look. It's a compound fracture."

Dear God. She'd seen pictures of compound

fractures in the textbooks Dylan had brought home when he was studying to be an EMT. With shaking fingers Molly dialed 9-1-1 and explained the situation. In her arms, Sierra started to whimper. "It's okay, honey. It's okay."

"Owie, Daddy. Owie," Sierra cried.

"Molly, I'm going into shock. Can you get a blanket from inside?" Even though he was gritting his teeth, Dylan might as well be talking about the weather. *Did you see those clouds? I think it might rain.*

Molly carried Sierra on her hip, trying to comfort her. "Daddy just needs a blanket because he's cold. It's going to be all right."

She pulled a blanket off Dylan's bed and rushed back outside. Molly covered him with it and then laid his head on her lap. She held on to Sierra's hand, not that she would go anywhere right now. Her little girl bent down and gently petted Dylan's head.

"Thank you," Dylan said before he passed out.

MOLLY TRIED TEXTING Emily a hundred times to let her know what had happened, but she hadn't responded in the past fifteen minutes. Probably because she was up in a plane again.

"Call me back when you get this, Em. I have a serious problem here and I need you." What should Molly do? What would Emily do?

Emily would fix this. She'd know what to do.

Or at least, she would have before she'd turned into some wacked-out version of Molly's big sister. Flying planes and acting like she'd lost her brain somewhere. Molly was supposed to be the wild one, not Emily. But Molly was here at the hospital with her little girl, waiting to hear news about her husband. Emily was hanging out with Mr. Studley and flying planes. Maybe even joining the mile-high club. It was like opposite-day around here.

Sierra's little head rested on Molly's shoulder, as though the ordeal had worn her out, too. The nurse had stated in no uncertain terms that Molly was not to walk through those double doors without an invitation. So they were both stuck in the ER waiting room.

"Where is he? Oh my darling boy, what has he done now? Why does he insist on climbing trees? It's like he's still seven." Violet marched up to the triage desk. "Excuse me, where is Dylan Hill? I'm his mother."

"Nana!" Sierra squealed and climbed down from Molly's lap.

"My baby girl! There you are!" Violet bent down to pick up Sierra, who rushed into her arms. She looked up to see Molly, right behind Sierra. "What did you do, push him out of the tree?"

"It's good to see you, too, Violet. He's going to be okay. It's a compound fracture."

"I might have known you'd be involved. Why

did you let him prune that tree? He should have hired someone to do it."

Naturally, it was always Molly's fault. Her fault when she got pregnant, her fault she refused to have an abortion and her fault that Dylan wanted to get married. The precious granddaughter Violet now cradled in her arms might not even be here today if not for Molly's choice. But never mind all that.

"Which one of you is Molly?" the triage nurse interrupted.

"That's me. I'm—I'm his wife." Molly swallowed. *Why are they asking for me? Are they contacting the next of kin? Please don't let me lose Dylan. Don't let Sierra lose her daddy.*

"He wants to see you."

"We'll both go. I'm his mother. I'm sure he mentioned me." Violet started to walk past the nurse, who held out an outstretched palm.

"One at a time. And the baby stays in the waiting room."

Molly followed the nurse past the swinging doors and three curtained stalls until they got to Dylan. "We have him on a drip for the pain, but knowing our Dylan, he's probably still as sharp as a tack."

The affection in her tone was palpable. Naturally everyone in the ER would know him. The nurse patted the bed, checked the IV drip and left them alone.

Molly was afraid to get too close, because she might be tempted to touch him again and that hadn't worked out so well the last time. "Are you okay?" A stupid question, as he most definitely was not okay.

He looked at her, his amber eyes faded. "It's not painful anymore. But I'm going into surgery."

"Oh, no."

"Easy. I'm going to be fine. But I have a few weeks of recovery ahead of me."

Leave it to Dylan to make it all sound so normal. "What can I do?"

"I'm going to need a lot of help with Sierra."

"I can do it." Molly moved closer to his bedside.

"Don't get upset, but I was thinking maybe she could stay at my mom's house for a while. Or my mom might move in with me temporarily."

But this was not going to go down this way or Molly would not just be upset, she'd create a scene. And oh, there would be blood. "No, Dylan. I'll do whatever it takes. She's my daughter, not Violet's."

Rather than protest, Dylan appeared to be studying her. "Are you sure? She can be a handful."

Violet or Sierra? "I know. I gave birth to her. Remember?"

"How could I forget?" He nearly cracked a smile. "You said you'd kill me if I touched you again."

"And I meant it. At the time."

"Where's Sierra?" he asked, eyes now at half-mast.

"She's with your mother right now. Of course, she wants to blame this on me, too."

"She's wrong and she's always been too hard on you. I should have stood up for you more."

"Right." It felt good, having him acknowledge that Violet had been so unfair. "It's not my fault you got hurt."

His words became slightly slurred. "But I probably shouldn't have been showing off for you."

What was that?

Time for Molly's prepared speech. She would have loved to get Emily's input on this, but for now, she'd have to wing it. "I appreciate everything your mother did to help you out with Sierra while I was gone, but I'm here now. She can take a break and just be Grandma for a while. Would you tell her that?"

Dylan's eyes were fully closed now and he didn't answer. Yep, he'd fallen asleep.

"I'll take that as a yes." Molly moved even closer and ran a hand through his thick dirty-blond hair. Covered his big hand with hers. The same hand that held hers for seventeen hours of labor. He was going to be all right, because he had to be. How could the world keep spinning on its axis without Dylan?

She wasn't even aware she was crying until

the nurse walked back into the room, put an arm around Molly and shushed her. "He's going to be fine. We've got one of the best orthopedic surgeons on staff here. Don't worry, my dear. He's in good hands."

"Thanks." The nurse was kind, but it didn't take away from Molly's concern. There were so many things to worry about: what if Dylan never woke up from the surgery? What if his leg was never the same and he walked with a limp?

What if she still loved him?

CHAPTER TWENTY-FIVE

EMILY DROPPED OFF her licensing paperwork at the post office. With every requirement to become a licensed pilot checked off her list, and Stone's A-plus on her final flights, now it was just a matter of the paperwork. She'd have her license as proof that she'd accomplished something significant. Major. Giving up a little bit of control to try something new and exciting. She just hadn't expected to get her heart bruised in the process.

Stone had stayed away, and she assumed he would take her at her word and leave without saying goodbye. He was good at keeping his word, despite what he wanted everyone else to believe. He'd managed to keep the airport open. Cassie and Jedd would keep their jobs. The Air Museum and Shortstop Snack Shack would remain as part of the town's landscape.

He was still in town, she'd heard, but he'd left her alone. It was for the best. What had she expected?

Apparently a lot more than what he'd given her. And dammit, she was pissed off with herself about that. The temporary nature of their relationship, her stupid rules, had all been her idea and he'd only gone along with it. Maybe it wasn't his fault that while her feelings had changed, his obviously had not. So why did she feel used when she'd been the one to do the using?

Maybe all we needed was one more time to get out of each other's system.

The problem being, she wasn't sure she'd ever get him out of hers. It stung to realize she was going to be so easy for him to forget.

Emily pulled into the Builder's Emporium parking lot. She needed more paint choices. Emily had already changed her mind about the color in her bedroom. It was going from pink to a light yellow because that might cheer her up.

In the paint samples section, she found her private utopia. This was where she'd picked all the colors for her house so far. One of each. But today the shades of yellow were so confusing they gave her a massive headache. Canary. Lemon, saffron, amber, golden. Maybe yellow wasn't the right choice after all. Blue? Cerulean. Navy. Morning Sky. Ink. Royal. Cobalt.

Stone's eyes were cobalt blue.

She took a sample of each one, determined to hold them up to her bedroom walls until something felt right. Genuine. By the time she had one of each shade of both blue and yellow, she must have had more than fifty cards in her hands. How on earth were there this many different shades of yellow and blue?

The whole thing made her want to cry right here in the Emporium painting section.

Too many choices. It was way too easy to make a mistake.

"Emily."

She whipped around at the sound of his voice. He stood behind her, like he'd purposely sneaked up on her. The man was stealthy. Dangerous. Lethal. He looked like he'd just come from the wood section and was, in fact, holding a two-by-four in his hands.

His cobalt blue eyes were narrowed. "Are you all right?"

Of course he would ask that. Probably because it seemed she was crying a little bit now. She brushed past him, paint sample cards cradled in her arms.

"I'm not crying over you. I'm only crying because there are too many colors to choose from."

Heartbeat lodged in her throat, she ran out of the store and was halfway across the parking lot when she heard his voice again.

"Wait."

She turned to see he'd followed her out of the store without his two by four.

"What do you want?"

"To talk to you."

"I'm a little busy here."

He took a step closer. "It will just take a minute."

Thank goodness she'd thought to take all these paint swatches with her. They felt like a barrier between them. She gave him a little sharp nod. "Go ahead."

"First, forgive me for being an idiot."

"No."

He frowned a little. "Fair enough."

"Is that it?" She clicked her key fob to open the truck and almost dropped a paint swatch. Ink Blue. "I need to go."

He dragged a hand through his hair. "Just hear me out. I got my orders. Germany."

Emily dropped her swatches to the ground. "When?"

Stone immediately bent down and proceeded to pick them up one by one. "Two weeks."

"W-what about your father's house?"

"My sister bought me out. I think she's going to stay awhile, fix it up and maybe sell it."

"And you're helping her."

He sighed then. "Yeah. While I'm still here."

"I'm glad you two are speaking to each other. It's about time."

"Because of you. You were right. I had something bothering me that I couldn't let go of. I hated to admit I was wrong, but it's true. I should have contacted Sarah and our mother. What I did, what he did…it wasn't fair, and I regret it. It isn't easy for me to say that."

"I know." She accepted the last of the paint cards he handed over. "But I think you're forgetting something."

He studied her. "I know you said to leave without saying goodbye, but I wanted my goodbye, Emily."

Seemed like her hands were shaking. This wasn't fair. How dare he ask for a goodbye with his blue—cobalt blue—eyes? She didn't want to say goodbye to him. She opened the driver's-side door to her truck, leaned in and threw the cards toward the passenger seat.

Then turned to Stone. "So long."

But Stone reached for her elbow and she couldn't leave without her elbow. She was tugged into Stone's embrace and had no idea how it happened so fast but somehow she was hugging him back.

She closed her eyes and breathed in that wonderful smell that was all his. Pushed her face into his warm neck and tried to memorize everything about him. He always smelled so amazing. If this was it, the last time she'd hold him, she wanted to remember every smell, every touch and every sound. Across the street, she could smell the stale oil from the French fries at the Snow White Drive-In, and heard the sounds of a shopping cart rolling across the asphalt. Someone honked a horn. The wind whipped through a tree's branches. Her heart made no sound as it broke.

"This thing between us was more than I thought it would be," Stone said and he squeezed her tighter still. "And it's the hardest goodbye."

Emily chocked back a sob. When he left, she had a feeling he wouldn't be back again so she wasn't even going to ask. Her heart fisted inside her chest as she considered all that could go wrong for him overseas and said a prayer that he'd at least be safe. Somewhere on the other side of the world, far away from her and Fortune but at least safe.

Stone released her and stood there and watched, hands shoved inside his jacket, as she slipped inside her truck.

She caught him in her rearview mirror when she exited the parking lot. Still staring.

Emily turned on to Monterey Street and headed home. In her purse, her phone buzzed incessantly but she wouldn't answer it now. Driving rules. Not to mention it was hard enough to drive when her heart was breaking. Driving and talking on the phone while her heart was breaking? Sorry, too many moving parts.

She was madly in love with a man who couldn't love her back. And he didn't understand that she'd love him whether he'd reenlisted or not. She could love him long distance or short distance or any which way till Sunday. Real love had the ability to stretch boundaries, and she'd already catapulted over a few.

When Emily finally had a chance to look at her phone, there was a flurry of text messages from Molly.

Call me!
It's important. Where are you?
I hope you know this is more important than your stupid pilot's license.

Emily pulled into her driveway and wasted no time in dialing Molly back. "What's wrong?"

"Finally. I need your help. I don't know what to do." Molly sounded weak, sad and almost wistful.

"Is it Sierra?"

"No, it's Dylan. He broke his ankle and they took him into surgery!"

"Oh, no. Did it happen on the job?"

"Emily, are you listening to me? They're taking him into surgery. Surgery! What if he never wakes up again?"

Sounded like maybe Molly had been beaten with the truth stick. She still loved Dylan, which didn't surprise Emily. She'd figured it was only a matter of time before Molly realized it.

"Breathe."

"I am breathing. Will you tell me what to do? Please? How can I fix this?"

Emily sighed. "You can't."

"Fine, if you won't tell me what to do, just say so."

"There *is* nothing you can do, but be there for him. Sometimes bad stuff happens, Molly. You just can't fix it. It isn't anyone's fault. I'm sure it's not your fault he's hurt. Please tell me it's not your fault." Emily squeezed her eyes shut. Molly had been known to lose her temper a time or two, but she'd never purposely hurt anyone.

"He fell out of a tree, the dummy."

"You were there?"

"Watching Sierra. He was outside doing yard work with his chainsaw. You know, 'I'm a man! I can make fire and operate hazardous machinery!' And then he fell."

Emily squelched a laugh. Probably the big lug had been trying to impress Molly, as he'd been doing as long as Emily had known him. "He'll be all right, Molly."

"But what if he's not? What am I supposed to do then?"

Emily could spend several minutes assuring Molly that Dylan had a 99.8 percent chance of being just fine. He was young and strong. But there was something else Molly should know.

"No matter what, you'll be okay, Molly. You're strong. And you have Sierra."

"When he gets out of surgery, I'm going to take care of him and Sierra both. If he'll let me." Molly sniffled on the other end of the phone.

"You still can't control everything."

"But you always said if I just planned better—"

"I was wrong, okay? You can't plan some things. They just happen. Some things in life are left up to chance." Like falling in love. Even when you had rules to control everything. Like crazy stupid love.

Rachel was right. Emily probably should make origami with her list for all the good it had done her. She was madly in love with Stone Mcallister, and there was no way it could end well.

LATER THAT NIGHT, the gathering of the Pink Ladies included a soon-to-be licensed pilot named Emily Parker.

"This calls for a drink!" Luanne said. "I'll mix up some of George's Po'man margaritas."

"I'm sorry, Emily, don't take this the wrong way or anything, but I still think you're dependable. Reliable." Marjory patted Emily's hand. "Sorry if that's boring."

"It's not." This whole embracing her inner wild woman felt like walking around in shoes that were a size too large. "I don't mind being reliable. It turns out I don't do wild."

"I'd say you did a fine job!" Julia said. She'd been apologetic for weeks about the genealogy mistake. "You know, this family history goes both ways."

"What do you mean?" Emily asked.

"What I mean is that sometimes we, as gene-alogists, get so preoccupied with the past that we forget we're making history right now. And one of us sitting here tonight just accomplished something that her great-grandchildren will someday hear about. As long as we keep a good record of it." She patted her book.

"Right. Can't forget the record keeping." Emily smiled and powered up her laptop.

"Also, if you don't mind my saying, dear, can't forget to have those children." Marjory patted Emily's hand. "Won't have any great-nothing without first having children."

"Now, now. Let her take her time and do it right," Grammy, bless her, said.

"Of course!" Luanne said. "But when you're ready, we'll fix you up."

"Great, Luanne! Is your nephew not married yet?" Marjory asked.

"Oh, no, not him. He's dating a nurse. So pre-dictable." Luanne tsked-tsked.

Emily wasn't ready now. She hadn't been ready two months ago, but that was humiliation talking. Now she thought she understood true love, that rushing overwhelming pulse she felt when-ever she saw Stone. It was a little bit of panic, a splash of helplessness and a whole pound of vul-nerability. The other day she'd seen his back as he walked into the coffee shop and her heart rate had sped up into what felt like the triple digits.

There wasn't anything quite like being in love, even if it was one-sided. That rush to the senses, robbing a person of rational thought. No way would she ever settle again. Never again would she have color-coded ties, assigned days of the week for making love and beige. No sir, not in her house.

"Unless you're seeing someone…" Luanne still seemed worried about Emily's impending spinsterhood.

Emily ignored her, navigating to the genealogy research site. But in the gaping silence, she looked up to find all three women studying her. "No. Not seeing anyone."

"I, however, am," Grammy said.

Emily froze. Every eye in the room turned toward Grammy.

"Am what?" Emily asked.

"Seeing someone. If anyone cares."

"Why, you old broad!" Luanne cackled.

"Who is it?" Julia and Marjory said at once.

"George," Grammy said as if she'd just announced what was for dinner.

But this was big. Huge. Momentous. "George, our employee?" Her friend George, handyman George. Po'man Margarita George. And Grammy? When? For how long? Emily's brain fired off too many questions at once and none of them seemed to formulate as a complete thought.

Grammy waved her hand. "Now please, don't

you all make this weird. I wouldn't have said anything, but now that Emily's moved out, he's probably going to take her loft, and I know how people talk. So I figured I'd just try to get ahead of it."

"Wait. You mean he's—he's moving in?" Emily finally stammered out.

"I wouldn't say he's moving in exactly."

"Sure sounds that way," Luanne said with a nod.

"Good Lord, Jean," Marjory said. "What will people say?"

"They better not say anything if they know what's good for them. I'm an old lady, but I'm not going to stop living until someone takes me to the crematorium. I'm not getting buried, you know. It's too expensive." Grammy turned to Emily. "Remember. The dining room."

Emily wiped a bead of sweat off her brow. "I'm—I mean, I'm—"

"I think she's trying to say she's happy for you," Luanne interceded.

"Sure, that's what I mean," Emily said. "We're all happy for you, Grammy."

"Of course we are!" Julia said.

"That goes for me, too. Why shouldn't old broads like us have fun? That's what I say!" Marjory lifted her glass.

"Thank you," Grammy said. "Actually, it's all because of Emily."

"Me?"

"Look at everything you've done with your life. You're about to be a licensed pilot. For a while, it seemed like maybe my life was close to being over, so I started doing a little housekeeping. You know, making sure my affairs were in order."

There was a collective gasp in the room.

"No, no! I'm not dying. I think I was just bored. Thought I'd already finished with my life. I've had a long and busy one, after all. But since I'm still here, still kicking, I thought maybe it was time to do something new. And I haven't dated anyone since Kennedy was president. Talk about trying something new."

"And—George?" Was this an attraction that had always been silently brewing right under Emily, Molly and Dad's noses?

"I've always liked him." Grammy smiled shyly.

"The truth is, it happened to me, too," Marjory said. "No, I'm not dating anyone! I mean, I started thinking and, of course, you all know my relatives on my mother's side came from Madrid. So, I started taking Spanish lessons at the local community college. And saving up for that trip to Spain. Someday. You inspired me, Emily."

Luanne stood. "Nobody laugh, but I'm writing a novel. Historical romance. I always said I would. Now I'm going to do it."

"Wonderful, Luanne!" Julia clapped. "All of you. You've done something you put off for a long time. And all because of genealogy."

"But actually, I never wanted to fly before," Emily said quietly.

"You've always tried a lot of different things on for size, Emily, and maybe this was just one of them. It seems like you do enjoy it, and Pilots and Paws is a worthy organization," Grammy said.

It was, and Grammy knew Emily had already volunteered to help as soon as she was able. They'd have one less pilot available to them soon.

"Is there something else you've always wanted to do?" Luanne asked kindly.

Fall in love. Crazy breathless I-think-I'm-going-to-die-without-him love.

But you couldn't plan that kind of thing, and it just had never quite happened for her. Until Stone.

For a long time, she'd made excuses. Thought maybe it could never happen to her like it had to Rachel. Because Emily was just too sensible to get swept up by a man like that. Which was another reason to stay away from good-looking men, because they tended to do most of the sweeping.

Everyone was waiting for her answer.

She cleared her throat. "Actually, yes. And I did it."

"What was it?" Luanne prompted.

I fell in love.

But instead it felt safer to say something else. "I learned to live."

CHAPTER TWENTY-SIX

ONE BABY WAS hard enough, but two were about to break Molly in half.

As far as she was concerned, Dylan was being a stubborn baby when he continued to act as if he could do everything for himself without any help from Molly. *Men.*

"Don't worry about me," he said for the hundredth time as he hobbled around the kitchen. "Just take care of Sierra."

She couldn't get too irritated with him. He'd sided with her against Violet when she'd come, bags packed, to take over the caring of both Dylan and Sierra. Molly had left it to Dylan to kindly explain to Violet that it would be Molly taking care of Sierra in his home while he recuperated. As for Dylan, he claimed he wouldn't need any help, but Violet would be welcome to come by any time she liked.

"Sierra's taking a nap. I can make you lunch. It's no big deal."

"And if I were an invalid, I'd let you." He propped his crutch on the kitchen counter, keeping the weight off his ankle as he reached for a paper plate.

"And you say I'm stubborn."

"You are."

"Right back at you, buddy."

"You want to make me lunch, go ahead. I'll do these dishes."

"No, Dylan, I was going to do those." Molly sidled up next to him. The man was crazy. Certifiable.

"I used to load the dishwasher with Sierra on my hip. This might actually be easier."

Either she let him do it, or she'd be forced to shove him out of the way, which wouldn't help his ankle any. With a big sigh, Molly made him a turkey sandwich and put it on the table just in time for Sierra's cry. Molly rushed into the bedroom and found Sierra with one leg over the rail, a big smile of triumph on her face. The girl was a climber for sure, with no fear.

"No, sweetie, don't do that. Mommy will get you out." They would need to transition Sierra to a child's bed and soon.

"Dylan, she did it again." Molly called out to him.

"What did you put down this sink?" Dylan yelled back.

Not exactly the flow of a good conversation. Molly rushed back to the kitchen, Sierra toddling behind. "What's wrong now?"

"The sink is stopped up." He hopped back to the table and sat down to his sandwich. "I'll take care of that after lunch."

"You will not. We'll call a repairman."

"Daddy!" Sierra said and climbed up his leg.

Dylan skillfully made sure she avoided his bad leg and settled her into his lap. "I can't afford a repairman. I'll do it myself. It's not rocket science."

"You're supposed to be recovering from a compound fracture." Why were men so damned stubborn? Why did Dylan have to act like being helpless was a curse for the feebleminded?

"I'm feeling a lot better." He took a bite of his sandwich and offered Sierra a bite.

"But Violet said to keep you off your feet. She'll kill me twice if she finds out I let you do this."

"Don't worry about it." He narrowed his eyes, like the subject was irritating him.

She didn't want to make him mad, but she would distract him if that was what it took. Distraction worked wonders for Sierra, and maybe it would work for Dylan. If she had to take her clothes off and parade around in front of him, that was what she'd do. It might even be fun.

A few hours later, it looked like the work would be done for her because, like she was in on the plan, Sierra wouldn't leave Dylan's side for hours. He had to sit with her and watch two episodes of *Dora the Explorer*, followed by the one-thousandth viewing of *Frozen*.

Finally, it was bedtime and Molly gave Sierra a bath and put her to bed. It was only eight, but she was ready to go to sleep with Sierra. First, she had to make sure Dylan was still watching TV on the couch.

No Dylan. When she walked into the kitchen, his toolbox lay on the floor beside the sink.

"Oh, hell no." Molly ran to the sink, put her back to it and blocked it. "No way."

Dylan limped over to the sink. "Get out of my way and stop being ridiculous."

Molly didn't budge, which meant Dylan stood directly in front of her, meeting her gaze. In his eyes, she read a resoluteness and intractability that pissed her off. "I'm not moving."

"You'll move or I'll move you."

How did he take a few words and make them sound so sexy? Molly took in a breath. She had to go all the way with this. Take one for the team. With that in mind, Molly reached up, grabbed his shoulders and kissed the hell out of him.

Strangely, even though he froze for a moment, it wasn't long before he kissed her back. Deepening the kiss and grabbing her ass, the way only Dylan could do.

"Molly," he growled. "What are you up to?"

There wasn't any anger in his voice, only fresh

and raw desire. Easy to recognize it since it coursed through her, too. "You'll find out."

She kissed him again, threading her fingers through that thick hair, and then pulling at the top of his sweats so he'd know exactly what she wanted. She wanted him. All of him.

Sink forgotten, somehow they made it over to the couch, removing layers of clothes as they went. She'd often fought with Dylan over who would be on top, but tonight there was no doubt she would win this battle. She pushed Dylan on his back and straddled him. This would be quick, but she had a feeling fast was what they both needed and wanted right now. It had been too long since she'd made love to her husband. She needed him inside her, like she needed oxygen.

Molly tore off her top, and let Dylan catch a glimpse of her red push-up bra before she took that off, too.

"You're killing me," Dylan groaned.

"I don't know if I can wait another minute." She moaned when Dylan took one breast into his mouth and then the other one, licking, kissing and nibbling.

"The condoms are in my bathroom," Dylan said between nibbles.

"Right." She jumped off him and took the opportunity to pull off the rest of her clothes and her panties. Then she ran bare-assed into his bathroom.

When she returned, Dylan wore his sailor-on-leave grin. "Please let me see you run like that again."

"Maybe later." Molly smiled because Dylan had taken his shirt off, and this time she wouldn't just have to watch from a distance and yearn. Instead, she took a tour of his body with her tongue, starting at his neck, working her way down.

"Damn, baby," Dylan groaned. "I missed you."

Molly wished she could say the same, but it was so much more than that for her. She loved him, pure and simple. And she was too afraid to think that this might be the last time they'd be together this way. One last hurrah. That was why she couldn't think anymore as he thrust into her again and again. She could only feel the ripples of pleasure through her body, taking her away, lifting her to another time and place.

A place in which she'd never left.

When Molly woke the next morning, dawn light was filtering through the vertical blinds and she was cradled in Dylan's arms, too afraid to move. Too afraid she'd burst this bubble they were in. What would he say to her in the light of day? Would he tell her this could never happen between them again?

Sometime during the night they'd moved to Dylan's bed for round two. And still she couldn't get enough of him, but the man needed to rest. He had a broken ankle; though, she certainly couldn't tell by the way he'd made love to her.

She kept her eyes closed and pretended to sleep when Dylan stirred. He kissed her forehead and then whispered, "Molly?"

She couldn't avoid it any longer. Sooner or later she'd have to wake up and face reality. "Hmm?"

"Would you get me some water, baby? I need to take my meds."

Baby. "Of course." Molly climbed out of bed and filled a glass with tap water from the bathroom.

"I could get used to this kind of service," Dylan said with a sleepy smile as he reached for the bottle of pills on the nightstand.

"Are you hurting?" She climbed back into bed. He'd probably given that ankle a workout when he'd insisted on being on top.

"A little, but boy was it worth it. Want to go for round three?" He smiled again, and Molly thought she would cry because she loved him so much.

"Oh, Dylan." She buried her face in his neck.

"Hey, what's wrong?" His arms came around her, squeezing her tight.

She didn't want to say the words and freak him out, but she had to do it. She chose to whisper them in his ear, maybe to soften the shock. "I just love you so much."

"I know," Dylan said, not sounding at all surprised. "I love you too, baby."

Molly couldn't stop the sob that ripped out of her throat. "I never thought you'd love me again."

"I never stopped, Molly. I've always loved you, and I always will." He kissed her shoulder. "We still have a lot to talk about. A lot of trust to rebuild. But I'm all-in. I'm not giving up on us."

Sierra woke up then with her usual morning cry. Molly disentangled from Dylan and jumped out of bed. "I've got to get her, and all my clothes are by the couch. I'm naked."

"I noticed." Dylan laughed. "Just grab my bathrobe. This is going to happen a lot from now on, and she'll get used to it."

Molly threw the robe on and fairly skipped to Sierra's room, Dylan's words ringing in her ears and in her heart. *This is going to happen a lot from now on.*

When Molly opened the door to her bedroom, Sierra once again had one leg over the railing and a big smile on her face. She turned her little face to Molly and said, "Mommy!"

And nothing on earth had ever felt so right.

"WHAT DO YOU THINK?" Emily sat across from Rachel at The Drip, her brand-new shiny license gleaming.

"I can't believe it. You did it, Emily. Just you. You're the first Emily Parker to get her pilot's license."

"I can't believe it myself."

For the past few weeks she'd been on a journey, but if someone had told her she'd get her license and fall in love with the pilot in the process, she'd have asked them what they were smoking. She'd been done with men, back then, unaware that the good ones were still walking around, oblivious. Of course, her timing couldn't have been worse. Falling in love with a man who had plans to get out of town as soon as he could.

Since the day at Builder's Emporium, she hadn't seen or talked to Stone. Seven long days and two hours. Every day she vacillated between hating him for leaving and longing for him to stay. But they'd already said goodbye and she couldn't go through that again. All the paint samples were still tacked up on her bedroom wall. Not one of the colors were right, and she didn't want to go back to the Emporium and risk seeing him again. She hadn't been back to the airport, either, since she'd obtained her sport's pilot license.

The door jingled and Emily did a double take because the man who'd walked in The Drip was dressed in a black tux and he looked an awful lot like Greg. *Oh. No.*

"Emily, I've been looking for you everywhere," Greg said, coming up to their booth.

Rachel spit out her organic decaffeinated green tea. "What the hell?"

Emily couldn't speak. Greg, dressed for his wedding day. Here.

"I can't go through with it. Look at this monkey suit. She made me wear this—to a courthouse wedding! What kind of a woman would do that?" Greg took a handkerchief out and wiped his sweaty brow. What a tiny, weak little man he'd turned out to be. This was the man who was supposed to take care of her, provide her a lifetime of security and give her two-point-five children?

"You mean the mother of your child? You mean that kind of woman?" Emily finally said.

Greg had the nerve to sit next to Emily. "Please, talk me through this. I need you to tell me why this is a good idea."

"Because if you stay here, I'm going to kill you?" Rachel said quietly, without the slightest hint of a smile on her face.

"Get out of my booth! Now!" Emily yelled.

Greg jumped up. "Aren't you going to help me? I thought you wanted Nika and me to get married."

Emily rose, too. "Hear me out. I don't care what you do, where you do it or who you do it with! You need to leave me alone and go live your life with Nika, or whoever you want. Send me a Christmas card but never talk to me again. I mean it, Greg!"

"All right. Relax. Wow, why do you have to be such a bitch?" Greg asked, laughing a little and turning to the other customers for support. "Right?"

Like a particularly gory horror movie, suddenly all Emily could see was red. Red everywhere she looked. Her red hands curled into fists. And as though it now worked independently of the rest of her body, a red right fist rose up and shoved its way into Greg's red stomach. Hard.

"Ooosh," Greg said and buckled over.

"Now I'm a bitch."

It would seem all eyes were now on Emily as Greg clutched his stomach.

"Why did you do that?"

Emily stared at her fist. "I don't know, but it felt damn good!"

Greg slinked out of the shop, muttering to himself. Something about angry ex-fiancées and his horrible lot in life.

Men! They were forever trying to ruin her life. No more.

Emily turned to look at her fellow customers, lifting a fist. "Anyone else?"

One woman ran out the door with her coffees and the rest of the patrons looked away and went back to their coffee, tea and sandwiches. Emily sat back down next to Rachel, holding her right fist in her left hand.

"You might have to take me to the hospital. I think I broke something."

CHAPTER TWENTY-SEVEN

"HERE'S YOUR COFFEE. I'm not going back there. Someone scared the crap out of me." Sarah put the foam cup down on the kitchen table.

"Who was it?" Stone looked up from where he was installing the new granite countertop Sarah had ordered. Now he would need the name and description of this person. Sarah might be a pain in the ass, but she was still his sister, and as such, anyone who threatened her would meet with his wrath.

"It was this weird girl. I thought I was watching *The Runaway Bride*, except it was a Runaway Groom. Anyway, the girl who hit him—"

"Hit him?"

"I'm getting ahead of myself. I know you like a short story, so this weird girl punched the guy in the tux right in the stomach. Then, if you can believe this, she looked around and asked if anyone else would like a punch. I ran out of there."

Guy in a tux? "Wait a minute. What did this girl look like?"

"Blond."

"And what else?"

"What am I, your dating service? I thought you liked a short story."

"Not in this case." He needed details. What he wanted was an Emily fix since he'd been deprived of her for seven lousy, excruciating days.

"If you must know, she was my basic nightmare. Freaking gorgeous, big tits, Cupid bow lips. If it wasn't for the fact I'm as straight as an arrow, I'd want to date her."

"And she punched the guy in the tux?"

Sarah laughed. "Actually, it was pretty funny. She yelled at him before she punched him out. Said something like, 'Get out of here, I hate your guts. Don't call me.' You know. The usual breakup drama."

"Huh." Sarah had either described Emily, or her dead ringer. He didn't say another word but went back to the counter.

But Sarah was gifted with every woman's ability to talk a subject to death, plus she was apparently a bit psychic. "Oh, I get it. The girl. She's your ex. Am I right?"

"Why would you say that?" he asked, avoiding her gaze. For all he knew, his feelings were buried somewhere in his pupils.

"You men are so easy. Give me something difficult for a change."

Just his damned luck his sister had once been a forensic sketch artist for the police department.

She claimed she had facial expressions down to a science.

"Matt will be over soon. You can read him. Leave me alone."

"I'll just go back to my cataloging."

"You do that." Sarah had taken it upon herself to document the entire history of the Mcallisters in photos. She had several albums to go through, and she kept finding more treasures in Dad's junk.

Stone reached down to the second tool belt he'd attached to Winston, who lay beside him. Helping.

The poor dog was depressed. Stone had tried everything—new brand of dog food (one with vitamins), daily walks, even letting Winston sleep at the edge of Stone's bed. He had to face the fact nothing was going to fix Winston but Emily, and anyone with half a brain would know that.

Sarah kept asking if it was normal for a dog to lie around like he'd been hit by a car. Stone didn't have an answer to that, except that somewhere along the way, Winston had begun to read Stone's thoughts, like he'd once read Dad's. And why wouldn't he lie around like an accident victim when Stone felt like he'd been hit by a truck?

One thing, at least, had gone right. For the past few days, he and Sarah had developed an easy kind of truce. The ability to sort of take up where they'd left off without much talking about how they got there. Then the blame wouldn't have to be laid at anyone's feet. It was the only way he could do it, and she finally seemed to appreciate that fact.

He'd spoken to his mother on the phone for the first time since Dad's death. She'd cried, which had made him cringe, but then she'd regained her composure and the conversation had taken an easier and less emotional cadence. She planned to visit Sarah for a couple of weeks. It wouldn't be easy, and wouldn't happen overnight, but somehow, between his mother and sister, he'd figure out Women Code. He was almost sure of it.

The problem was, he didn't think he could wait that long.

He was either going to Germany next week or leaving the air force.

Six months ago this would have been a no-brainer. Not so much any longer, because of Emily.

It was clear he loved her; though, he almost couldn't admit it to himself. He loved the way she'd tried to control everything but then finally let go for him. Took a risk even if it meant she'd be hurt again. That he'd been the one to do the hurting killed him.

A few minutes later, Matt was at the door as expected. "Hey. Sarah here?"

"You know she is." Stone was going to try like hell and continue to ignore the fact that he often caught Matt lingering a little too long on Sarah while she did the same to him.

None of his business.

Matt followed him into the kitchen. "Heard you got your orders."

"You heard right."

"Does Emily know?"

"She knows." He went back to measuring.

"How'd that go over?"

Stone slid him a you-must-be-a-dumb-ass look. "About as well as you'd expect."

"Yeah. Got some news of my own," Matt said, then waited a beat. "I'm not going back."

"What the hell?" Stone had first met Matt in the air force, unaware until later that they each shared a connection to the small town of Fortune.

And if there was anyone that epitomized loyalty to the air force besides Stone, it had to be Matt Conner.

"You heard me. I'm out. Hunter is growing up, and I'm tired of seeing him once a year. This last time was two years. I hardly recognize the kid."

Unlike most of the men in their wing, Matt already had a son. He'd been practically a child himself when he'd become a father and joined up to help provide for the kid. He'd never married his now ex-girlfriend and by all accounts they still had a strained relationship.

"So that's it? You're out? Just like that?

"Just like that."

"What did I miss?"

"Nothing. Maybe some things are more important than the air force. At least for me." Matt lifted a shoulder.

"So what are you going to do with yourself?"

"What else? Get hired on somewhere as a pilot. It's what I do."

Some things are more important than the air force.

Not like Stone hadn't realized the same thing. His father had been more important. Stone hadn't thought twice when he'd been needed here in Fortune. But he wasn't needed here any longer.

Or was he?

"I could get work teaching at the aviation school, though I'd rather work for the new charter service. Truth is I'd rather work for you if you hadn't sold the place."

"Haven't yet. We got stuck in some airport regulations paperwork but it should happen soon."

"Before you leave?"

"Sarah said she'd taken care of the particulars. Anything gets held up, she'll take care of it."

Matt nodded. "Sorry to leave you, man, but you've still got Levi."

"Yeah."

It wouldn't be the same, of course. But maybe nothing would ever be the same. Was he seriously going to tell himself that he'd come back for Dad, stayed as long as he had needed to for Dad, but wouldn't do the same for Sarah? For Matt.

For Emily.

Face it, genius. She's your heart.

"Hey, ground control," Matt said. "Did you hear a word I said?"

"Nothing wrong with my hearing. You're leaving the AF. Got it."

"I said, 'Dumb-ass, are you seriously just going to leave Emily?' The best thing that ever happened to a fool like you?"

"Tell me what you really think. Don't hold back."

By the look in Matt's eyes, Stone was about to get an earful. "You got it. Truth is I've never seen a woman play hockey puck with your brain before this. You always had the upper hand. Easier to walk away. Believe me, I get it. But face it, this is different."

"I always planned to go back."

"But you didn't plan on her."

"Hell, no."

Matt chuckled. "Serves you right."

"Sarah just saw her at The Drip. Apparently Emily punched her ex and scared Sarah out of the shop. Emily will be all right without me. I'm sure of it."

"Not my point. Will you be all right without her?"

He had no freaking clue at the moment because

the truth was he hadn't been all right for a long time. Not since Dad died. Not since Sarah called him out on everything he'd done wrong, and not since Emily walked into his life and asked him to follow her ridiculous rules for one night.

God, he was a certified idiot.

If he wanted her, he'd have to go to her. He'd have to eat crow. Grovel like he never had before. He'd have to put his poor pitiful heart in her hands. There was no plan and no way to know if she'd come with him to Germany and leave this little town. Or whether any of her family would survive without her.

Whether he could survive without the air force: his home, his life.

But he had to go to her anyway because right now, the only thing that made any sense to him was getting his woman back. Now. "Tell Sarah I'm going out for a while."

But she was standing in the hallway and heard every word. "I'll alert the media."

Good to know the smart-ass thing ran in the family.

THE SWELLING IN Emily's hand was just starting to come back down, thanks to the ice pack the barista had given her. Her hand might hurt like hell, but her spirits were soaring. "I can't believe I did that."

"You and me both. In a million years I didn't

see it coming. Nice right hook, by the way," Rachel said.

"Stone taught me." Emily turned her hand over, inspecting for damage.

Rachel made a face. "Okay, I won't even ask, but let's just say I'm curious."

"Are you sure I don't need an X-ray?"

"I'm sure. Though, we might want one of your head."

"My head?"

"Why won't you admit you love that man? Why be so hardheaded about it? So what if it wasn't part of the plan. It happened."

"Fine, I admit it. You happy now?"

"But he's still here," Rachel said. "Why not enjoy what little time you two have left?"

"I'm sorry, but I can only say goodbye to him once. And I already did. Face it, I tried to be a wild woman, but I can't do it. I fell in love."

Rachel leaned forward. "Em, it's okay to be who you are. A nice girl. It's no crime, last time I checked. I only wanted to see you grow a backbone. And I believe your fist just proved you did."

"It did, didn't it?" Emily couldn't help but smile. Her fist had certainly done some talking today. "Sometimes words are just not enough."

"Nope."

Rachel was right. It was okay to be a nice girl. And this nice girl loved Stone. Loved how he cared about her little town, even though he was leaving, cared about his father's wishes and even cared for Winston. Mostly, she loved the way he looked out for her. He wanted to make sure she'd be okay when he was gone. But she had to stay in Fortune, and Stone had to go to Germany. End of sad story.

She glanced up and her gaze slid to the customer who'd just walked in.

Stone.

He walked over to her and Rachel's booth.

He looked so good and so terrible all at the same time. His hair was mussed up, and he had what looked like several days of beard growth. Bags under those beautiful blue eyes. On the other hand, he wore low-slung jeans, a tool belt and a Henley shirt with the sleeves pushed up, showing off the cords of muscles in his arms. He looked like he'd just jumped off the pages of *Home Depot* magazine, Stud Edition. A magazine which existed, of course, only in her imagination.

She went for stating the obvious. "You look tired."

"I haven't been sleeping. I need to talk to you. If we could, uh, talk privately."

"Dude, I wouldn't if I were you," a young man in the booth next to them said. "Chick has a mean right hook."

Stone glared at him.

The guy threw up his hands. "Just saying, man."

"Emily—" Stone said.

"No! We already said goodbye, and I'm not going to say it twice." Damn it, she was so not going through that again. She stood up and walked past Stone and out the café, but Stone followed.

"You're not getting away from me."

"What is it you want now, Stone Mcallister? A pint of my blood?"

Another parking lot. Different location, same town. Morning now, instead of afternoon. And all she could hear right now was the sound of her own heartbeat thudding in her ears triple time.

"I hurt you."

"Yes," she breathed out. "You did."

"It's the last thing I wanted to do."

"You could have fooled me."

He looked at his hands "Damn. I'm no good at this."

"At what?"

"Expressing my…feelings." He said the last word like it was salt on his lips.

But suddenly Emily considered that maybe this was about more than saying goodbye again.

"*Feelings* is not a four-letter word."

He didn't look convinced. "I asked you to forgive me for being an idiot. Now I want you to forgive me for something else."

She folded her arms across her chest. No paint chips today. "You don't ask for much, do you?"

"True enough. This time I want you to forgive me for forgetting something. Something pretty big."

"You. Forgot something." Strange. He never forgot anything.

"I forgot to tell you that I love you."

"W-what?"

He closed his eyes for a second, raked a hand through his hair and sighed deeply. "Here's the thing. I'm not great with words, and you know that. Not good with the touchy-feely stuff. But I'm trying. How am I doing so far?"

"Um, I'm sorry. Did you say you love me?"

He cracked a smile and took her hand in his large one.

"I didn't think it would be this hard to go. When I first came here, Fortune felt like a place I would leave soon enough. I could just bide my time here. I'd go back home to the air force and whatever part of the world they'd send me next. But when I wasn't looking, you became my home. What I'm trying to say is, I don't think I can ever get you out of my system."

"Really?"

"As long as you're with me, I already feel like I'm home no matter where I go." That made her heart jump in her chest and her body and feet followed as she went into his arms.

"I love you, too."

"You make me feel everything, even when I'm trying hard not to feel a thing. You woke me up."

"And you're doing so good with the talking." Emily buried her face in his neck. When she glanced up at him again, he was smiling widely, his rare double dimples showing. He didn't smile like that nearly enough. Something she'd have to fix.

"I don't have all the answers yet. But I do know I want you with me wherever I go, whether it's in Germany or right here in Fortune. Are you on board?"

"I'm so on board with that, Sergeant Mcallister." Then she kissed him in the parking lot of The Drip, simply because she was a woman in love.

"That went well. I didn't know I had so many sweet words in me."

"You have a lot more in there." She pointed at his hard chest. "I'll just have to slowly tease them out of you over the years."

"Sounds sexy." He traced the curve of her jaw, and then her lips. Then he kissed her again, like there was no one else. Like they were the only two people in the world.

Because in a way, at that moment they were.

EPILOGUE

Two months later

"DON'T WORRY MR. EDISON, we'll be there soon."
With two minutes left to her ETA, Emily went
through her mental checklist as she prepared for
landing, eyeing the county airport strip below her.

Today the skyline was a heartbreaking rush
of aqua blue on this beautiful May morning. She
lowered the landing gear. Mr. Edison sat strapped
in and rock still behind her as he'd been throughout the entire forty-minute flight, not making a
sound or false move. She turned to briefly look
over her shoulder and found puddles of drool
gathering on his seat.

"Uh-oh. My boyfriend won't be too crazy
about that, Mr. Edison. He's pretty anal about
his planes."

Mr. Edison didn't care much, judging by his
grim expression. Then again, the Rottweiler-
Boxer mix had just been rescued by the San
Martin Shelter and Pilots and Paws. His forever family would be waiting for him when they
landed in Fortune. Maybe he was nervous, hop-

ing for a good fit. That was the important thing, not whether or not he'd drooled a little bit.

The Hughes family, she'd heard. They were coming from Palo Alto to pick up Mr. Edison. "Great name, by the way. I hope they don't change it." Emily landed, possibly her smoothest one to date. She taxied to the hangar named Mcallister's Charters.

Her heart swelled as it had every day, seeing Stone on the tarmac, waiting for her. It had nothing to do with a lack of confidence in her piloting ability, she understood, but only his protective instincts that sometimes worked overtime.

Something she'd learned to live with.

She wasn't going to see Germany after all, at least not anytime soon. After much discussion, it had become obvious to both her and Stone that they both wanted to be closer to family. She to hers—Grammy and George, Dad, Molly, Dylan and Sierra—and Stone to his sister, Sarah, and his best friend, Matt.

Stone and Sarah had reconciled and it was a sight to see. Emily had listened in on some of the talks about their father, and noticed Stone used telling stories about his father to ease some of his grief. He didn't seem to be aware he was doing it, but every day his eyes were less edgy and strained.

Or maybe that was love.

Two months ago, he'd decided to separate from

the air force and pulled out from the sale of Magnum Aviation. He'd started the flight charter business, too. It was an idea he said had been brewing the entire time he'd run Magnum. He'd seen a need and filled it. Now, the charter was available for skydiving trips, small vacation hops and pulling banners every now and then. Now Emily split her time between working for Fortune Family Ranch events and flying as a pilot for her boyfriend's company.

And spending long and warm nights with Stone, who had moved into her duplex. Even Pookie and Winston were getting along after the initial territorial bark-fests, and were learning how to coexist.

It turned out that while searching for her past Emily had found her future.

That future was with Stone. She felt sure of it, even if they'd never talked about making forever official and on paper. She, Emily Parker, self-confessed control freak, had learned to take life one day at a time. No more self-imposed rules, either for living as a wild woman or just plain-old Emily. That girl had wanted a man to provide safety and security. A solid and unshakable future, even if it lacked the passion she might have hoped for at one time.

She no longer sought safety and security from a man. That she had found within herself. At long last.

Emily took off her headset and leaned back to snap the leash on Mr. Edison, easing him out of the plane.

Stone walked to meet the plane, took the leash from her and pulled Emily into his arms. "The family got caught in traffic on 101, but they're on their way."

She lifted up to her tiptoes to brush a quick kiss on his lips. "Did you miss me?"

As usual, he yanked her back to deepen the kiss. "Always."

Their private joke. Sometimes Emily would walk out of the room and back again two minutes later, asking Stone whether or not he'd missed her. The answer was always yes, even if it was occasionally accompanied by a quirked eyebrow and a sideways smirk.

"I have some bad news," she said as they walked hand in hand from the tarmac to the hangar. "We had another drooler."

She waited for the tension to hit Stone's stride but it didn't. He appeared to be slightly distracted which was unusual. Was his palm sweaty?

He shook the bad news off. "Ah, it's okay. It happens."

Something was off. Different. "It—happens? What's wrong?"

"Nothing's wrong." He stopped walking, and drew her in for a long, deep sensual kiss.

At their feet, Mr. Edison moaned.

I hear ya, buddy.

Stone broke the kiss and grinned. "Everything's right. Yeah?"

"Oh, yeah." Everything in that kiss told her that nothing was wrong at all, in fact everything was damn near perfect. Just as it had been for the past two months. Almost too right, too good, and Emily kept wondering when she was going to see a side of Stone that she couldn't live with.

But so far she'd found that she could handle his minimalist approach to talking, as long as he continued to show her how he felt.

He was ever so good about showing.

She could also live with his anal attitudes about the planes. Doing the bookkeeping for his business made her hyperaware of the cost and upkeep of those planes and she had newfound sympathy.

But if nothing was wrong, why was her former air force pilot–adrenaline junkie–cool-as-steel boyfriend's hand sweaty?

Stone opened the door to the hangar for her and she walked through it.

Someone had decorated their office in airplane- and heart-shaped balloons. Red, white and blue confetti lay on every available flat space. Cutout cardboard cupids hung from the ceiling. But it was way past Valentine's Day.

The first two people she noticed were Grammy and George sitting nearby. Cassie and Jedd, still working for Magnum, were standing in the hall-

way of the hangar which led to their office. Molly
and Dylan, Sierra on his shoulders, were to the
right. Stone's sister, Sarah, and their mother, who
was visiting, were next to them. And to her left—
Dad, sporting a wide grin.

What was almost everyone she knew doing in
Stone's little chartered flights' office?

"I decorated," Molly said. "Hope you like it."

"Are we having a party I don't know about?"
Emily asked.

"I hope," Stone's deep voice came from behind her.

She turned to see vulnerability in his blue eyes
that she hadn't ever seen there before. He didn't
say another word, but dropped to one knee.

Emily's heart hop-skipped into her throat.

"Everyone is here today because I couldn't do
this without their support. Sorry, I'm a little nervous."

She put a hand over her mouth, and then lowered it. "You? Nervous?"

"Yeah. Never thought I'd do this, but when
it's right, it's right. I love you, Emily. Would you
marry me?" He fished inside his pocket and drew
out a beautiful solitaire diamond ring.

Emily couldn't breathe. Nearby, Molly squealed
and so did Sierra, since she imitated everything
Molly said and did these days.

"Yes!" Emily said, tugging him back up to
his feet.

That brought on a whine from Mr. Edison, followed by another squeal in stereo sound from Molly and Sierra. Claps and shouts from everyone else.

"Thank God!" Grammy said.

As if there were any chance Emily would say no.

Dad clapped a hand on Stone's back. "Good on ya, son. Good on ya."

Emily went into Stone's arms and, fingers running through his hair, kissed him with everything she had.

Because he was everything to her, from the moment she'd discovered that sometimes the right man is the one you'd least expect.

* * * * *

If you enjoyed this book, you'll also love these Superromance stories with heroes and heroines who get an education in more than just love: TEMPTING THE SHERIFF by Kathy Altman, MOLLY'S MR. WRONG by Jeannie Watt and THROUGH A MAGNOLIA FILTER by Nan Dixon. And watch for Heatherly Bell's second book in the Heroes of Fortune Valley, coming June 2017! All available at Harlequin.com.

LARGER-PRINT BOOKS!

GET 2 FREE LARGER-PRINT NOVELS PLUS
2 FREE GIFTS!

◆ HARLEQUIN®

Romance

From the Heart, For the Heart

YES! Please send me 2 FREE LARGER-PRINT Harlequin® Romance novels and my 2 FREE gifts (gifts are worth about $10). After receiving them, if I don't wish to receive any more books, I can return the shipping statement marked "cancel." If I don't cancel, I will receive 4 brand-new novels every month and be billed just $5.09 per book in the U.S. or $5.49 per book in Canada. That's a savings of at least 15% off the cover price! It's quite a bargain! Shipping and handling is just 50¢ per book in the U.S. and 75¢ per book in Canada.* I understand that accepting the 2 free books and gifts places me under no obligation to buy anything. I can always return a shipment and cancel at any time. Even if I never buy another book, the two free books and gifts are mine to keep forever.

119/319 HDN GHWC

Name	(PLEASE PRINT)

Address	Apt. #

City	State/Prov.	Zip/Postal Code

Signature (if under 18, a parent or guardian must sign)

Mail to the **Reader Service:**
IN U.S.A.: P.O. Box 1867, Buffalo, NY 14240-1867
IN CANADA: P.O. Box 609, Fort Erie, Ontario L2A 5X3

Want to try two free books from another line?
Call 1-800-873-8635 or visit www.ReaderService.com.

* Terms and prices subject to change without notice. Prices do not include applicable taxes. Sales tax applicable in N.Y. Canadian residents will be charged applicable taxes. Offer not valid in Quebec. This offer is limited to one order per household. Not valid for current subscribers to Harlequin Romance Larger-Print books. All orders subject to credit approval. Credit or debit balances in a customer's account(s) may be offset by any other outstanding balance owed by or to the customer. Please allow 4 to 6 weeks for delivery. Offer available while quantities last.

Your Privacy—The Reader Service is committed to protecting your privacy. Our Privacy Policy is available online at www.ReaderService.com or upon request from the Reader Service.

We make a portion of our mailing list available to reputable third parties that offer products we believe may interest you. If you prefer that we not exchange your name with third parties, or if you wish to clarify or modify your communication preferences, please visit us at www.ReaderService.com/consumerchoice or write to us at Reader Service Preference Service, P.O. Box 9062, Buffalo, NY 14240-9062. Include your complete name and address.

HRLP15

LARGER-PRINT BOOKS!

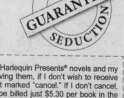

HARLEQUIN *Presents®*

GET 2 FREE LARGER-PRINT NOVELS PLUS 2 FREE GIFTS!

PASSION GUARANTEED SEDUCTION

YES! Please send me 2 FREE LARGER-PRINT Harlequin Presents® novels and my 2 FREE gifts (gifts are worth about $10). After receiving them, if I don't wish to receive any more books, I can return the shipping statement marked "cancel." If I don't cancel, I will receive 6 brand-new novels every month and be billed just $5.30 per book in the U.S. or $5.74 per book in Canada. That's a saving of at least 12% off the cover price! It's quite a bargain! Shipping and handling is just 50¢ per book in the U.S. and 75¢ per book in Canada.* I understand that accepting the 2 free books and gifts places me under no obligation to buy anything. I can always return a shipment and cancel at any time. Even if I never buy another book, the two free books and gifts are mine to keep forever.

176/376 HDN GHVY

Name	(PLEASE PRINT)

Address		Apt. #

City	State/Prov.	Zip/Postal Code

Signature (if under 18, a parent or guardian must sign)

Mail to the **Reader Service:**
IN U.S.A.: P.O. Box 1867, Buffalo, NY 14240-1867
IN CANADA: P.O. Box 609, Fort Erie, Ontario L2A 5X3

**Are you a subscriber to Harlequin Presents® books
and want to receive the larger-print edition?
Call 1-800-873-8635 today or visit us at www.ReaderService.com.**

* Terms and prices subject to change without notice. Prices do not include applicable taxes. Sales tax applicable in N.Y. Canadian residents will be charged applicable taxes. Offer not valid in Quebec. This offer is limited to one order per household. Not valid for current subscribers to Harlequin Presents Larger-Print books. All orders subject to credit approval. Credit or debit balances in a customer's account(s) may be offset by any other outstanding balance owed by or to the customer. Please allow 4 to 6 weeks for delivery. Offer available while quantities last.

Your Privacy—The Reader Service is committed to protecting your privacy. Our Privacy Policy is available online at www.ReaderService.com or upon request from the Reader Service.

We make a portion of our mailing list available to reputable third parties that offer products we believe may interest you. If you prefer that we not exchange your name with third parties, or if you wish to clarify or modify your communication preferences, please visit us at www.ReaderService.com/consumerchoice or write to us at Reader Service Preference Service, P.O. Box 9062, Buffalo, NY 14240-9062. Include your complete name and address.

HPLP15

REQUEST YOUR FREE BOOKS!
2 FREE WHOLESOME ROMANCE NOVELS
IN LARGER PRINT
PLUS 2
FREE
MYSTERY GIFTS

🌸🌸🌸🌸🌸🌸🌸🌸🌸🌸🌸🌸🌸🌸🌸🌸🌸🌸🌸🌸🌸🌸

H E A R T W A R M I N G™

Wholesome, tender romances

LARGER-PRINT BOOKS!

GET 2 FREE LARGER-PRINT NOVELS PLUS 2 FREE GIFTS!

◆ HARLEQUIN®

I N T R I G U E

BREATHTAKING ROMANTIC SUSPENSE

YES! Please send me 2 FREE LARGER-PRINT Harlequin® Intrigue novels and my 2 FREE gifts (gifts are worth about $10). After receiving them, if I don't wish to receive any more books, I can return the shipping statement marked "cancel." If I don't cancel, I will receive 6 brand-new novels every month and be billed just $5.49 per book in the U.S. or $6.24 per book in Canada. That's a saving of at least 11% off the cover price! It's quite a bargain! Shipping and handling is just 50¢ per book in the U.S. and 75¢ per book in Canada.* I understand that accepting the 2 free books and gifts places me under no obligation to buy anything. I can always return a shipment and cancel at any time. Even if I never buy another book, the two free books and gifts are mine to keep forever.

199/399 HDN GHWN

Name   (PLEASE PRINT)

Address   Apt. #

City   State/Prov.   Zip/Postal Code

Signature (if under 18, a parent or guardian must sign)

Mail to the **Reader Service:**
IN U.S.A.: P.O. Box 1867, Buffalo, NY 14240-1867
IN CANADA: P.O. Box 609, Fort Erie, Ontario L2A 5X3

**Are you a subscriber to Harlequin® Intrigue books
and want to receive the larger-print edition?
Call 1-800-873-8635 today or visit www.ReaderService.com.**

* Terms and prices subject to change without notice. Prices do not include applicable taxes. Sales tax applicable in N.Y. Canadian residents will be charged applicable taxes. Offer not valid in Quebec. This offer is limited to one order per household. Not valid for current subscribers to Harlequin Intrigue Larger-Print books. All orders subject to credit approval. Credit or debit balances in a customer's account(s) may be offset by any other outstanding balance owed by or to the customer. Please allow 4 to 6 weeks for delivery. Offer available while quantities last.

Your Privacy—The Reader Service is committed to protecting your privacy. Our Privacy Policy is available online at www.ReaderService.com or upon request from the Reader Service.

We make a portion of our mailing list available to reputable third parties that offer products we believe may interest you. If you prefer that we not exchange your name with third parties, or if you wish to clarify or modify your communication preferences, please visit us at www.ReaderService.com/consumerchoice or write to us at Reader Service Preference Service, P.O. Box 9062, Buffalo, NY 14240-9062. Include your complete name and address.

HILP15